WORK-LOVE BALANCE

AN OUT & ABOUT NOVEL

ALLISON TEMPLE

WORK-LOVE BALANCE

Recently divorced, Nash is a busy man. He's got a film festival to run and a new life as a single dad to navigate. He doesn't have time for delays or complications, which is why he relies on Brady to keep the festival IT in top shape.

For IT consultant Brady, the customer is always right, but the way Nash makes him feel is so very wrong. Brady's given up everything for his business, from friends to a love life. It shouldn't be surprising when boundaries between professional and personal get blurry, especially with Nash.

A summer fling is exactly what both Nash and Brady need. There's no time for anything else. But as external pressures mount, they'll have to decide what tips the balance. Will it be work, or will it be love?

Work-Love Balance is a 70k contemporary MM office romance. It's hot enough you'll want to make sure the air conditioning is on in your cubicle, and heartfelt enough you'll want to smack both characters before the end. HEA guaranteed.

Cover Design: Samantha Santana, AMAI Designs
Developmental Editing: Posy Roberts, Boho Press
Copy Editing: Manuela Velasco, Tessera Editorial
Proofreading: Kiki Clark, LesCourt Author Services

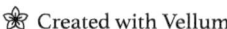 Created with Vellum

This one is all for me, from Brady's shirts to the tapas, but I'm so happy to share my city with you.

For news on future releases, join the A-List at allisontemplebooks.com/newsletter.

1

BRADY

*T*he number on my desk phone's call display makes my heart skip. If he's calling first thing in the morning, nothing good can come from this conversation, but I'm such a slut for punishment that I'll talk to him no matter how pissed he is.

I settle the headset over my ear, waiting for the call to connect. "Good morning, Brady speaking."

"Brady!" His voice cracks over the speaker, and I can't help the way I sit up a little straighter.

"Oh. Good morning, Nash. Everything okay?"

"No. It's not fucking okay." It's never fucking okay when he calls before ten in the morning. After that, he's calling because they have someone new starting, or the printer isn't working, or someone left the projector on again and burned out the bulb. Before, though . . .

"Something I can help you with?"

"What the hell did you do to my phone?"

I take a very long, slow breath and let it out on the count of nine. I've learned if I start talking too quickly, he thinks I'm trying to cover something up and jumps all over me. If I pause, he thinks I'm trying to find a solution.

Not that I'd mind if he jumped me.

"Your phone?" I set up his new cell phone yesterday. He can't possibly have broken it since then, can he? Nash is hard on his hardware. Two laptops this year, and he's never managed to outlast his phone contract, but twenty-four hours would be a new record.

"Yes." His voice drops low in a way that should be a warning but lately has been doing strange things in the general area of my crotch. "My phone. The phone you set up yesterday."

I lean back in my chair, wrapping my hands behind my head. "What seems to be the problem?"

"My contacts are gone."

I almost make a joke about whether he has a spare pair of glasses in his desk, but that way lies a verbal flaying I am not ready for on a Friday morning, so instead I say, "Did I send you the email about importing them?"

"I don't check email."

He doesn't. He says it wastes time. But wasting my time is perfectly reasonable.

I close my eyes. "Did you plug your phone in last night?" As far as I can tell, he works a lot and has no social life at all. When I first got the queer film festival contract, I expected an office full of beards and torn T-shirts. Women in plaid and with long hair pulled up in messy buns. I was not expecting the festival director to come to work every day in pressed pants and a button-down. He's even been in a tie on more than one occasion when I had to stop in. And he's uptight and abrupt, but it's hard for me to ignore the spark in his eye, the jaw that could cut glass, and the flecks of silver that pepper his dark hair.

Plus, he pays his invoices on time, and that is basically the only criterion for being my BFF these days.

"No," he says. "I didn't need to plug it in. It was fully charged when I left work last night."

Right. Except plugging in a phone does more than charge it. But he'll get his back up if I tell him so.

Ramona comes through the office door and grins at the exasperated look on my face. She mouths, "Nash?" with wide eyes and waggling brows. I flip her off.

"Okay. Do you have the charger?"

"Of course I do."

"And your computer is on?" I am leading the mountain to Mohammed, but it's what keeps my lights on.

"Brady, get over here and fix my goddamn phone," he growls. I have to bite back a shudder at the sound.

"Okay, so plug your phone into the computer."

The line goes quiet. He fumbles with something and curses softly. I wait.

"Nothing's happening," he snaps.

"Nothing?" When I finished my degree, I never envisioned this was how I'd be putting it to use.

"Nothing. The damn wheel is spinning and spinning."

Thank God for that. Sometimes technology can be unpredictable, and I'd have to hop on the streetcar and go down there to walk him through something that should have happened automatically overnight.

"Still spinning?" I say.

"No." His voice has lost some of its earlier fury. "Now there's a menu."

I do a quiet fist pump, and Ramona giggles. "What does the menu say?" I ask, trying to keep the glee out of my voice.

"Do you want to import contacts?"

Which is exactly what we talked about last night. When I showed up to help him finish getting his phone set up, he'd been on a call. I wound up waiting for almost forty-five minutes. Finally turning his attention to me, he'd said, "You have me for five minutes, and then I have to go."

I would take him for any time he would give me, but not in

3

his office, and not like he meant. So instead, I'd scrambled to get his email pushed over, synced up his calendar, and given him the very simple instruction of "plug your phone into your computer tonight so your contacts will download automatically."

Which he had obviously completely forgotten.

"And do you want to import your contacts?" I say, unable to stop the grin that slides over my face.

"Don't get smart with me, Brady," he snarls, but his words only make me smile more.

"No, no, sir. Not smart." Never mind that I run my own company. I am the lowly IT consultant, and he's the big, bad, big-city executive.

And also, never mind that he's in charge of a queer film festival, not a bank or a real estate conglomerate. We all have our roles to play.

"Is it syncing?" I say.

His pause before his sheepish yes tells me everything I need to know. I have fought the dragon and lived to fight another day.

"Is there anything else you need this morning?"

He grumbles for a minute. "The new marketing intern is starting on Monday."

"Harpreet has his laptop."

"But he doesn't get a phone," Nash says.

"No, sir," I drawl. "The minimum wage intern does not get any perks." Frankly, I'm glad Nash is paying him. He's probably nineteen and has an unlimited data plan on his own phone. No sense giving him company collateral on top of that.

"It's done," Nash says.

"And are your contacts there?"

In the silence, I can picture him, the frown he gets where his whole forehead wrinkles and his lower lip pushes out.

"I think so." He harrumphs, and for a second, I expect him to call me a whippersnapper. He's older than I am, for sure, but he's not my grandfather. "Okay. This looks better. If it's not, I'll be in touch."

"Of course. I'm a phone call away." I'm smiling so hard my cheeks hurt because Nash O'Hara would be lost without me, and Ramona's making kissy noises.

He never says goodbye when our calls are over. The line goes quiet, and I'm supposed to take that as a job well done. I groan as I stretch, and Ramona laughs.

"Nash again?"

"Who else?" I scrub my eyes with my hands. "Oh my God. That guy. He's so old-school about tech, it's adorable. Sometimes I can't decide if I want to call him daddy or if I want to call him *daddy*."

She gasps theatrically. We've been making variations of this joke for months.

"What was it this time?" she asks.

"Hello?"

My heart does a record scratch in my chest.

"Hello?"

My face must look like death because Ramona freezes, mid-giggle.

"Brady?" The voice is decidedly male and decidedly coming from the headset over my ear, not from somewhere else in the office.

Like a slo-mo horror movie, I slowly glance down at the phone, where the red light for line one is still solid.

Motherfucking Oedipal Christ. He's still on the line.

I throw the headset off like it's on fire and push away on my swivel chair so hard it sends me crashing back into the wall behind me.

"What? What's going on?" Ramona says.

I gasp, pointing a shaking finger. "The phone. Hang up the phone." My voice is a strangled whisper.

Ramona, excellent employee and wingwoman that she is,

5

does as commanded. She stabs at the button on the phone over and over until the red light disappears.

Oh my fucking God. I am so fucked.

"What happened?" Ramona looks scared, probably because I'm still cowering in the corner of my cubicle like the monster from *The Ring* is about to come through the phone and tear me into a million bloody pieces.

I'm fucked. The film festival isn't my biggest client, but they're one of my steadiest. And they're exciting to work with. So many of my clients are law firms and accountants who pay me a ton of money for encryption and security, but I never get the same thrill seeing their numbers on my call display as I do when Nash's number comes up.

And now it's over.

"He heard me."

"He heard—" Ramona gasps, putting her hands to her mouth. "He heard you call him daddy?"

I can only nod, running through the conversation in my head, trying to figure out how to talk my way out of it. I didn't say *daddy*, I said *maddy*, like he was mad when he called, and I talked him out of it.

Yeah, no one is going to buy that, least of all the film fest boss with the flinty eyes that see way too much.

On cue, my phone starts ringing.

Ramona and I stare at it like it's a bomb.

"Is it him?" she whispers. We find it's best to split the client portfolio, but it means she doesn't know the phone numbers for the Out & About Film Festival the way I do, just like I don't know her clients' numbers on sight either.

The phone rings and rings. I can't bring myself to pick it up. Because he's either calling to chew me out for my unprofessionalism then probably fire me, or he's calling to laugh it off, pretend it was no big deal, and the very idea of that is so humiliating I want to wheel myself out of this office and right into traffic.

When it finally goes silent, we both breathe a sigh of relief.

"Oh my God." I put my face in my hands. "This is a disaster."

The phone starts ringing again. On a Friday in the summer, when the co-working space that we rent our office from is practically empty, the ringing is impossibly loud. Every chime is the sound of my doom coming for me.

"I'll answer it," Ramona says. I hide, holding my breath as I listen. "Hello, Ramona speaking. Oh, hello, Nash, yes, how are you? Brady? No, uh, he's on a call with another client right now. Is there something I can help you with?" Her voice is brittle in a way you probably can't hear if you don't know her, but I know she's lying for everything she's worth. "Uh-huh? Well, I'll let him know, but, uh, he's got a few meetings this morning. Sales calls, actually, so he'll be out of the office. Might be a while before he can get back to you. Okay. I'll let him know. Goodbye." When she hangs up, she gives me a smug smile punctuated by jazz hands. "You're welcome."

Kissing your employees is highly inappropriate, and since I've already violated too many professional boundaries today, I'm going to draw the line at that one.

But that doesn't mean I can't fling myself at her feet. I have no shame, and the floors here are reasonably clean.

"Oh my God," I grovel. "We don't have enough revenue this quarter for me to offer you a raise, but I will pay for the Starbucks run for the next month at least."

"I like a venti PSL with extra whip," she says.

I snort. "It's not even PSL season."

"You would put conditions on my loyalty? Next time, you can answer your own damn phone."

She's kidding, but I'm so screwed. I should probably call him back and apologize, but with every minute that passes, it gets harder and harder.

The decision is made for me when the phone rings and it's a prospective client with a million questions. I talk to him for over an hour then have to leave immediately for a sales call at a small manufacturer near the train tracks. By the time I'm done there, it's already midafternoon.

I should do the right thing. Nash has been a good client, and even if he can be a jerk, he's never unreasonable. I'll apologize, maybe offer to let Ramona handle his account from now on, and hopefully clear the air.

Except when I call, his number goes to voicemail. And I can't really leave a "sorry for being a pervy weirdo on a Friday morning" message, so I hang up and catch the streetcar back to the office.

I'll call him on Monday.

2

NASH

I have to stop scheduling meetings on Fridays. Especially Friday afternoons. But we're getting ready for the family film weekend and I want to go over the schedule with Doug, the programming director, one more time. After that, I have an interview with *Reel Magazine*, which is only marginally painful, and then two hours with the accountant because Canada Revenue Agency seems to think our nonprofit status means we must be hiding money in our desk drawers. Or maybe it's because we're all queer. I've spent the past two weeks compiling every receipt and every spreadsheet. I will drown the CRA in paperwork and make them regret ever questioning our bookkeeping.

The point is, by the time I shut my laptop down, I'm exhausted and wondering why I ever thought Friday meetings were a good idea. Except I look at my schedule for next week and see next Friday is as full as today. And the Friday after that. And after that.

My phone rings. My cell phone. The new one I got yesterday. Not the desk phone that has stayed annoyingly silent since—

Right. Phone is ringing. It's Dominic.

"Hey, I'm finishing up," I say.

"Take your time," he says.

"I'll be there by six." Maybe six-thirty. Twenty minutes to get back to my apartment and pick up the car. The highway will be a nightmare for traffic by then, but once I'm north of the city, I can run the toll road until I get to Markham, to our house where—

I stop. To Markham, to Dominic's house. Not mine anymore. Someday, the little twist of pain will be a memory. Someday, I'll stop slipping up.

"So, would it be okay?" Dominic says.

"Would what be okay?"

He sighs, and the pain in my chest goes to dread, because he makes that sound when he's annoyed and doesn't want to say it. He made that sound a lot in the last two years of our marriage.

In this case, it means he asked me something and I was too busy missing my old custom kitchen with the walk-in pantry to hear him.

"I'm sorry," I say, as he sighs again. "Can you repeat that?"

"My mom called." He says it like it's no big deal, but now I'm not sure I want to hear him after all.

"And?" I ask stiffly.

"And Miranda's bringing the kids up to the cottage for the weekend."

I close my eyes. I know what I missed. "And you want to take the boys up too."

"You could come," he says, like he's only just thought of the idea, but if I know anything about Dominic, he's been working on this speech for hours. "It worked okay the last time."

It . . . was not okay. In fact, it was awkward as hell. Miranda, Dominic's sister, didn't speak to me once, and Dominic's mom would hardly look at me. Apparently once the ink is dry on the divorce papers, you stop existing to your former in-laws. At the end of the night, when I went to sleep in the stuffy bedroom the kids called "the Harry Potter room" because it was essentially built under the stairs, I heard Jacob ask Dominic, "Why isn't Daddy sleeping with you?" and nearly broke down.

So, no. It wasn't okay. That attempt at normalcy failed spectacularly.

And besides, "If I come, where is Miranda supposed to sleep?" Last time, she'd shared a room with her mother and bitched endlessly over breakfast about how badly Rosa snored all night.

"There's always a hotel. Or an Airbnb."

"For Miranda?" I ask.

"No." Dominic sighs, disappointed I'm not playing his game. "For you."

Of course. Sometimes I can barely believe we were married for almost ten years, and together for six before that. The guy has the emotional intelligence of a beaver.

"It's my weekend to have the boys," I say firmly.

"I know, but Miranda—"

"And instead of honouring our agreement . . . " I lean on the last word. I'd been perfectly happy to keep things informal and amicable. Dominic was the one who'd insisted on getting the custody agreement formalized. *So the boys don't get confused. They need structure.*

"Nash." But apparently that structure doesn't apply when Dominic's family snaps their collective fingers.

"Instead of honouring—" I say again.

"You can have them next weekend," he says with the same tired sigh.

"I'm at a conference next weekend."

"Then the weekend after."

"That's my weekend to have them anyway!" I'm yelling now. I catch nervous glances from two members of our event team as they scurry by my office door. Harpreet, head of marketing, follows and gives me a dirty look. I grit my teeth. I'm supposed to be a role model. Nash O'Hara, Executive Director. The nameplate is fixed to my door, and certain expectations come with it. Yet too many people on my staff have already been witness to the dissolution of my marriage. I do my best not to bring this shit with me to the office, but it's impossible to keep it completely insulated.

I didn't think it would be like this. We worked so hard to be a couple. And then the boys. Every part of bringing them home was a struggle, but we were happy, the four of us together, in our three-bedroom home on a subdivision cul-de-sac where every house looked like ours.

Except sometime between the first visit with the social worker and that evening last year when I came home to find my stuff in boxes by the door, Dominic decided it wasn't enough. I wasn't enough. For him or the boys. I did my best to be a father and husband and run the festival, and in the end I had to admit I could only manage two out of three.

"Fine." Even if I hop in the car right now, Friday afternoon traffic means they'll be long gone before I ever get to Markham. And what would I do then? Call the police? *Help, help. My ex-husband has taken our children to his mother's lavish lakeside cottage so they can play hide-and-seek with their cousins all weekend.* I do not want to be the asshole. We have said too many things to each other that we'll never be able to take back. For the boys' sakes, if nothing else, I don't want to add more to the list. "Have fun up north. Make sure Jacob wears sunscreen and Karter doesn't eat too many—"

"Okay, perfect, thanks for understanding!" The phone goes dead. One thing I will say for Dominic: he doesn't gloat. He gets what he wants and then moves on.

As an ex-husband, he's a jerk. As a dad, he's great, at least. It's the only peace I've been able to make as I find myself forty-two and single again. Dominic and I both want what's best for our kids. We just can't give it to them together anymore.

Doug's lurking at my door as I hang up. I scowl at him. "Eavesdropping's rude, you know."

He hunches a bit, making me think of a mole or a badger, even though I've never seen one in real life, just in the story-books I used to read to Jacob and Karter at bedtime.

"You shouldn't let him push you around like that," Doug says. "They're your kids too."

They are. But somehow, exiled downtown as I am, they feel like they're another life away. "Well, now I have a weekend to myself. Freedom to do whatever I want."

"Yeah." Doug's smile is wry. It's nice to see him smile. He's had as tough a go of it lately as I have. "But you'll spend it all working."

"I won't!" I say. "I'll—" My brain goes blank because, yeah, that's what I'll do. My inability to stop bringing work home is why Dominic said he was done. Bringing the laptop on our Algonquin Park canoe trip was the last straw, apparently. Not that we had Wi-Fi out in the woods, but I figured I could at least work on drafting a new set of fundraising requests once the kids were asleep. Dominic and I were well past the blow jobs under the stars phase of our relationship by then.

Meanwhile, Doug's smile is growing, like he knows exactly what I'm thinking. "You'll what?"

I wish we hadn't gone paperless at the office, because I really need to wad something up and throw it at him. "I don't know. What are you doing?"

His smile fades. "Calvin and I have a cake tasting."

For a guy who's supposed to be getting married in a few months, Doug is not nearly as excited as I think he should be. But maybe that's for the best. When Dominic and I got married, I completely bought into the *biggest day of my life* crap, and look where that got me.

"Stick with vanilla," I say. "Go with coffee buttercream if Calvin insists on being fancy."

"Feels like everything Calvin is doing for this wedding is to make it fancier than his last decision made it. I told him we should just skip it all and go to city hall, and he—" Doug shrugs. "Coffee buttercream. I'll remember that."

I try to look encouraging. No point in dumping my baggage on Doug. It'll be two years this fall since his dad died, and for a while I thought we were going to lose Doug too. He was ghostly on the odd days he did come to the office. But since he and Calvin got engaged, he's been doing better. Hopefully married life will help him turn the rest of the corner.

"Don't worry about me," I say. "I'll take the weekend to relax." In fact, I was going to take the boys to the aquarium. Jacob loves the shark tunnel.

"There's always that gift certificate Harpreet gave you last Christmas."

I snort. Hot yoga. I don't know what she thought I would do with it. Yoga's not really my thing.

But when I get home, the apartment feels impossibly huge and empty. It's too big for me, but I chose the two-bedroom plus den so the boys would have somewhere to sleep when they came. I didn't realize how infrequent every second weekend would feel when it got down to it.

I browse my phone for new movies. My secret guilty pleasure is anything with Jason Statham. I told Doug once, and he looked like I announced I'd laced the office coffee maker with cyanide. When you work at a film festival, people have a lot of opinions. And while most of Jason's work is hardly a masterpiece for the ages, you can't knock a shaved head and that jaw.

I wake up—or rather, I fall asleep on the couch, somewhere in the middle of *Snatch* and *then* wake up—in a puddle of my own popcorn-scented drool. The couch is a cheap one I bought from a warehouse on Dupont, and it's slippery under my spit.

The apartment is too quiet.

My life is too quiet. I miss my boys. I miss their gappy smiles as they lose their baby teeth. Once, in the days between dropping them back at Dominic's on a Sunday evening and picking them ten days later, Jacob and Karter lost three teeth between them.

"Look!" Karter had beamed. "The tooth fairy brought me five dollars! Isn't that awesome, Daddy?"

His question is followed by another voice in my memory.

"I can't decide if I want to call him daddy or if I want to call him daddy."

Brady. Fucking Brady. The idea of trying to meet someone new shrivels my dick like a week-old raisin smushed into a car seat.

Except for Brady. He's been the one tempting distraction as he struts into the Out & About office in skinny jeans and skate shoes, his floppy hair saying he doesn't give a shit about being a professional, when I feel like I have to keep up appearances for every sponsor and every member of the media who comes through our door.

Or maybe it's that he's so much younger than I am. When I watch his fingers fly over my keyboard, I'm reminded how much more technologically literate his generation is than mine, and I had mastered the art of programming a VCR before I could fully read.

His generation. Shit. I wouldn't mind finding someone to call me a certain kind of daddy, but Brady's not it. For one, he works for me—more or less. And two, he was probably still in high school when Dominic and I met. No, shit, maybe middle school. Either way, a relationship between us would be completely inappropriate.

I wipe the drool off the couch, throw the rest of my popcorn out, and go to bed.

I'm awake again way too soon. Too many years of early wake-up calls. For all of Dominic's complaints that I wasn't there as much as he needed, he has never been a morning person, so breakfast duty was mine from the minute the boys came home.

My cupboards are mostly empty. These days, I'm as likely to take Jacob and Karter out for a pancake breakfast as I am to make food at the apartment. I tell myself it's because we should do something nice—make special memories as the three of us. In reality, Dominic is right, and I still work too much to reliably go grocery shopping.

I find a packet of instant oatmeal and heat it up in the microwave. I stare at the fridge as I eat the mushy, faintly apple-cinnamon-scented paste. The gift certificate is there, stuck behind a magnet. *One free class. Hot Yoga. Curling Lotus Studio.*

I have never done yoga in my life, but in a fit of annoyance, I grab the certificate. Fuck it. I can't wallow all weekend, and I don't want to turn my laptop on. Even without the boys, I'm not going to get sucked back into work.

I reserve a spot in the hot yoga class online that starts at nine. At the back of my very bottom drawer, I find an old pair of shorts and a T-shirt. So much of my wardrobe has become about wooing donors and putting on a good impression for the festival. I miss the days when I picked my shirts based on which one had the least amount of toddler spit on it.

The yoga studio isn't actually all that far from my building. I'm greeted by a perky instructor in flowing pants and a loose top. She lends me a mat and gives me a whole stack of blocks, straps, and blankets.

"Why do I need a blanket if it's hot yoga?" I say.

She grins. "Some people find it soothing as we cool down."

I'm strangely nervous. Yoga isn't really my thing, but maybe it could be my thing in this new single, part-time dad life I'm living.

A few people have already arrived, and they're setting out their mats and stretching. I set mine off to the side and toward the back, where no one will notice if I make a complete ass of myself, but not so far back that I can't see the instructor.

By the time she starts, the class is full. The instructor says a few words and invites us to lie down. The room is warm, but not uncomfortably so. I do my best to follow as she tells us about our breathing and talks about spreading awareness through our entire body. I'm very aware that my right big toe itches, but reaching for it feels against the rules somehow.

Eventually she gets us to stand. Oh. The room is definitely warm now. When I glance around, most people are wearing a lot less than I am. Women in sports bras and tight shorts. The men around me are in loose cut out tanks. One guy even has his shirt off. He has to be at least sixty, and his skin is flushed pink, but he arches back with a control that says he does this often.

In my T-shirt and old basketball shorts, I feel like a mummy, and as we work through the positions, I realize my mistake. Sweat is flowing down my face and back. Everyone around me has brought what must be a gallon of water, and all I've got is the Captain America water bottle we bought for Jacob's lunches that we had to stop using because it leaked if you didn't keep it standing all the time.

"Now wheel around and look over your other shoulder," the instructor says. It takes me a minute to figure out what she means, but after I watch the people around me, I adjust the placement of my arms and legs before finally turning my head so my chin is in line with my back shoulder.

My sweat freezes when my eyes meet Brady's.

3

BRADY

*H*oly fuck. It's Nash. Nash is in my yoga class.

Hot yoga is my Saturday morning retreat. Technically, we're on call 24/7. No one told me when I started my own business that I'd basically be sleeping with my cell phone. But Saturday mornings are off-limits. Ramona gets to carry the nuclear football phone—the after-hours phone that never leaves our side—on Saturdays while I run errands and maybe have lunch with my dad, then I get it back for the rest of the week.

I started hot yoga about a year ago, when the anxiety dreams —the ones where clients never pay their bills, or demand laptops that don't exist, or refuse to admit that I've already delivered the same phone twice—became so chronic I was only getting a couple hours of sleep a night. These Saturday morning sessions are a chance to wipe the slate clean and let my body and brain go blank. If I squeeze in a little meditation a few other times a week, I can get four or five hours of sleep most nights, instead of two or three.

Hot yoga is a place for me to forget about work, and now I'm staring down the client I most want to avoid.

I noticed him, of course. It's the dead of summer, so only the really regular people are showing up for classes, while everyone else is at the cottage or chasing their kids around. The new guy on the mat in front of me stood out, particularly because he was dressed for a game of pickup basketball and only brought a tiny Captain America bottle for water. Still, he's fit, with nice calves and a great ass. The hair on the back of his head is dark brown, with flecks of silver in it.

I've been into older guys lately. I mean, in theory I've been into older guys. My schedule hasn't really set itself up for any kind of love life. But I don't know. Maybe it's because I'm working so much, while most guys my age are still navigating first jobs, or talking about going back to grad school, or still living in their parents' house while they save up for a mortgage. And I've got employees—well, I've got Ramona—and clients, and I may never be able to afford a mortgage, because right now I'm just trying to get clients to pay me in a timely manner. I don't have much in common with the other twenty-somethings I know.

So, maybe, instead of focusing on my breathing and finding the length in the pose, I think about the guy in front of me. About those strong calves and the swell of his ass as he stretches one leg out behind him. His hair is cut short as it fades to his nape, and I picture the feeling of it if I were to brush my fingers along it.

And then he turns around, and it's motherfucking Nash O'Hara, and all my peace and mindfulness dissolves into a puddle of sweat.

I almost run out of the room, except that won't be obvious at all, will it? The way his eyes widen and his nostrils flare shows he's just as surprised to see me. His face is flushed, and his hair is matted down onto his forehead. His scruffy U of T T-shirt is mottled with sweat, and now I'm thinking about his chest and whether he might be hairy and—oh God—whether that chest hair might be a little silvery too.

Before I can smile or say hi, or apologize for objectifying him on the phone yesterday—oh my God, was that only yesterday? The universe is fucking with me—Fiona, the instructor, sends us into a tree pose that has him turning back toward the front.

He's strong. His foot is up in the crease of his groin—*don't think about his groin, don't think about his groin*—and he doesn't even wobble. The line of his spine is straight, accentuated by the way his shirt is sticking to him. His left leg, planted on the floor, is a solid pillar of muscle that would make my throat dry if it weren't already parched from the heat in the room.

My concentration is shot. No matter how many times I try to find the balance point, I'm hopping around on my mat like a pogo stick. It's a relief when Fiona lets us out of the pose, except then she sends us into another sequence of standing warrior poses, and Nash seems to flow through them like water. His whole body melts from one posture to the next, and I don't know if I'm centered or grounded, or even still on this planet, because all I can do is watch the way his body moves and stretches, highlighting the tension in his legs or the veins in his forearms.

Fiona approaches him and gives him a smile. "Can I make a small correction?" she asks. He nods a little, so she gently puts her hands on his hips, and I watch, mesmerized, as she gives them a soft push, turning him more fully into the pose. And I can't help myself when I think about my hands on his hips, turning him the way I want to, fitting him just so, so that his muscles are straining as he sinks into—

I'm hard. Holy shit, I'm wearing stretchy shorts and a tank that leaves more of my body open than covered, and now I have a motherfucking erection in the middle of hot yoga and—

I drop to my knees so fast that pain radiates up my shins. Abandoned marionettes have more grace than me right now as I curl in on myself, trying to hide my raging hard-on while wearing next to nothing.

A hand settles on my back, and I flinch, but it's Fiona's voice that says "Brady, are you okay?"

"Yeah," I say hoarsely. "Just a foot cramp." I curl my toes under my feet as if I might be stretching them out.

She rubs a little circle on my damp shirt. "Okay. Stay in child's pose if you need to. And remember to hydrate. Cramping is a sign of dehydration."

And the ache in my dick is a sign I have lost all self-control. I need this yoga mat to melt and swallow me up.

I try to calm down, pressing my forehead into the floor. But, without the visual stimulation of Nash's long body in front of me, my brain gloms on to the sound of him breathing. Of his soft grunts as he settles from one posture to the next, and oh, Jesus, that is so not better than watching him move.

Get it together. I am not a teenager. Awkward public boners are not a thing I should be dealing with anymore. I can get control of this. When I was in high school, I'd think about sports or the smell of the henna my mom would boil before using it to hide her grey hairs. Now, I think about work. About clients calling to complain their internet is down, even though I can't do anything when the provider has announced an outage throughout the entire southwest end of the province. But that train of thought leads me to the way Nash growls my name on the phone when he's pissed and about how much I'd like to hear him growl my name in other contexts, ideally while he pulls on my hair and—

In total, I stay on my knees for about twenty-five minutes of the hour-long class. Fiona comes by every so often to ask me if I'm okay, and I nod or give her a feeble thumbs-up. She asks if I need water, and I somehow manage to take a few drinks from my big two-litre bottle without drowning myself or getting off the floor.

But there's no plausible way to stay on my knees when she tells us all to lie down and begin to relax. I've gotten my erection under control, although I don't trust that control will last, but really, if I stay locked in child's pose while everyone else is spread out on the floor, Fiona will worry.

I cover myself in a blanket I always bring and never use, because the room is kept at thirty degrees, and who wants to be warmer than that after an hour of exerting themselves? But today, modesty and a giddy sense of losing my grip on reality drive me to cover myself, even though the blanket plasters my clothes to my skin.

The room goes quiet. I can't even hear Nash anymore. Fiona walks us through a final meditation, and I do my best to focus on my breathing the way she tells us to. Usually, this is my favourite part of the class, when my body thrums with heat and I can practically feel the blood pulsing through my veins like an endless river. Today, I'm aware of how much the bliss I normally feel is like the high after the most amazing orgasm. That fucked-out floaty feeling where you're aware of your whole body but also can't really feel your limbs. And that awareness makes it impossible to ignore the man ahead of me who drives me nuts and turns me on, even when we're both supposed to be in our own personal yoga bubbles.

The class ends. Normally I need six cups of coffee to feel this buzzed. I stay lying down as long as I feel is reasonable without Fiona worrying I've passed out. Except, when I sit up, Nash is still there, sitting on his mat ahead of me. His shirt is so wet the grey fabric is nearly black, the skin at his neck is flushed bright red, and he's swaying a little as he sits.

"Are you okay?" My voice is a croak. He keeps swaying. I glance around for Fiona, but she's at the back of the studio, talking to a few of the other students, so I scramble forward on my hands and knees until I can see Nash's face. It's flushed, but his gaze glassy. He's breathing hard. "Nash?"

He blinks when I say his name. His dark eyebrows knit together in a frown. "It's really hot in here."

Touching him is presumptuous, but I'm glad I do, because when I put my hand on his forearm, his skin is hot to the touch when it should be cool under his sweat.

"You're overheating." I reach for his water bottle, but it's empty, so I grab mine and push it into his hands. "Here."

He shakes as he lifts it to his lips, but the second the water hits his tongue, his whole body turns back on and he sucks it down in big gulps.

"Take it easy," I say. He wouldn't be the first newbie in this class to overdo it and have to rush to the studio's small bathroom to throw all that water right back up.

"Is he okay?" Fiona crouches down next to us.

"Yeah," I say. "Think he's just too hot."

"Do you need to lie down again?" Fiona asks.

Nash has nearly polished off the rest of my water, but he shakes his head. "No." He gasps. "I'll be okay."

"Are you sure? Lots of people overexert themselves the first time."

He plucks at his T-shirt before giving me a once-over that makes me shiver even though the air around us is still hot. "Guess I wore the wrong thing for yoga, eh?"

Fiona looks around us. "There's another class coming in a few minutes. Are you okay to stand up? It's cooler in the lobby. You can sit there until you feel better."

"I can stay with him." The words are out of my mouth before I think about it.

"Really?" Fiona says.

"Yeah." In for a penny, in for a pound, even if Canada doesn't have pennies anymore. I give her my best confident smile. "We know each other from work." Right now, whatever strain I've put on our professional relationship is less important than making sure Nash doesn't collapse.

He's still a bit wobbly as he gets to his feet. I keep a hand on his back as we walk out of the room. We both sigh as the cooler air of the front lobby hits us. Nash's body is still a furnace under my palm, but his breathing is easier. When he's seated, I refill both our water bottles, then pull up a chair next to him.

"Thanks," he says as he takes a drink. The action is less desperate than it was before. The flush on his skin is receding. "Guess I should have done a little more research before signing up for my first class."

"It's okay." I pat his knee, noticing the way he's cooling down there too. "We had a guy who came in a full tracksuit once. He made it about fifteen minutes before Fiona had to help him out and call the paramedics."

"So I don't win the lowest spot on the wall of shame?"

"Nah," I say, giving him a grin. "He had the hamstrings of an eighty-year-old man too. Nowhere near your flexibility."

I snap my mouth shut so hard I bite my tongue, but I can't even whimper because every single one of my brain cells is focused on the slow flush pushing itself back over Nash's cheeks and the way my whole body is going hot for reasons that have nothing to do with yoga.

His eyes drop. "Thanks," he says with a soft laugh.

We sit in silence for a few more seconds, drinking our water. When I can't take it anymore, I say, "Nash, I—" but he's already pushing to his feet, running a hand over his hair.

"Sorry if I'm keeping you from anything," he says. "I should get going."

"What? Oh. Yeah, of course," I babble as I rise too. "No worries. I didn't have anything planned." Another white lie. I don't have any social plans, but I've got a wicked fun afternoon of webinars about the new collaboration suite Microsoft is launching—and which two of my clients are already clamouring for—waiting for me.

He gives me a tight smile. "Still. Sorry. I'll . . . I'll talk to you next week."

He leaves before I can say anything else. I still haven't apologized for the incident yesterday.

But I kinda saved his life in yoga class, so that has to count for something, right?

4

NASH

*W*ell, that was embarrassing. Going to the cottage and making small talk with my former in-laws would be less awkward than nearly fainting in front of my IT guy.

My hot-as-shit IT guy. Jesus, he was beautiful today. I've always thought Brady was kind of cute, in that fluffy casual way that millennials all seem to have. He likes to wear skinny button-down shirts in pastel colours with bananas and dachshunds—not together—on them.

Today, though. I was so glad I was ahead of him, because it meant I only got to see him on the odd time we turned around. But in his loose tank, with his tanned skin glistening with sweat and his whole body curving gracefully—even when he was crouched on the floor—he was nearly impossible to ignore.

I haven't been especially attracted to anyone besides Dominic in a long time. Not with all the work it's taken to get the festival off the ground and all the effort that went into adopting the boys and then being dads to them. Not when Dominic said he didn't love me anymore. But Brady . . .

As he's kneeling next to me, asking me if I'm okay and looking up at me with those big brown eyes, part of me is pretty sure I'm dying, while another part of me is thinking, if I survive, I'd like to see him on his knees again sometime, looking up at me while he asks if everything is okay. And it would be. Because he's perfect, with his long lashes and soft lower lip and—

I haven't wanted anyone in a long time, but maybe in this moment, I want Brady.

If I could, I would run all the way back to my apartment, but my body still hurts. So my progress is more a shuffle as I desperately suck down the rest of my water. The water Brady poured for me as he took care of me.

Gratitude. I'm feeling gratitude, not attraction. I've been adrift since the divorce. Maybe lonelier than I want to admit. After the final months of fights and cold shoulders, I don't really miss Dominic per se, but I miss lying in bed at night, talking with him about the boys and school, about where they're struggling and how we can make it easier for them. Being adopted twins with two gay dads is not the easiest way to blend in. And I miss running problems at the festival by Dominic and getting his take on things. I miss knowing someone cares about the things I care about.

Although there weren't so many of those nights in the last few years, even before I knew we weren't going to patch things up. There were more nights of me coming to bed late or bringing my laptop with me to map out business plans and long-term vision statements or research new ways to promote the fest. It was so big and exciting, that time as the festival took off, but somewhere along the way, I forgot about my husband, and he stopped caring about the things I care about.

Just gratitude. Not attraction. Brady's too young for me, too young to be really interested in me, no matter what he said on the phone on Friday.

———

The intern starts on Monday. His name is Patrick. He looks like he's about twelve and tells me he's from somewhere called Grizzly Falls when Harpreet brings him by my office for an introduction. He also thanks me about a hundred times for giving him this opportunity. I wish I could tell him we're paying him to play on Facebook all summer, but it feels unprofessional. Also, the way he looks at me with naked awe, as if he's meeting the prime minister, makes me feel about a million years old.

"How old is he?" I mouth to Harpreet as she leads him away, but she only shrugs.

His laptop doesn't work. Or, maybe it does, but he can't log in. Harpreet's on the phone with Brady, their conversation audible through my open office door. Somehow, I neither want him to solve the problem over the phone nor come to the office to fix it. Because despite all my good intentions about gratitude and everything else, I can still feel the imprint of his palm on my knee and the cool trickle of his water down my throat. And not far behind that is the purr of his voice as he says he can't decide if he wants to call me daddy or *daddy*.

Would it be so bad? Maybe not with Brady. The work thing makes it complicated. But maybe it's time. The divorce has been final for six months and Dominic asked me to leave six months before that. Would it be so bad if I met someone new? It doesn't have to be serious. Just an itch to scratch with someone willing and moderately attractive.

"Hey there." Brady's voice makes my head snap up. I glance at the clock on my laptop. It's after noon. For the last two hours, I've been mindlessly scrolling between reports and spreadsheets and some mock-ups Harpreet put together last week.

"Hi," I say, feeling guilty, like he's caught me watching porn at the office.

"How you doing?" He gives me a grin that draws my attention from the dimple on his cheek to the diamond stud in one earring. Has he always had that?

"Fine. You?"

His grin spreads, and with every fraction of an inch it grows, my heart beats faster too. "No, I mean. How are you doing? After Saturday."

My skittering heart wobbles to a sloppy stop. Because maybe on Friday he wanted to call me daddy, but now I'm the idiot who nearly passed out in a yoga class.

"Oh. Yeah. Fine." I lift the mug on my desk. "Staying hydrated."

He frowns. "Coffee dehydrates you."

It's actually chamomile and peppermint tea, but correcting him feels fussy, especially while my ego is still licking its wounds, so instead I say, "You here for the laptop?"

"Yeah." He jerks a thumb over his shoulder. "We got it worked out. I gave Harpreet the wrong password. My fault." His grin is cocky, but after meeting Patrick the intern, today Brady looks like an actual adult to me. He must be almost thirty, right? Old enough that he could—

"How's your phone? Still got your contacts?" he says.

Old enough that he knows how to be a professional—something I am failing at today.

"Yeah. It's great. Thanks."

We're not usually this stilted. I'd even go so far as to say we have a certain kind of banter. We had another IT service before I hired Brady's company, but every time I called them with a problem, the guy on the phone sounded like he was about to burst into tears. Brady's no-nonsense, and he's been able to work with us as the organization continues to grow. We're up to sixteen full-time employees and an army of short-term staff and volunteers when the festival rolls around.

"Well, call me if you run into any other problems." He's backing away, hands in his pockets. They pull the front of his Bermuda shorts tight across his crotch, and suddenly I'm wondering what he looks like in his underwear.

When I blink back to the present again, he's gone, and Harpreet is standing in his place. "The marketing team and I are taking Patrick out for a welcome lunch. Wanna come?"

"No. I still haven't finished going over the quotes for the new website."

Her mouth pinches. She wanted to have a web designer picked out by the end of June, but I got behind. She's offered more than once to go with the lowest bidder and be done with it, but I'd rather be methodical and know we're getting the best value we can. I just have to find the time to make a decision.

The rest of my week is pretty much par for the course. I talk to the boys every night. Dominic's got them in some kind of sports camp this week, since they're off school for the summer. Jacob scored a goal in soccer. Karter helped hand out water and animal crackers. They may be twins, but they're so different. Jacob is rough and tumble. He can out-talk me on a good day and is a champion negotiator. Karter is the caretaker. Not super coordinated, but he's got a heart of gold.

I'm speaking at a conference this weekend. It's a gathering of queer creators. When they asked me to give the keynote speech, I was pretty sure they'd called the wrong number. The more I work on my presentation, though, and as I explore some of the lessons learned as we've taken the Out & About Film Festival from little more than me and my roommates swapping DVDs in our dorm to an event with international contributors from—I double-check my notes—twenty-seven countries this year, I'm reminded we've really built something to be proud of.

But my presentation isn't ready yet. I'm preparing my fiftieth slide at ten o'clock on Friday night. There hasn't been time this week to put it together at the office. Also, I'm pretty sure fifty slides is at least twenty too many for a forty-five minute talk, but I'll figure it out.

Outside, a summer storm is raging. A good one. A fork of

lightning splits the sky, highlighting the skyline. The air shakes as thunder booms so close it might be in the unit upstairs.

And the lights go out. It's only for a few seconds, long enough for my heart to rattle in my chest and my eyes to strain in the dark, and then everything is back on.

Except my computer. It sits on my desk, inert, with a black screen.

I fight down the first fluttering of panic as I press the power button.

Nothing happens. Not on the second time either. Or the third. I stab at the little button over and over, waiting for something, anything. A flicker of the screen. The hum of a fan.

Nothing

My slides. All fifty-something of them. They're gone.

Acid bubbles in my esophagus, and my vision wavers. That was hours of work, and I'm giving this talk tomorrow. Outside, another clap of thunder shakes the building and makes me flinch. I scramble, trying to find a solution. My phone? It's not set up for slides. The office? I have a key, but no one else will be there, and I have no way to get into anyone else's computer, even if the slides weren't on my hard drive. Harpreet's always nagging me to save my things on the cloud, but no one ever uses my slides but me, so what's the point of putting them in a shared location?

The answer is pretty obvious right now. I'm fucked. Another weekend I committed to my job instead of my family, and now it's all gone to hell.

With shaking hands, I dial the only number I can think of.

5

BRADY

*T*he thunderstorm outside is so intense that, even though I'm exhausted after the work week, I'll never be able to sleep while it's going. I'm debating whether to pick up a new book or surf social media for a while when the football phone at my hip vibrates. I must be half asleep, because the sensation is so startling I nearly leap off the couch.

My heart only beats faster when I see the name and number on my screen.

"Brady." Nash's voice has none of its usual gruff impatience. He sounds breathless and maybe even a little panicked.

"Hi. Everything okay?"

"I need you. I'm so fucked right now."

He gives me an address for a condo downtown, not far from the festival office. I don't own a car, and normally I would take transit, but he sounded so unlike himself that I call an Uber instead.

When I arrive, Nash has his front door open, and he's wide-eyed and messy haired.

"It's gone," he says, not wasting time on greetings. Once I'm close enough, he lets go of the door and strides up the hall, leaving me to catch the damn thing as it swings toward me.

"It's fine. I'm sure we can get it back." Or at least part of it. I've set up all the festival computers to autosave every few minutes, but God knows what will happen if the computer really did manage to melt down in some kind of surge.

The condo is nice, if a little stark. If you asked me—but why would anyone ask me—I'd say Nash probably lived in a townhouse on the waterfront. I'd have expected a lot of chrome and leather. Granite countertops. I know running a queer film festival probably doesn't pay anywhere near as much as working on Bay Street, but I'd have thought Nash was one of those people who likes the finer things in life.

By comparison, this place is basically builder's beige. The countertops are whatever people make countertops out of these days when they can't afford granite, and the furniture must have come straight out of an IKEA catalogue. Not that it looks bad; just not as upscale as I would have expected.

Nash is pacing by the laptop that's currently on the dining room table. At least it's one of mine and not his personal computer. If he fried it completely, it's still under warranty, and I can get a new one.

He's pressing the power button over and over and shaking his head. "See? Totally done. I have to be at the conference in less than ten hours. What the hell am I supposed to do?"

"Okay. Okay." I drape my wet rain jacket over the back of a chair, since he obviously isn't in a state to offer to hang it up. Nash's isn't the first emergency call I've responded to on a Friday night. Most of the time I can find a way to work around the problem. "So the lights flickered, and then the laptop died?"

"Just gone. All my slides. Gone."

I step in front of him, trying to claim some space between him and the laptop. Nash doesn't really take the hint. He's set up the computer on the side of the table closest to the wall, and we could probably both fit in the space if he pressed himself against the drywall and didn't mind my ass in his crotch.

Despite his distress, I can't say I'd mind that very much, but that's not what I'm here for. If I get done fast enough, maybe I'll see if I can find someone online who is looking to let off some steam tonight. It's not the classiest way to get laid, but with the schedule I keep, it's the most expedient one.

I start with the power button, ignoring Nash's growled, "I already did that," behind me, because really, truly 90 percent of IT consulting is asking, "Have you tried turning it off and turning it back on again?" When in doubt, reset. In this case, though, nothing happens.

Another 8 percent of IT is unplugging the device and plugging it back in again. Most users don't know how many functions need more than a quick ten count to reset. I shimmy onto my knees, trying to maintain some dignity, and unplug the cord from the wall.

"You should really have a surge protector, even for a laptop," I say, mostly to make conversation.

"Well, you can order me one on Monday, can't you?"

I chuckle softly to myself, hoping he can't see my smile down here. I feel for him. Almost everything can be recovered these days, but there is the occasional situation where work is lost and not even my wizardry can salvage it. And while I might like to poke Nash occasionally to watch him scowl, I know he takes his work seriously, and I can sympathize with the amount of effort he puts into something he's clearly passionate about.

Which is why I'm going to save his presentation for him.

After giving it a solid minute to reset, I plug the cord back in.

"Try it now?" I say as I stand, brushing nonexistent dirt off my knees. Nash's apartment may not be as fancy as I would have expected, but it is immaculate. Not a dust bunny to be seen.

Nash swears softly. "Still nothing. Oh my God." His hands are in his hair as I straighten fully. "This can't be happening. First time I ever get asked to speak at one of these and—"

"Okay. Okay." I press a palm to his chest. He's still in his button-down from work, although at least he's taken off his tie. His heart is pounding under my hand, and his eyes are bouncing around the room in budding panic. "It's okay. I'll figure it out."

I press the power button again. Still black. It really is possible that the storm short-circuited something, but it seems so unlikely with a modern unit and in a building this size. What are the odds that only his computer would have died? There should be malfunctioning kitchen appliances or a larger power outage.

I run my hands along the unit, trying to think. Nash is still too close, muttering and cursing. I almost wish he'd pace so I could have a little breathing room, but he's rooted to the spot.

My heart skips when I bump against the charger in the back corner of the laptop. My fingers barely brush it, but it falls to the table with a soft sound.

No. It couldn't be that simple, could it?

I keep my hands where they are, trying to stay calm. If I laugh, Nash might deck me; he's that wound up.

"Could, uh—" I clear my throat while my lips tremble. "Could I trouble you for a glass of water?"

"What?"

My fingers tighten. "A glass of water?"

He pauses, and he's so close I can almost feel the tail end of his exhale as he sighs. "Yeah."

I wait until he's in the kitchen before I sit up. Quietly, I plug the cord back into the port and wait. Within a few seconds, the small light that indicates the unit is charging begins to flash.

Oh my God. What are the odds? But Nash has the right kind of single-minded intensity that he very well could dismiss all of the warnings letting him know he needs to plug in his computer. The timing that would finally shut it down right at the height of an electrical storm is a little too precious, but if it's something else, all my other solutions involve taking the laptop back to my place, and I don't think he's going to appreciate that option.

"Well?" he says. He's got a glass in each hand.

I randomly press a couple keys on the keyboard. "Just doing a reset, and then we'll see."

"What?" Nash nearly drops the glasses as he sets them down. "No. A reset? No. You can't reset it, I need my slides!"

"I know. I'm doing my best. This will clear whatever you were working on so we can get it turned on again. We might have to revert to an auto-recovered version, but better than losing the whole thing, right?" In truth, when I look down, I'm holding the Function and L keys. I don't think that does anything, but Nash is still so strung out. I shouldn't laugh at him.

He glowers while he sips on his water. If I wasn't feeling so sympathetic, that glower would have me halfway hard in my pants.

"We have to give it a minute. Why don't you have a seat?"

"I don't want to have a seat, Brady. I need to finish my slides!"

Okay, okay. I stand, taking the water and heading to his couch. Nash trails after me forlornly, but if we stay there while we wait for the battery to pick up enough of a charge to turn back on, one of us is liable to spill our water all over it, and then my clever diagnosis will mean jack shit.

"What are the slides for?" I say.

"For a queer arts conference this weekend."

"Oh, where's that happening?"

He drums his fingers distractedly on his glass. "Westin Harbour."

I whistle softly. Stuff like that always makes me happy. You put a queer tag on anything and it becomes niche and marginalized, the sort of thing that happens in coffee shops and hipster community spaces. This nice hotel means Nash has hit the big time.

"What are you talking about?" I say.

His smile twists a little bitterly in the corners. "Mistakes made. Lessons learned. Things I wish I could do over again."

"You?" I say. "Mr. Prepared. What do you wish you could do over?"

He shakes his head. "So many things. I wish—"

The computer beeps and whirs softly to life. Nash is off the couch like a shot. "Did you fix it?"

I wait, holding my breath, while he rounds the table. His ears are up around his shoulders as he hunches over the keyboard. The screen lights his cheekbones and the hard line of his jaw and makes his eyes flash. He makes a soft clicking noise with his tongue as he watches it boot up and has to retype his password three times because his fingers shake.

"Don't lock yourself out," I say, biting back a laugh.

"Up yours, Brady." But there's no heat in it.

The seconds as he scans the screen and clicks around are agonizing, but then he shouts and throws his fists over his head in victory. "It's here! It's all here!"

I stand, confident in the knowledge of another satisfied customer. "You're welcome."

His smile is blinding relief. "What did you do?"

"Oh, nothing. Just a little IT slight of hand and—"

"No, seriously." He takes a few stumbling steps away from the table, like he's afraid to let the laptop out of his sight while he talks to me. "Is it going to stay on? Should I get you to check it on Monday?"

I shrug, reaching for my jacket. "I think you'll be okay. Keep it plugged in and you'll be fine."

"Plugged in? Why? Is something wrong with the battery?"

"No." I don't want to embarrass him. Between my phone call last week and then the hot yoga, we've done enough of that to each other lately.

"But then how—" He gets in front of me. What does he want

me to do? Sit next to him for the rest of the night while he finishes putting his slides together?

"Because it wasn't plugged in when I got here."

Some of his elation vanishes. "What?"

I want to smack him. Punch him in the arm. "Because you let the battery die." I leave the *you overanxious diva* unsaid.

"What?"

I sigh. Apparently I'm not getting out of here until the whole story is told. "You didn't plug it in fully, and the battery drained."

"The battery? But what about the storm?"

I shrug. "Dramatic irony?"

"Dramat—" His mouth snaps shut, and a storm of its own passes over his face. "Then what did you do?"

I saved his ass. If I wasn't surgically attached to my phone, he might have spent all night freaking out about a problem that had the simplest of simple fixes. "I plugged it back in for you."

"But . . . but the reset?"

Ah. How to explain that without sounding patronizing. "We needed to give the battery a minute to pick up a charge."

"So there's no reset?"

I shake my head.

"And all you did was plug it in?"

"Sometimes the smallest solutions are the most effective?"

He opens and closes his mouth a few times before he finally stabs a finger into my chest. "You better not charge me for this."

My jaw drops. "Excuse me?"

He scoffs. "Any idiot can plug a laptop in."

"Yeah." Now I've got *my* finger in his face. "Any idiot."

Calling your favourite client an idiot is probably not a smart professional move, but I'm suddenly angry. If it's so obvious, why did I have to come over here?

"Don't be a brat, Brady," he snarls.

"A brat?" I crowd into his space. "I am a saint. I am here at eleven o'clock on a Friday night because you called me in a panic. I could have been in the middle of anything, but I dropped it the second I saw your number on the phone. So don't patronize me, and don't for a minute think I'm not going to charge you for every single second that I—"

My head hits the wall with a thump that has me grunting, and I realize in the fraction of the second before his mouth comes down on mine that he pushed me. Shoved me up against the wall and followed right after me.

And now he's kissing me.

Well, then.

6

NASH

*A*drenaline. Colossal lapse of judgement. Frustration. God only knows what possessed me to kiss Brady. One minute I'm the biggest idiot in the world, and the next he's in my space, lecturing me about how much I've inconvenienced his Friday night, and all I can see is the fury in his normally laughing eyes and the color rising in his cheeks, and I want him. I *want* him. And as he spits angry words at me, he gets closer and closer, and his mouth is tight and firm, and all I can think is that I want to touch those perfect lips and find out if they're warm and slick the way I think they will be.

So I do.

Brady's still fighting, still spitting as I crowd against him, taking him to the wall. He makes a surprised noise against my mouth, but before I can second-guess, the noise turns to a moan, and his lips relax under mine.

I didn't realize how much I needed this until he makes that sound. I growl as I press into him, lips working. Fuck, he tastes good. His mouth is warm as I slip my tongue inside, and he moans again, pulling at my shirt.

"I can't decide if I want to call him daddy or daddy." He wants me. Fuck, it's been seconds, and already I can feel the ridge of

him pressing against my hip. Maybe I've always known he wants me. Have I wanted him too? He's too young for me, but now, with my eyes closed and my hands working to tug his shirt out of his pants, he's clearly a man, and that's all I need to know.

"Nash." His voice is rough as his fingers tangle in my hair.

I don't want to talk. Just want to kiss. Touch. Grind—God. My dick is pressing against my fly, and I'd be totally happy to hump against him until I come inside my pants. He smells amazing. His hair is soft, and I'm pretty sure I can feel the shape of a ring or other jewelry on his nipples as I push up his shirt.

"Oh God." His hips rock against me, and I skip his chest to explore lower. Could I get his pants open? Touch him? He feels thick, hefty in my hand behind denim. So unlike Dominic, who was long and thin from head to toe and—

Ice water pours down my spine at the thought of Dominic. I haven't been with anyone since the divorce. Or while we were together. No one but him in seventeen years.

Brady doesn't fight me when I step back. Instead, he sways, blinking rapidly. His hair is pushed to one side, and his head is cocked, exposing his neck, and I could easily drag my mouth along the tight cord there. I know the noises he'd make, and even the idea of them has my erection throbbing.

We stare at each other in silence for a long time. His hand comes up to his chest, thumb stroking over where his nipple probably is. I have to lick my lips, but my momentary lapse of judgement is retreating, and in its place is disappointed-but-firm conviction.

This is a bad idea.

As I say, "Thanks for coming over," Brady says, "I should go." Except we stand there for a few minutes longer. Somewhere along the way, it stopped raining, and the apartment is incredibly quiet. It will get quieter when he leaves. But he *needs* to leave.

I go back to the coffee table in the living room and pick up the two glasses. They're still half-full. I keep my gaze down as Brady tucks his shirt back into his pants. I should send him to the bathroom so he can fix his hair in the mirror, but he really can't stay.

We share the usual pleasantries as he heads to the door. He says I can call him if I have any more problems, and nothing about his tone or the way he won't meet my eyes speaks of any kind of double entendre. I say I'll be fine, even though something inside me shouts that I haven't been fine in more than a year.

———

The talk goes according to plan. Doug and his fiancé, Calvin, are there, and they take me out for dinner afterwards. They're so in love it's disgusting, but I can't blame them. I remember that nervous sense that we were really going to do it, and how much I wanted to tell literally everyone who would listen that I was going to marry the beautiful man at my side.

Calvin's like that now. Attentive. Constantly checking in to make sure Doug is okay. Doug's always been quiet, and he's shrunk in on himself even more since his dad died, but Calvin is all patience and caring with him, and it's nice to see. Calvin even orders dinner for him when Doug gets flustered over the menu.

"So, how you been?" Calvin says.

"Yeah, fine," I say, poking at my Caesar salad.

"You getting out more? Trying anything new?"

"Calvin," Doug says, looking uncomfortable. "Don't bug him about it."

"What?" Calvin puts his hand over Doug's. "I'm just asking. I'm worried. We're worried, aren't we?" Doug gives him a nervous smile.

"I'm fine," I say again. "I went to yoga last week."

"Yoga!" Calvin gives me an encouraging smile. "That's great.

We tried yoga a few times last year, didn't we, babe?" He pats Doug's hand again. "Anything else?"

I kissed my IT guy in a fit of desperation, loneliness, and poor judgment?

"Nope." I shake my head and chew vigorously on my salad. "That's about it. I've been busy lately, you know? And I'm trying to make sure Doug's not working too hard so he has time for wedding planning, right?" If I keep talking, they won't notice that I'm lying through my teeth. That I can still feel the warmth of Brady's hands on my body, feel the rasp of his skin on my cheek.

Ridiculously, I want to call him. Not to restart what I should never have started in the first place. Maybe to apologize? Make sure we're still okay? Everything about last night is a sexual harassment lawsuit waiting to happen. Or worse, there will be a tersely worded email on Monday telling me that Brady is canceling his contract with the festival, and I can't have that. He's great. Responsive, affordable. I can't screw up that relationship.

And also, I like him. I know I can be a lot to deal with, especially in the last few years while my marriage fell apart. Brady gives as good as he gets and—

I really need to stop thinking about him.

There is no tersely worded email on Monday, which is a relief. Brady does write, though, asking if I will be a reference for a prospective client. The idea that he has other clients leaves me unexpectedly uncomfortable, and I try not to think about why. I write back a short, "No problem." I almost say, "You have my contact information," but of course he does. He basically told me he knows my number on sight, and that thought makes me equal parts pleased and embarrassed. I need to back off. Dominic used to criticize me for not being around enough, but I also don't want to be needy. Jesus Christ, I called Brady in the middle of the night because my battery died. I'm better than that. I used to be better than that, anyway.

I finally get to see the kids the weekend after. When I arrive at Dominic's, the house is chaos.

"Daddy!" Karter throws himself at me.

"Hey, bud. How are you?"

"Jacob! Daddy's here." Dominic's gaze swings back to me. "You're late."

"Traffic." I stand my ground. We aren't married anymore. I don't have to be on the defensive.

"Coming." Jacob's voice comes from the direction of the basement, and Dominic shoots me a nervous look. The basement is where the TV is, and Dominic has always been very concerned about how much time the boys spend in front of screens. I know the parenting blogs say it's bad, but honestly, Dominic and I both grew up in a generation practically raised by TV, and we turned out okay. We sucked at being married, but otherwise, we're both pretty functional.

"How was sports camp?" I say.

Karter wrinkles his nose. "It was okay."

"You had fun, didn't you?" Dominic ruffles his hair, but Karter only shrugs. "You'll like next week better. It's theatre camp."

"Theatre is dumb." Jacob comes around the corner, scowling for all he's worth.

"No, it isn't!" Karter says. "Papa, it's not dumb, is it?"

"No. Theatre is an important art form. Right, Daddy?" He gives me another pointed look, and I'm not even sure why. I run a film festival. Who am I to argue against encouraging my kids' creative endeavours?

"Sure is." I glance at my watch. "And speaking of art forms, we need to go." Out & About has started offering programs outside the main festival, and this weekend they're running a kids queer film festival. Finding family-friendly cinema with queer rep has been a task, but Doug and the rest of the programming team have done an outstanding job. "Movie starts in forty-five minutes. Come on, guys, time to go."

"Oh," Dominic stands. "But, Nash, I wanted to talk to you."

I almost say, "Send it to my lawyer," which is how he ended so many arguments. Instead, I say, "No time." I've got my best Daddy smile on. Everything from here until the time I drop the twins back here on Sunday afternoon is going to be an amazing adventure. We are no longer on Dominic's turf and don't have to play by the rules.

He glances at the boys and says, "On Sunday then?"

"Sure. Where are their bags?"

Karter gasps. "I forgot Henry." Henry is the stuffed raccoon he brought from his foster home. Karter and Henry are almost as inseparable as Karter and Jacob.

"Well, go get him," I say before tugging at Jacob's sleeve. "Come on, let's get in the car."

Dominic trails after us. "I put some books in their backpacks. If you could try to do some reading practice . . . The tutor said—"

"School's out," I say, making sure Jacob has clipped himself properly into his booster seat. "No more homework until the fall, right, buddy?"

"No more homework!" Jacob crows.

"But—" Dominic looks stressed, and I'd feel more sympathetic if he hadn't pulled the short-notice cottage quick change two weeks ago. This weekend is on my terms.

"Papa!" Karter's standing in the front door. "I can't find Henry."

Dominic goes to say something else, but I jump ahead of him. "Can you go find the raccoon, please? We're going to be late."

We aren't late, but despite it being my festival, we get three seats in the very back of the auditorium. I should be grateful.

New programming is a risk, and it's great these families are embracing the idea. Getting so many people to see queer representation on the big screen should totally be worth being seated so close to the door I can hear the two kids working at the concession stand arguing over who is going to go get more butter out of storage.

Jacob falls asleep, and maybe a movie on a Friday after a week of sports wasn't a great idea, but whatever. Karter is rapt through the whole thing. I take them for ice cream when it's over.

I've lived in my apartment for almost a year, and the boys have their own room with a bunk bed they picked out themselves. And yet, every time they come over, there's a fight over who gets to sleep in the top bunk.

"It's my turn!" Karter insists.

"You had it last time!" Jacob pushes him out of the way as he lunges for the ladder.

"Hey," I say. "No pushing. Jacob, what does the calendar say?"

The great bunk bed debate has gotten so heated that I put a twelve-month calendar on the wall at the start of the year and wrote out whose turn it was on every night they're supposed to be here from January until Christmas.

Jacob rolls his eyes, but he shuffles over to the calendar. He stares at it, hands on his hips, then glances at me. I arch an eyebrow, and he goes back to the calendar, tugging on his lower lip as his gaze darts over the days. Finally he spins and returns to the bed. He snatches Henry out of Karter's arms and throws him up in the air, where the raccoon bounces off the ceiling before he lands on the top bunk.

"Hey!" Karter whines.

"I didn't want the stupid top bunk anyway," Jacob says, crawling into the bottom.

As far as bunk bed standoffs go, this one is relatively incident-free, unless you're Henry.

"Good night, guys," I say. "We're going to have fun this weekend."

They're asleep quickly, if the snuffling noises coming from their room are any indication. When the boys were small, this would be the time of night on a Friday where Dominic and I would crack open a bottle of wine and put our feet on the coffee table. Usually we had big plans about watching a movie or slowly seducing each other over a glass of Syrah. Inevitably we fell asleep and woke up after the sun went down, then we stumbled to bed where we'd be asleep just as fast.

Tonight, I'm alone and far too awake. The apartment still makes sounds I'm not used to, and with no one's shoulder to fall asleep on, I pull out my laptop. The family weekend looks like it will be a success. Time to start planning the next one.

This single life is imperfect, but I'm getting used to it.

7

BRADY

I don't think about Nash or the way his mouth tasted or the scrape of his stubble on my cheeks or the hardness of his dick as he ground against me in the hallway.

Nope. Not for a single minute.

Except once again, I spend the following Saturday morning yoga class on my knees because of mysterious "foot cramps." Because I may not get to gape at Nash's perfect quads or the way his body strains from one pose to the next, but it's been a week and I still I can't get the memory of the desperate way he kissed me out of my head or the smell of his sweat as I buried my nose in his neck.

On Monday morning, an email comes in that I am not expecting. It's from Bill Immerchuk, who is opening a bunch of new after-school tutoring centres. He's got six locations throughout the city. I sent him a proposal for services, but I didn't expect to hear from him again. With a company that size, a lot of businesses will have their own in-house IT, but on Monday, Bill emails me to say he wants some more details on my pricing.

I choose to take Bill's email as an indication that everything is returning to normal.

Normal lasts until Harpreet from the Out & About office calls on Wednesday. "The internet isn't working in Nash's office."

I sigh. Out & About is located in an old repurposed factory. It's cute and spacious and gives the office a modern feel when you walk in, but the internet is a bitch. Everything is brick and concrete, which makes reliable Wi-Fi nearly impossible, yet Nash seems to think using cables when people are working at their desks somehow hurts their professional credibility.

Nash really is a bossy jerk. I need to remember this.

Except he's a bossy jerk who pays the bills, and Harpreet is pretty awesome too, so I tell her I'll come over in an hour.

The place is quiet when I arrive. The intern, Patrick, is sitting at the office's central table.

"How's the laptop working?" I say. "Any more password problems?"

"What?" He stares up at me from behind big Coke-bottle glasses that are partially obscured by a mop of hair that tumbles into his face. "Yeah, it's good. Way nicer than the one I have at home." He gives me a toothy smile that makes him look like he's seven. He's probably only a few years younger than I am. Definitely in his twenties.

Did I ever look that eager?

I figured out pretty quickly that working for someone else wasn't for me. That I was never a great student should have been my first clue I wasn't cut out to be someone else's employee. All the things that didn't work for me at school also didn't fit when it came to the corporate life. Too many stupid rules, too many forms to fill out, and no one ever seemed interested in making things run better. I had three different managers tell me, "You have to learn how we do things before you can change it," and every time, I was done with that job a month later. Working for myself is hard, but I never have to do anything just because it's the way it's always been done.

But I do have to do things the way Nash likes them.

"Is he in his office?"

Patrick's eyes widen. "Nash?" He whispers it like if we repeat it three more times, Nash will burst out here and eat our souls.

I smirk. "Yeah."

Patrick nods vigourously, and I decide not to tax him anymore. I give him a casual wave and head toward Nash's office.

"He's on a conference call." Harpreet pokes her head out of the office's boardroom. Her hair is braided over one shoulder in a long tail, and she's wearing a T-shirt with a dancing unicorn on it, along with the words *Bitch, I'm Fabulous.*

I freeze, trying to understand what she means. "Nash?"

She nods. "With the screenwriter mentors. They were supposed to do a video call but . . . " She shrugs.

"But the Wi-Fi's not working." I can picture it now. Nash would want everything to be perfect. He'd log in early to get the right angle on the camera. Then, when he couldn't connect, he'd huff and stomp around his office, cursing instead of doing anything to fix the problem. No wonder Patrick looks nervous.

Harpreet's eyes rise to the ceiling. "I think it's the extender."

I growl. We've got extenders in every corner of this building, trying to make a signal stretch in ways it was never meant to. I'm going to have to talk to Nash about hardwiring again. The bump to his ego and the cost of installation would be cheaper than my fee to come once a month and climb ladders until I find the faulty signal.

"Can I borrow this?" I ask Patrick, grabbing a chair from the long table he appears to be using as a desk.

"Oh. Oh, sure," Patrick stutters. "Do you need a hand?"

I sigh. The kid is cute. "Do you know much about internet connections?"

His gaze drops, and he clicks his mouse, pulling up the network options on his laptop. I smother another sigh. Helpful people are great, but Patrick will strain something if I don't let him off the hook soon.

"It's fine. Just don't report me to the health and safety committee for standing on this chair, okay?"

His face scrunches up like he's about to ask if they actually have a health and safety committee, so I hurry back to work.

The extender is mounted on the ceiling outside Nash's office, and it does seem to be malfunctioning. The power light is on, but there is no connection. I stretch up to reach overhead toward the three spindly antennas that stick out from either side.

"God dammit, Harpreet! It's still not working! Where the hell is Brady?"

The door to Nash's office swings open, and before I can say anything, he barrels into the chair I'm standing on.

"What the—" he says, as his shins bang into it, and the whole thing tips dangerously. I shout and pinwheel my arms, but I'm going down, the chair lurching out from under me. Guess Patrick better call that health and safety committee after all—except then strong hands grip my thighs, digging into flesh.

For a second, the world blips in and out. My heart is pounding in my ears, and I'm breathing so hard I can't focus on any one thing. Finally I settle enough to realize my hands are also tangled in crisp fabric covering solid, warm muscle. My eyelids flutter, and when I look down, I'm staring into Nash's breathless face. Stunned, I watch as he licks his lips and opens and clothes his mouth a few times, before he finally rasps out, "Are you okay?"

My voice is also hoarse when I say, "Fine."

His gaze drops, and I am very aware of the fact that his face is directly in line with my crotch. He's still got his hands on my legs, and the whole position is very . . .

I glance over my shoulder. Patrick is watching us, eyes gigantic behind his glasses. He's half-stooped, like he was about to leap into action and got stuck. Harpreet and a guy I've met before but don't remember his name are standing in the door of the meeting room, looking startled, while a few other people can be seen gawking over cubicle walls.

Quietly, I clear my throat and unclench my fingers where they have a death grip on Nash's shirt. Nash appears to have the same thought, because he drops his hands, although maybe his fingers run down the backs of my thighs for a second longer than they should. I wobble as he lets go of me, but at least he doesn't reach for me again.

"Sorry," he says, taking a step back. His eyes are on the toes of his polished shoes. "Guess I should have watched where I was going."

I stare up at the ceiling, grimacing at the mangled extender. I must have ripped one of the antennas off when I started to fall, and the whole thing is twisted. For a second, I'm pissed, because technically I broke it, but then I remember that the jackass currently standing six inches from my dick literally ran into me, so he is going to pay the bills.

"I think I found your problem." I give Nash a weak smile. Our fingers brush as he takes the busted extender from me. He's still looking uncertain as he makes some odd noises that sound like he's working to find words. When I check over my shoulder again, everyone is still frozen.

"Can I—" I swallow as my head swivels back around to Nash in slow motion. "Can I talk to you for a minute?"

Nash nods jerkily. "Sure."

The loudest thing in the office right now is the rattle of the air conditioner through repurposed ductwork.

"In private?" I say.

Splotches of color are spreading over Nash's face. He takes a stumbling step backwards through his open office door, bumping against the desk. The extender drops from his hand. I climb off the chair and take one last look behind me. Harpreet and the other guy—Doug, my brain helpfully reminds me, his name is Doug—are very dutifully staring at the carpet. Patrick, though, is watching us with naked awe, his mouth open, his fingers poised over his laptop keyboard like he's been live-tweeting this whole debacle. I give him a dirty look before I follow after Nash, closing the door behind us.

Nash is still agitated as I sit. He's holding the extender between his hands on his desk, playing with the two remaining antennas. His brows are furrowed as he stares at them with a focused intensity that gives me a second to study him. His shirt is pearly pink, his tie grey. His office may have unreliable internet, but he's still wearing silver cufflinks. For the first time, I notice subtle lines on the fourth finger of his left hand. He wore a ring there, and now he doesn't. Have I ever seen him wear a wedding ring before? His apartment certainly showed no other signs of human habitation, but there's a picture on the wall behind his desk of two smiling boys.

Whatever. My job is not to make guesses about his personal life. My job is not to think about the warmth of his body under my fingertips or the brush of his breath over my fly. I am here to fix his internet, keep his computers running, and do my best not to roll my eyes when he cracks another phone.

So I'm going to do what I should have done weeks ago. I clasp my hands between my knees and say, "Nash, I need to apologize."

8

NASH

*H*e needs to apologize? I'm the one who just tried to keep Brady from falling by groping him in my office.

Fuck, the shape of his ass . . . The muscle fit so perfectly in my palms.

But while I'm replaying the highlight reel, Brady keeps talking.

"I know you heard me. On the phone."

"Brady, I—" I falter. His face is so serious, I can't think of what to say.

"No." He waves me off. "It wasn't okay. In fact, it was hugely unprofessional. I shouldn't have . . . Even if you hadn't heard me, I should not have said it. I apologize if I've made things uncomfortable or"—his eyes rise to mine, making my breath still—"if I gave you the wrong idea. About me and . . . what I'm interested in."

Oh. Heat floods my face, pumping over my cheekbones and around my ears. I did assume. Have I been that wrong?

But he kissed me back. In my apartment, he kissed me back. And what was that in his pants, if not interest?

Still, everything about his voice and posture, hunched

forward like he's been called down to the principal's office, screams sincerity, and everything he's said about what is and is not appropriate is true. Whatever this thing has been between us, it's got no legs. A workplace crush, a desperate divorcé. We're going to stop now.

"I understand," I say, though part of it feels dishonest on my tongue. "Thanks for clearing the air."

He nods, curly hair bouncing. "Sorry about the extender," he says. "I'll get a new one and bring it by tomorrow."

I give the twisted antenna a wiggle. "There's got to be a better solution than this thing."

He gives a short laugh, upper lip curling, and in a heartbeat, he's back to the Brady I know, instead of the uncomfortable serious one who is trying to do the right thing for both of us.

"Is this the part where you start nagging me about running miles of ugly cable through this office?" I say.

His grin spreads, loosening something in my chest. "Sometimes the old ways are the best ways."

We argue about the cabling for a few more minutes.

"I can run it through the ceiling."

"You can't be trusted on a stepladder."

"You can't afford to keep calling me in to reconfigure your extenders."

"We got approved for another operating grant. Name your price."

The rhythm is familiar and comforting.

"How's your phone?" he says. "Contacts all still there?"

I lift it, showing him the cable plugged into my laptop. "Battery's charging too."

Something wordless washes over Brady's eyes, and for an instant, I'm sad. Because the thing that was happening between us was never going to be real, but for a few days it was exciting and distracting, and I'll miss that.

"I should . . . " He jerks his thumb over his shoulder toward the door.

"Right," I say, getting to my feet.

"You'll have to find somewhere else to work this afternoon if you need the internet." He pushes his chair back slowly.

"Yeah, no problem," I say. "The screenwriters are waiting on some follow-up details from me. I can send them from home." The festival is introducing a new mentorship program for queer screenwriters. We've received almost a hundred applications, and I'm really excited to work with them. It's been tough finding the time to get the program kicked off, and not being able to do today's video call with the mentors who have agreed to help is going to set us back a bit more.

"I'll be back tomorrow with the extender," Brady says. Something makes me rush toward him, like I'm being rude by staying behind my desk.

"That would be great. Thanks for coming by."

"I'll . . . " He swallows. "I'll see you later."

"Sure thing." I reach for the knob to open the door, and he does too. His knuckles brush against the back of my hand, and the graze of his skin on mine is lightning all the way up my arm. He must feel it too, because he snatches his fingers back, gasping. For a second, our eyes lock. My limbs are shaky, and my throat is suddenly dry. I swallow hard.

Just as I'm about to start with the pleasant and professional goodbyes again, Brady lunges for me. I must have left the door ajar, because it's not solid as I stumble back against it, and those few inches leave me falling as Brady grabs at my shirt in bunches and his mouth slams up against mine.

I don't even have time to gasp before his tongue is pushing against my lips. He feels feverish and desperate, and he tastes like coffee and mint, and as quickly as I taste it, I forget about it because his teeth graze my bottom lip, and I moan at the sting.

"Nash," he breathes against my cheek. I drag one of his

earlobes between my teeth, snagging against the stud there, and his breath hitches as he melts against me. He's hot, and his hands are starting to move over my shirt and around my body.

Sometime, not too long ago, we were having a conversation about how stuff like this can't happen, and it all seemed very reasonable, but clearly one or both of us was lying, because how can we not when it feels this good? I grab his ass with both hands, finding the round, firm muscles I only had a chance to feel for a split second when I desperately tried to keep him from falling and instead found myself face-to-face with his crotch. It was all over so fast, but it was still long enough for me to wonder how he looked under his clothes. What he'd feel like in my hand. In my mouth.

I growl as I turn us, and he bangs against the door.

"Yes," he hisses, tangling his fingers in my hair. He's so responsive. The shaky sensation has become a trembling through my body. It's scary. I haven't felt this out of control in a long time. This needy.

Fuck it, I'm horny. I've been horny ever since I heard Brady's secret words on the phone that morning, and now he's here, and his hips are arching against mine while I massage his ass, and I don't think I can stop.

He's wearing one of those tight button-downs he likes. Navy blue with pink palm trees. Turns out it's held together with snaps, because when I go to undo the top one to more easily suck at his throat, it comes open with a pop. His skin is smooth, nearly hairless. He has a freckle on his sternum, a few inches below his clavicles, and I brush a thumb over the line of bone. Even that soft touch makes him shiver, so I dive in as I work the rest of the snaps open, running my tongue along the hard cord of his neck, then lower, finding his pierced nipples, sucking at them as he whines.

"Oh, fuck. Nash. You—" His head bangs softly against the door. Brady's eyes are closed, and his lips are slick and puffy. Our hips are pressed together, rolling into each other in a way that leaves no questions about what we're feeling. The rock of his erection, trapped between mine and the crease of my groin, is like a magnet now instead of a pleasant distraction.

I give him one last kiss and drop to my knees, running my mouth over his flat stomach before nuzzling at the trail of hair that runs from his belly button to his waistband.

"Nash." His eyes are hazy, dark under the tangled curls that fall over his forehead. For a second, I remember he's so much younger than me, and a flutter of fear squeezes my heart. What does he see when he looks at me? A middle-aged man, sad and alone, and now desperately waiting for permission on his knees?

"Say yes." I palm his cock, running my thumb over the hard length stretching the fabric in front of me. I want to taste it. Touch it. I'm so close now. "Tell me you're okay with this?"

He pants as I stroke him through his clothes, hands on my shoulders. I'd catch him if he fell. Take him right down to the floor, then strip him out of his pants to see how beautiful he is.

"Say yes," I say again, kissing the soft skin above his belt buckle. I'm dizzy, drunk on the sight and smell of him, but I know what I'm risking here. If he tells me to stop, I will.

His hand finds mine, and he presses it over his erection, grinding and squeezing. "Yes. Fuck, yes. Whatever you want."

My hands shake as I undo his belt and pants. They fall to the floor with a clink and a hiss of fabric. His hip bones jut out over periwinkle boxer briefs that have a telling wet spot on the front.

I nose at his dick through the fabric, breathing in the scent of him. "Wanna taste you." The words are barely coherent.

"Oh fuck," he breathes, whole body going pebbly with goose bumps. I run my thumbs over his hips as I mouth at his erection, darkening the fabric further until spit and pre-come are indistinguishable.

"Can I taste you?" I need this. On my knees, with him

looking down at me, expression full of lust and feverish desire, I need him to say he wants this from me. Wants me.

His hands go to the waistband of his underwear, but I stop him. "Say it."

Brady swallows, Adam's apple bobbing as he nods jerkily. "Yes. Please, Nash. Please."

I peel the elastic down. His dick bobs out, free, and smacks my cheek, leaving a wet smear that makes me so hard I think I'll burst. I press my mouth and nose into his groin, inhaling him, learning him. He's clean and musky, the hair at his groin so dark it's black. It tickles my skin as I run my tongue over the base of him and then slowly trace the underside of his cock from root to tip, lapping at the slit when I come to it. He lets out a strangled whine as I tongue him, tasting pre-come. We could do this for the rest of the afternoon. Me in front of him, licking at him like a popsicle on a summer day until he comes all over my face.

His hand is in my hair, though, and despite him not pushing, I know what he wants. I want it too. Want the taste of him in my throat, want to know what sounds he makes as I take him apart.

I swallow him slowly, inch by inch. The hand on my head is steady, telling me he wants more but not forcing it. I slide back up, sucking gently, and he lets me, but his fingers tighten as I'm about to release him.

"Do it again." His voice is gritty, and he's watching me, eyes half-closed. "Oh fuck. Yes."

We go slow. When I try to pick up the pace, the door rattles a bit too tellingly, and I have to slow down again. He whispers encouragement, though, and he's hard and salty on my tongue, so I know he's enjoying it as much as I am. He never lets go of my hair, and as my jaw starts to ache, he takes over, thrusting gently into my mouth. Yes. This. I need this. Need him to take control and do what he wants.

Once, he thrusts a little too far. I gag and push back to sit on my heels, trying to find the space to breathe, but my retreat gives him more space to move. He's thrusting in earnest now, taking a few tiny steps away from the door so he can fuck my face and not give away what we're doing to the people outside.

The people. I groan around him at how this must look. I'm still fully dressed, while he's completely pulled open and exposed above me. There's inappropriate comments on the phone between colleagues, and then there's risking being discovered by your employees while you let the IT guy shove his dick down your throat.

The thought of it, of what we're doing and how much risk is involved, makes me feel giddy. Turned on like I haven't been in years. Decades even. Not since I was Brady's age.

I struggle to undo my belt. I'm going to come. I still haven't touched myself, but the thrill of this whole situation is enough that I'm about to blow all over the inside of my pants.

"No." Brady's voice is ragged, and I still, looking up at him. "Not yet."

I frown, but he takes another step toward me, forcing me to crawl back another few inches.

"Me first," he says. The greedy light in his eye has me squeezing the base of my dick for all I'm worth, trying to hold off my orgasm, because, yes. Him first. Him, that's what I want.

"Good," he purrs, and my whole body is going to go up in flames, but I hold still as he works, letting him take what he needs from me. His breath is uneven, and his thighs shake under my hands. Pre-come trickles steadily from his slit over my tongue. I hollow my cheeks and try to relax my throat, blowing him, watching him, trying to tell him how grateful I am for this one time, even if it's the only time we ever have, because I needed to feel this, something, anything but the regret that has plagued me for the past year.

"Nash. I—" Brady squeezes his eyes shut, and his body bows over mine as he comes. His fingers go tight, pulling at my scalp, and the pain nearly has me coming too, but I squeeze and count and swallow the semen that coats my mouth and spills over my lip as he pulls out, breathing in great gusts.

I sit on my knees, hand pressed over my desperate erection, waiting for him. His eyes are still closed as his face breaks out into the sweetest smile. Brady laughs to himself as he runs his hand through his hair, then finally glances down at me.

"Wow," he says, almost as if he's talking about something else other than the come that I can still feel on my chin or the way my knuckles are going white as I try to hold off the orgasm making my dick shudder in my palm.

"You look good like that," he says.

"Brady, I need—"

"I know." He leans over, running a thumb along my bottom lip and then sticking the digit in his mouth as he reaches across to my desk. There's a familiar sound, and then he's placing a couple tissues in my free hand. "Go ahead. Let me see."

I pull my dick out from my underwear, smoothing fluid over the head, trying to decide how much of a show I need to put on. I'm so horny I'm not sure I'd even be able to manage buttons if he wanted me to.

Brady is tucking his softening dick back into his underwear, but he waves an indulgent hand toward me. "Go on."

Yes. My palm is hot and rough, and it takes all of about four jerks before my balls seize, and I gasp as they empty themselves, my dick bucking and pouring itself out into the tissues Brady gave me. I bite my lip to keep from making any noise while my body trembles and shakes.

When it finally stops, Brady is in front of me, also kneeling. It takes a while for me to remember how to make my limbs work as I sag back, nearly banging my head on the edge of the desk.

"That was so hot," he says. All I can do is nod.

I manage to drop the soggy tissue into the wastepaper basket, and I can't stop my hands from shaking as I slip my dick back in my pants. Brady moves in, touch gentle, mouth sweet on mine as he does up my fly and puts the belt back into its buckle. I want to wrap my arms around him and pull him down to the floor, so we can lie next to each other for a few minutes. I need the world to stop spinning.

Instead, he helps me to my feet and sets me against the desk like a forgotten mannequin. He goes about the business of doing up his own pants and fastening the snaps of his shirt. His hair is a mess, but a few fingers into it and the curls settle down again. He leans into me, kissing some more, and somehow I still can't get my voice to work.

Finally, he gives me a soft smile that would be sweet—except he ends it with my lower lip caught between his teeth, eyes roaming up and down my body, making me flush.

He reaches around me, invading the tatters of my personal space, and just when I think he's going to force me onto the desk, he stands up again. The twisted extender is in his hand, and he gives it a friendly wiggle in my direction.

"I'll be back tomorrow," he says.

I'm so afraid of what he means by that.

"Okay," I say, voice hoarse, and I know part of that is adrenaline and a lot is the remembered burn of his dick in my throat.

He gives me another once-over, then points at my chest. "You've got a little . . . "

I glance down, and my cheeks heat at the drying smear of come on my tie.

"Oh shit." I reach behind me for another tissue, wiping madly at the mess. "Damn. I'll have to get this dry-cleaned."

The sound of the door closing makes me realize Brady has left.

9

BRADY

"*Where'd you go?*"

I blink back to reality, and I'm standing at my desk. Ramona is leaning over the cubicle wall with a big smile on her face.

"What?" Was I daydreaming?

Okay, yes, I was daydreaming. What the fuck else am I supposed to do? My whole body feels radioactive, and all from the memory of Nash's mouth on my dick.

"I'm here." I give Ramona a smile. Even I know it's weak.

"But where did you go?"

I can't help the way I tense up. "Where?" Does she know? How can she? Who could possibly guess how my afternoon has gone? Not me, that's for sure.

"You went over to solve another Nash crisis, and then you just disappeared. I called when I didn't hear from you after an hour. Where did you go?"

"I went to get an iced coffee." And then I got on the streetcar to come back to the office. Except somewhere between the memories of the hungry look in Nash's eyes as he sucked me off and the taste of my spunk on his lips, I completely missed my stop and got halfway to Etobicoke. If the streetcar hadn't been short-turned in the west end, I'd probably still be on it.

Ramona frowns. "Are you okay?"

"Of course!" I straighten, trying to pull myself together. "Yeah. Things took longer at Out & About than I thought they would."

So much longer. My head spins. As Nash scrubbed come off his tie, I was overwhelmed with the need to get out of there. To avoid the awkward conversations. The *"Hey, man, thanks for letting me come my brains out down your throat. Should we do it again sometime?"* I don't even know if I wanted him to say yes or no. I just know I never felt more in control of anything in my life than I did in those moments after Nash dropped to his knees.

When I go back the next day, I'm sweating in my shirt, and my throat is dry. Nash's door is open as I walk into the festival office, and I falter for a second.

"He's not there," a voice says, and I turn to find Patrick looking up at me from his computer.

"Where'd he go?" I say before I can stop myself. At least I manage not to whine, but what was I expecting? An encore performance seems unlikely.

Patrick shrugs. "There's no internet in his office. Harpreet said he was working at home today."

Of course he is. What a perfectly logical answer.

I get the new extender installed and am testing the connection on my phone when Harpreet appears.

"All set?" she says.

"Looks like it."

"And it works in Nash's office?"

My confident smile fades. "It should."

Harpreet looks uncomfortable. "Would you mind double-checking? I told him I'd give him the all clear. I'd hate for him to show up and something's still not working."

The request is reasonable. But still, as I stand in Nash's office doorway, I feel shy. I glance over my shoulder and Harpreet is watching me, so I lift my phone, like I've been running some kind of diagnostic. "Still good."

The office is silent. The desk orderly. Garbage can empty. Nothing out of the ordinary has happened here. Gently, I lower myself into Nash's chair. For Harpreet's sake, I make a show of disconnecting from the Wi-Fi and reconnecting it. No problem. When I look up again, she's gone back to her office.

I should go. Ramona is taking a long weekend, so I'll be on call by myself until Monday. But I can't make myself get up yet. I glance at the door, open now, but closed yesterday. I'd been all set to leave then too, but Nash had touched me, obliterating my resolve at the last second. I couldn't not kiss him, and then once we'd started . . .

I rock back in the chair, the leather creaking, and the motion makes me think of what it would be like, the two of us in this chair. Hands, mouths, my cock in Nash's ass as he pleads for more, his gaze full of that needy gleam it had yesterday.

I could wait until he comes back . . .

Except of course that's a terrible idea on nearly every front. But it's so tempting. The thought of going back to work, of calling more clients, of sending more emails . . . In the heady memories of what we've already done in this office, it's hard to escape the desire.

But Nash and I have no understanding on what happens next, and I don't just have a job, I have a business to run, so I give myself one last second to soak in the scent of Nash that lingers in the air and the remembered sound of his soft grunt as he came in his fist, before I put my grown-up socks back on and get back to work.

My dad calls that evening, just as I'm digging into my take-out curry.

"Hello?" I say around a mouthful of coconut rice.

"Hey, sport. Am I catching you at a bad time?"

I grimace. I try to see my dad every couple weeks, but lately we've communicated more by phone and text than face-to-face. Even the phone calls have gotten spotty.

"No." I stuff a fresh roll in behind the rice and chew quickly. "Just finishing dinner."

"How you been?" I can hear the smile in my dad's voice, which only makes me feel guiltier that I've been out of touch the last little while.

"Yeah, good. Busy." I wince, knowing how insufficient it sounds.

"Busy." Dad snorts. "Brady, I'm going to outlaw that word from your vocabulary. You use it every time we talk. It gives me no new information."

My dad is my biggest supporter in every way imaginable. When other people's parents would have thrown up their hands in disgust after I quit my fourth job in three years out of school, Dad shrugged and waited for me to make my next move. He reviewed my business plans, introduced me to my first client—a tiny travel agency down the street from his house in Greektown —and even fronted me the money on my start-up costs when my credit cards were done and I still didn't have the cash flow I needed to keep going.

"Yeah, it's good," I say, scrambling for work-related details that aren't Nash's shining eyes and the wet suction of his mouth on my dick. My dad and I are close, but there's close and there's weird, and the line is a pretty obvious one. "I'm working on a quote for a new client. He runs a bunch of tutoring centres."

We talk about a few other clients—very specifically not Out & About. My dad's a great listener and gives good advice. He's a teacher. He's been teaching middle school students about integers and Canada's role in World War I for longer than I've been alive. The man has more patience in his little finger than I do in my whole body, and if he can get bored thirteen-year-olds to care about the Somme, then he can find a solution to almost any problem.

Except the one problem we always come back to, somehow.

"You've been getting out?" he says.

I pretend I don't understand what he means. "Sure. We've had the co-working space for nine months now. You came by right after we moved in, remember?"

"Brady," he says in that "we both know you're bullshitting me, but I'm not professionally allowed to say *bullshit*, so let's cut to the chase" way that only career teachers have. "I mean are you getting *out*? Seeing friends? Anyone?"

"Friends?" I roll the word over my tongue like I'm a Muppet. "What does this mean? Friends?"

He laughs, but I can't distract him. "You work a lot. I haven't seen you in two months."

"Sure you have! I saw you . . . " I do the math. It's July . . . June we did the install for the pharmaceutical tech start-up in Vaughan, and Ramona was away for a weekend to go to a wedding. May . . . in May I lost three clients who all went out of business in the same week, which meant I spent all of May hustling to find new clients to fill that revenue gap. But the long weekend, I would have . . . Oh. No, I spent the long weekend in a virtual summit for IT specialists and finishing the last assignment in a certification course I needed. So . . .

"Have I seen you since Easter?" I ask, suddenly horrified.

Dad laughs again. "We came over for your birthday."

My birthday. Did we go out for dinner? I don't remember a party.

"Your mom and I brought meatloaf and strawberry short-cake," Dad says helpfully, and suddenly I remember. The sight of them, standing together in the apartment door. My first thought was that I was dreaming. The second was that they had come to stage an intervention. And maybe they had. We got as far as opening a bottle of wine when the football phone went off. It was Nash. The festival website was down. Web hosting isn't even part of my service, but I spent two hours on the phone with some hosting provider I had undoubtedly woken up in Ukraine before I managed to get it resolved. When I finally came back to the living room, my parents were gone, the cake was in the fridge, and the meatloaf was staying warm in the oven.

At least they had the good grace to drink the wine. I felt bad enough as it was.

Still, was that the last time I saw my dad?

"I'm sorry," I say.

He sighs. "It's fine. You're an adult. But I worry. There's working hard and then there's . . . "

Whatever I'm doing.

I poke at my curry. "Did Mom tell you to call me?"

"I haven't spoken to your mother since your birthday. She said something about doing a silent retreat. Maybe it went long."

I snort. "Sounds about right."

We talk more. Nothing consequential. The NHL draft, a family friend who announced he's retiring.

"I've got Spotify on my phone twice," Dad says.

"What?"

"I don't know how I did it, but one of them has my free account with all my saved playlists, and the other one has my credit card, and I want them to be in the same place. Do you know how to do that?"

"You can't download the app twice."

"Well, I did. Do you think you could come by and figure it out?"

I close my eyes and smile softly. Dad's prowess with mangling technology is pretty impressive. He's old enough that a lot of twenty-first century tech is a bit of a mystery, but he's just savvy enough to be dangerous. Somehow, though, I suspect he's now going to spend the next week trying to figure out how to download two instances of the same app on his phone so I can pretend we both don't know this is an excuse for us to get together.

Which . . . I owe him.

"Yeah. I'll come by next week."

"I look forward to it." The pleased tone of his voice makes my chest warm. "And try to maybe go have a drink with the guys sometime, okay?"

The guys. Do I even have guys? I'm sure there are a few friends from school and old jobs who would let me tag along if I randomly texted and asked what they were up to. But my social life has basically become Grindr hookups and text messages with Ramona.

And sucking off Nash in his office.

After I hang up with my dad and am stuffing lukewarm curry in my face, I stare at my phone, lying black and shiny on my table. Easy enough to find a little company, but the idea of logging into a dating app makes me uneasy. I don't just want any company.

I know his phone number, of course. I can dial it by heart, even if it weren't saved in my contacts. But it's in there for use in a strictly professional capacity, and it's not even like I'm thinking about calling him to see if he wants to do something as innocent as go out for a drink. None of the images in my head are innocent.

I clean up the remnants of my dinner. Leftovers in the fridge. Curry makes good breakfast. Dishes in the dishwasher, even though it takes me at least a week to fill it enough to make it worth running.

My phone is still on the table when I walk back.

Would it be so bad to call him? We don't have any boundaries left to cross. What's the worst thing he can possibly say?

With shaking hands, I dial his number.

10

NASH

I don't see the missed call until Saturday morning. After a lot of negotiating, Dominic finally agreed I'd get a makeup weekend with the twins, and I've plugged the phone in to navigate us to the zoo. It's about a million degrees outside, but I promised Jacob and Karter we could go.

Missed call from Brady Jansen.

It came in last night about the time I was popping popcorn and getting the boys set up on the couch for their first viewing of *Star Wars*. Dominic was never a fan, but it's way past time for the kids to be indoctrinated. Jacob was enraptured. Karter hid behind a pillow for all the lightsaber battles. We might have to wait another year before he's ready for *Empire*.

Without thinking, I connect to voicemail, and Brady's voice, tinny on the speakers, fills the car.

"Hey. It's . . . it's Brady. I guess you probably know that."

Something about the way he says his own name makes my face heat and my throat go dry, and I punch frantically at the screen, popping the phone off its holder. It tumbles into the wheel well at my feet, but at least the recording cuts out.

"Daddy? Who was that?" Karter asks from the back seat.

My knuckles pop as I squeeze the steering wheel, but I give both boys a big smile. "Just a friend from work."

A friend. Fuck. Why was he calling? And why did I think playing his voicemail for my children was a good idea?

Of course, he didn't say anything that could be misconstrued. He might even have been calling for some perfectly professional reason, but seeing as how I've barely had a birds-and-bees talk with my kids, I'm sure as hell not introducing the idea of Brady and random office hookups to them.

We have a few tense minutes as we finally get on the highway, where Jacob suddenly announces he has to pee and absolutely can't wait, and then I have to navigate my way over eight lanes of traffic to the next off ramp and find us a McDonald's where I can rush both boys inside. Predictably, this detour leads to pleas for french fries and McNuggets that I would normally say no to, especially since it's only ten o'clock in the morning, but I've really pushed that this is a special bonus weekend with endless fun, so it's McNuggets and fries for everyone, followed by another trip to the bathroom, before we get on our way again.

And that's how our morning goes. We park a million miles from the front gate, because we're later than I wanted to be, and I join the legions of parents trying to cajole their kids into putting more sunscreen on as we make our way inside. But, finally, we're there, at the zoo like I promised. The sun may try to bake us into the concrete, but we're going to have a good time.

Jacob wants to see the cheetahs. Karter wants to see the raccoons.

"Buddy," I laugh. "We have raccoons at home. And you have Henry. You don't have to come to the zoo to see them."

He looks up at me with curious eyes. "You have raccoons at the apartment?"

My smile freezes. When I said 'at home,' I meant the house in Markham. God only knows Toronto's raccoon army is ubiquitous and cunning enough that I wouldn't be surprised to find one on my nineteenth story balcony, but I hadn't been picturing that image as I'd spoken.

"Just Henry," I say slowly. "I meant at your house. With Papa."

Their house. This separateness. It's a loss of identity, and here I am, trying to buy back time with them using fast food and orangutans.

We're still full of McDonald's, but we stop for lunch around one, finding a picnic bench in the shade. I packed a cooler of carrot sticks and cheese and crackers, which the boys inhale between busy gulps on juice boxes. They chatter about the animals they've seen so far. Karter is still on the hunt for his raccoon, eyes roaming around us continuously in case one could pop out of a garbage can at any minute.

It's only after we've packed up lunch and headed to the zoo's splash pad to cool off for a little while that I remember Brady's voicemail. The boys are chasing each other around a fountain shaped like a killer whale, laughing and kicking up water. Keeping one eye on them, I fish my phone out and play the voicemail.

"Hey. It's . . . it's Brady. I guess you probably know that." For a minute he seems uncertain, and the sound of it is so at odds with the image of the man standing over me, telling me I can't come until he does, that I wonder if I made the whole memory up, but then he coughs to clear his throat, and his voice deepens. "I was . . . I was wondering what you're up to tonight. If . . . if you wanted to get together. Um. Yeah. You have the number. Call me."

The longer he speaks, the more trouble I have breathing. Thank God I've got an Avengers towel in my lap, because every word drains blood from the rest of my body and sends it south where my dick perks up eagerly.

Except the voicemail is eighteen hours old, and I'm sitting at a splash pad in the middle of a damn zoo where I'm supposed to be watching my children.

As if on cue, Jacob runs up to me. He's soaked, his hair plastered to his head, eyelashes making spikey triangles.

"Having fun?" I say.

"My stomach hurts."

"How much—" But before I can even get the whole question out, his face twists, and I wind up with a lap full of nugget- and carrot-stick-scented vomit.

Our zoo trip is effectively over. The drive back into the city is subdued, and I'm disappointed that our day was cut short. For a second, I consider going north instead of west and taking them back to Markham. Dominic will be beside himself when he finds out Jacob's sick, but inevitably the story about the trip to McDonald's will come out, and I'll get a lecture about not feeding the boys crap.

I can't get the smell of puke out of my nostrils. I don't need Dominic's nagging on top of that. If he had his way, they'd live on macrobiotic yams and free-range protein powder.

And it does seem to only be an unfortunate combination of processed chicken, fruit punch, too much sun, and tender seven-year-old stomachs, because we get back incident- and vomit-free. Jacob's still feeling pretty low, though, so I get the boys installed on the couch and put on some of the animated *Clone Wars* series to let them chill.

"I'm just going to call Papa and let him know what happened," I say. Now that everything is under control, I can call without fear of screaming.

Except Karter says, "You can't!" before I even turn.

I pause. Karter's not one to object to very many things, especially something as innocuous as a phone call. "Why not?"

The boys give each other nervous looks.

"He's not home," Karter says.

"Did he go to Aunt Miranda's?"

"No." Karter looks really uncomfortable now, and even Jacob sits up.

"He went hiking," Jacob says.

"Oh." Something prickles along my nerves. Dominic's never been very outdoorsy, but hey, we're both getting to know ourselves outside our relationship, so maybe he's trying out new hobbies. I should let him know I took up yoga.

"He went hiking with Karim," Karter says.

My heart stutters. "With who?"

"Dr. Karim." Jacob shrugs and lies back down.

Karter grins at me. "His name is Karim, and I'm Karter. That's pretty funny isn't it? If he and Papa get married, we're going to get our names mixed up all the time." He flops next to his brother, giggling.

Except I'm not sure what's so funny. Who is this person? A friend? A boyfriend? Never trust a seven-year-old with critical details, and I don't want to upset them by pushing. They aren't responsible for who Dominic meets or introduces them to.

But is he dating? Is it serious? It sounds like the boys have met this person, so it damn well better be serious.

I nearly call him, demanding answers, but my role is the uncaring workaholic ex-husband, not the hysterical one. That's Dominic. He's always good for making a scene. But I should have some say in how my kids meet future prospective partners, but the truth is, I don't. Because they aren't only my kids, and I have no control over Dominic's choices or his love life anymore.

We've been split up for a year, divorced for six months. He wanted a partner who was there more, who worked less, so I can't really be surprised if he doesn't want to be single.

Do I want to be single?

I glance at the kids before I pull my phone out.

Brady is the first person I've so much as touched since my marriage ended. I know there are ways to meet men, but my knowledge is pretty academic. I met Dominic before smartphones became widespread, when online dating was the sketchy thing you didn't talk about, and before swiping left and right were part of our vocabulary.

I feel old.

But it doesn't have to be that complicated. No need to wade into the swamp of apps and hookups. Because there's a voicemail on my phone that sounded like it could be something.

I can't call while the kids are here, but I can text.

Hey, sorry I missed you last night. If you're not doing anything later . . .

11

BRADY

*A*s far as booty calls go, this one has to be the most meticulously planned one I've ever been a part of. Of course, it's Nash, so I'm not surprised. Also, I haven't been this nervous to have a guy to my place in the whole time I've had a place to have guys over to. Again, that it's Nash probably plays into my anxiety.

And because I have a whole other day to stress about it. I'd already been pretty busy beating myself up for misreading the signs—and maybe getting caught up in my dad's good intentions —when Nash didn't answer my voicemail. And when he finally does and he says he wants to come over, my heart skips then does a whole tap dance, because he can't come by until Sunday. So I get a bonus twenty-four hours to worry that this could all go off the rails at any moment.

For once, the football phone is quiet. Where are the client crises that will keep me distracted when I need them? By lunchtime on Sunday, I'm scrubbing the grout in my shower— like Nash is going to care about my fucking grout.

I try meditation. Hell, I even consider jerking off, but I tell myself to have a little self-respect and hold it together.

When the knock comes on my front door, I nearly jump out

of my skin. Inviting him over was a terrible idea. I should have dodged and weaved the way I've been doing until the tension between us reached another breaking point. Except God only knows where we'd be next time. We were lucky his office can't be seen into when the door is closed. Next time, we might be in the yoga studio or randomly run into each other on a streetcar and collide in a spontaneous eruption of sexual need on Queen Street.

I'm being dramatic. Also, he's knocked again. With a little too much force, I throw it open and breathlessly say, "Hi!"

His eyes glitter as he says, "I was starting to think you gave me the wrong address."

I blink as I finally calm down enough to take him in, only the sight of him gets my heart racing again.

Oh my ever-loving flying spaghetti monster. Whereas I have made an effort to dress up a bit for Nash's arrival—which is to say I got out of my usual Sunday afternoon sweats and put on a pair of jeans skinny enough to be club-worthy if clubbing were still a thing I had time for—he has actually dressed down— which is to say he's out of his button-downs, cufflinks, and khakis and into a pair of slim-fitting shorts and a soft-looking black T-shirt that clings to his chest in just the way an obliging T-shirt should.

Holy shit, is this guy actually here to fuck me? Or to be fucked? I can't even—but he's smiling expectantly at me, his face tanned and his eyes crinkling a little in the corners. The silver shines in his dark hair, and for one last second nervousness rattles around in my chest before it's overwhelmed by a tsunami of relief and lust that has me burying my hands in his still-so-obliging shirt and hauling him through the door.

He laughs softly, a rumble in the back of his throat that vibrates over his lips as they press against mine. Nash runs his hands down my sides, more gently than the way I'm crushing his shirt in my fists, but doesn't resist as I pull us around until we're back to where we always seem to be these days and I can cover his body with mine while I make the wall do all the hard work.

"Hi," he says against my lips.

"Hi."

"How was your weekend?"

I blink, stepping back. Are we supposed to talk first?

He frowns. "I wasn't sure? Seemed polite."

Oops. I asked that out loud.

"I don't know," I say, but I don't give him any more breathing room. "Did you come here for conversation?"

He slides his hands over my waist to my ass, pressing us together. "Not really, I guess."

Except it turns out he's chatty. The only time Nash isn't talking is when our lips are locked together. Other than that, anytime his mouth his free, words are coming out of it.

"Yes. That. More. Oh God. Brady. More."

We're still in the hall, and I'm half-crouched to tongue what I think is a nipple under his T-shirt.

"You're bossy," I say, glaring up at him.

"Well, I am the boss." He glares back down, but he can't hide the way his heart is thumping in his chest.

Oh, we're playing that game, are we? I straighten, crushing my mouth against his. When his lips soften under mine, I find his cock, lengthening in the front of his shorts, and give it a squeeze. He freezes, going completely still under my grip, and our eyes lock.

"When we're together, I'm the boss," I say, and the shudder that rolls through his body is almost as gratifying as the way his erection jerks in my hand.

He licks his lips, his cheeks going pink. "Yeah. Like before."

A thought occurs to me. I grin as I push a hand under Nash's shirt, caressing the warm skin beneath. His stomach flexes, and as his eyes start to close, I say, "You don't really expect me to call you daddy, do you?"

Nash's nostrils flare, and the hazy expression gathering on his face evaporates. He scowls in a way that I haven't been able to admit until now is a complete and utter turn-on for me. But the scowl deepens as he says, "What? Fuck no. I have kids."

Oh. Oh, I hadn't thought of that. I've seen pictures on his desk. Two boys. And yet, the other night, at Nash's apartment, there was no evidence of kids. The whole place was sterile and empty and—

Nash stirs against me. "Are we doing this or not?"

What am I supposed to say to that? Besides *hell yes*, obviously. I'm a red-blooded man in his late twenties. I did not invite Nash over to see photos of his kids and talk about soccer practice. If he doesn't want to go there, I am more than fine with this arrangement.

"Take your clothes off," I say, stepping back.

He arches an eyebrow. "Just like that?"

"This isn't our wedding night. It's a hookup. Clothes off." I lift my own T-shirt up from the waistband of my jeans and then wait, staring pointedly.

The black T-shirt comes first. He steps out of the brown leather Top-Siders and unfastens the button of his shorts. His gaze is on mine as he peels off both shorts and underwear.

I take a minute to look. The last time, in his office, he had every single stitch of clothing on, and I only got the tiniest glimpse of his dick as he jerked himself off into a Kleenex. To be fair, his O face alone would have filled my spank bank for probably close to the next decade, but now—

"You should only be naked," I say.

Oh, daddy. Nash O'Hara is . . . Well, he's real. He doesn't have rippling abs and pecs on the verge of needing support garments to stay upright. But he's long and toned. His stomach is flat, and his chest is covered in curling dark and silver hair that I really want to drag my nose through before I suck on his flat brown nipples. And his dick is perfect. Cut and jutting straight out from his body. He strokes it as he holds my gaze.

My brain goes blank, watching him. I feel a lot of pressure, suddenly.

"You want it like last time?" I say.

He takes a stumbling step forward. For a second, I think he's going to drop to his knees right there in the hall, but instead he pulls me forward, fingers in my belt loops, until our mouths are a fraction of an inch apart.

"Want you," he says. "Want to fuck."

I kiss him, my brain going from blank to a panicky stretched feeling. His hands are on my waistband, making quick work of the button and fly. When his fingers graze the tip of my cock, helpfully already peeking over the elastic of my boxer briefs, I gasp and jump.

"What's wrong?" Nash says.

Fuck. Fuck fuck fuckity fuck. This worked last time. Why am I so jumpy now?

Maybe because last time he had his mouth on my dick before I had time to overthink everything?

But he's here. He came to my house, my turf. Nash got naked without questioning my words. And now he's watching me with impatient silver-dark eyes, and if I don't get my shit together, I'm going to fuck this up.

"Do . . . Do you bottom?" I say, ignoring the false start.

His lip curls up in a way that has my whole body going hot.

"Always." The word is a promise and a threat, and it takes all my fear away with it, blowing down the hall with the hum of the air conditioner.

My hips roll on their own as I slide my hand inside my underwear, stroking, watching as Nash does the same.

"You want me." I make it a statement, and the stretchy feeling in my head tightens and rolls over me, gravitating to where my hand is working my cock.

His nostrils flare. "Fuck yes."

I shape the words carefully. "Want me to fuck you."

"Brady, did we have a miscommunication somewhere? I thought I was here for—"

"Bedroom," I say quickly and jut my chin over Nash's shoulder. "Down the hall. Get on the bed."

He looks down the hall, then back at me. Because I have not actually planned any of this, the lights are all out, and my curtains are pulled tight, making the bedroom like a tomb. The smart thing would be to hurry ahead and turn some lights on, but I press the soles of my feet into the hardwood and wait.

Nash gives a soft laugh. He definitely knows I'm faking this for everything I'm worth, but he turns and strolls down my hall, letting me stare at the perfect round swell of his ass as he slowly disappears into shadow.

I only move when I hear the creak of the mattress, and then I hustle forward so fast I bang my big toe off the baseboard as I make the turn for the hall. I open my mouth in a wordless shout but keep moving forward.

Nash is sitting on the edge of the bed, and I curse myself for not telling him to get on his knees and face away from me so he can't see the way the wheels are turning in my head.

I slept with this other guy, a few times. He didn't identify any particular kinks on his profile, but he was bossy enough I'm pretty sure he was some kind of Dom slumming it among the normies. He had this tone in his voice as he told me to suck him off that still makes my dick drool.

And Nash certainly seemed down with my bossier side in his office. No reason it won't work again.

I take a deep breath, concentrating on filling my chest, and say, "Spread your legs."

Nash cocks an eyebrow, but he leans back, bracing on his elbows, and spreads his knees apart. I lean to the side and turn on the bedside lamp before I drop to the floor between his legs.

As I run my palms over his thighs, he sighs, and I can feel him relax, now that we're touching again.

My tongue on his tip makes him hiss, and he grips himself tight. "I thought we were fucking."

I give him a glare. "We will."

"Brady."

I flick the inside of his thigh with my thumb and index finger, and he yelps. "Who's in charge here?" I ask.

He rubs the skin where I touched him but lets go of his cock. "You are."

"Yes. When we're at work, we can do things your way." I lick him again, tasting the drop of clean, salty pre-come that drips from him. "I like your way, anyway. You on your knees with my dick in your mouth. You liked that, didn't you?"

His throat bobs as he nods. "Yes."

"So there, you're the boss. Here, though, this is my place. So they're my rules. You want to get fucked, I'm going to suck you until you're ready to come. Then you get fucked." My heart is beating fast in my chest, but every word grounds my focus and my need. "You ready?"

He grunts as I drag my tongue around the head of his erection, but when I look up again, he's watching me, eyes hooded. Won't take much to get him going. I want to know what he smells like when he's sweaty and wrecked.

I think it's time to find out.

12

NASH

I've known Brady was a smart guy from the first time he sat across from me and answered all my questions with this rapid-fire confidence that said he was unequivocally the guy for the job.

Turns out he is the guy for many jobs.

Teasing my sanity to within an inch of its life using only his lips and tongue, for example.

He's always had a smart mouth.

Right now, my dick is exploring the back of his throat, and he's swallowing like a champ, and all I can do is stare up at the ceiling and repeat his name.

"Brady. Brady. Fuck. Don't stop."

Except every time my balls tense and my orgasm is on the verge of erupting, he slides off me, the air cold where it hits his spit on too-sensitive skin, and I whine in frustration.

"No. No, please."

His smile would be enough to make me come, except he's got a grip on the base of my shaft that would stop a tidal wave in a disaster movie.

"Not yet," he says. "Thought you came here to fuck."

"Then fuck me already," I say through gritted teeth.

He licks a line up my cock, making me shudder. Then he presses out his lower lip in a pout that would be annoying if I weren't so aroused I can't think straight.

"Mmm," he says, like he's considering it. "Not yet."

He goes back to sucking my entire consciousness out of my dick.

Fuck. Fuck, if I'd known it would be like this, I would have . . .

I would have what? What have I done lately but wallow in my anger and guilt that I couldn't be what my husband needed me to be? That my kids continue to lead their lives without me under the same roof on a regular basis?

This. With Brady. It's exactly what I need, even for a little while, to get me back on track.

Speaking of on track, Brady tongues my slit, and the pressure is building again. But instead of tensing, instead of panting and whining his name and begging again, I relax. Go limp. I spread my arms out over the mattress and exhale, waiting for the soft warm burn that will erupt all on its own.

Except just as it starts, as the trembling threatens to take over even as I fight to stay still, Brady slides off me again with a slurp and a wink before he swats at my thigh and says, "You're ready."

"For what?" I grouse, annoyance flooding back even as semen and ecstasy recede again. Fuck him. Fuck his teasing mouth and his sly smiles. I can get off at home without all this effort.

He's still on his knees at the side of the bed, and he drags one dry finger between my legs, behind my balls and over my taint until he finds the crease of my ass and the tight muscle of my entrance. He hardly brushes it, but it's enough to send my hips off the mattress, my dick lurching up like a rocket.

"Roll over," he says. I glare at him, and he smacks my leg again. His lips are swollen and slick, but they make his smile even more perfect. He raises his palm a third time. "Go on. On your stomach."

I help myself to one of the two pillows at the head of the bed and put it under my hips as I turn. He may be in charge, but my lower back isn't what it used to be. For a split second I wonder— not for the first time—if he sees an old man when he sees me, but the question flutters away at the sound of his zipper, and when I glance over my shoulder, he's pulled off his shirt and is stepping out of his jeans.

I expect him to go straight for my ass, but instead he crawls up the bed behind me, knees on either side of my hips. He spreads his body over mine, covering my back with his warm skin.

"You're so hot," he says as his mouth moves over my shoulders and the back of my neck.

I don't know what to say to that, so I rock against the mattress, groaning when his erection settles into my crease.

He grinds against me as he nips at my ear. "You want that?"

"Stop teasing," I say.

"Uh-uh." His teeth at my earlobe go from playful to painful before his tongue swirls around it, and I melt under him again. "My terms, remember?"

He flattens his palm on my ass, squeezing and exploring, while his hips continue to pump, long and slow thrusts that promise things I want so badly.

"Please." The friction is dry and would be uncomfortable, but the more he rocks, the more I start to move with him, until we're flowing together in a way that makes me think of his body, glistening with sweat as he moved through the poses in that yoga class.

"Yeah." His voice is rough in my ear. "Yeah, there you go." And the praise warms me unexpectedly.

He glides down, leaving me exposed, but his thumbs spread my cheeks apart, and I arch toward him, trying to find his touch.

"Shit, you really want this, don't you?" he says.

I really do. More in this moment than when I walked in the door, or when I drove over to the address he had texted me, or when I replied to his message yesterday, hoping the whole time we corresponded that neither of my kids would ask me what I was doing. Right now, I need him so much I—

His tongue swipes over my hole, and the single wet caress is enough that I have to bury my face in the quilt on his bed. The second pass has my whole body going hot and my brain going white. With each lick, I get further and further away from reality, until the only thing I know is the dribble of spit from my ass to my balls. The room fills with a whining moan that I don't immediately recognize as coming from my chest, but his breath on my slick skin cuts it off in a strangled mewl.

"So pretty." He rubs his thumb over me and slips inside without much fuss.

"Please. Brady, please." I'm wet and open, and I need him so badly.

"Soon." He moves away, and I'm too edgy and already too blissed out to turn my head to see where he's gone. But the slide of a drawer and the snick of a bottle cap are familiar, even though it's been more than a year for me

His fingers are cool to start, and I shout at their first invasion, but within minutes the warm slick has me writhing. "Please, please, please," I babble.

"Nash." He kisses my shoulder. "You're going to feel so good."

Another pause. Another click of the bottle cap, along with the crinkle of foil. I wait, so heavy and aching I can barely keep my eyes open. I roll when he pulls me onto my side, letting him position me how he wants. All I need is to feel the stretch as he pushes into me.

He grimaces as he pulls the pillow I've been lying on out of the way. A wet spot has spread over the cover, where I've leaked pre-come throughout his careful attention.

"Gonna have to wash this," he says absently, and if I were more with it, I'd complain that he's clearly not into this as much as I am if he's got the wherewithal to plan laundry. But before I can protest, he stretches himself alongside me. We're spooning. Not my favourite position, but he lifts my top leg and presses into me, and I really don't care what position we're in as long as we're finally fucking.

"You're tight," he says against my neck, and I'd protest, but the feeling of him, the burn and slow slide says he's right.

He retreats, and I growl, reaching behind me to grip his hip.

"We've got time," he says, but I've waited long enough. I rock against him, driving him in, gripping his hip so tight it might bruise, but I'm done waiting.

The room goes quiet, except for the both of us panting in unison.

"You okay?" he says, one hand roaming over my stomach.

I don't want to talk anymore. Don't want to wait. I rock my hips, fucking myself on his dick, searching for the feeling I had before, because what I feel now is new. Foreign. A body I don't know, moving in ways that aren't familiar. His thrusts are short, not nearly as deep as I like. Brady pressed against me is different, supporting me in ways I'm not used to, the angles hard and soft in places I have to learn for the first time, which is something I haven't had to—

Fuck you, Dominic. I don't want to be thinking about you right now.

"Fuck me," I say through gritted teeth. "Please. Stop being nice and just fuck me." I roll, and he protests, but he comes with me until I'm back to being face down on the bed. He slides out of me as we go, but I'm only empty for a minute before he's lifting my hips, pulling me back on my knees, and driving into me in one long thrust that has me knuckling the sheets.

"Like that?" he says.

"Yes, fuck yes. Thank you."

If he was nice before, he's brutal now. The careful caress, the soft exploration is gone. Our only point of connection is the pistoning of his cock in my ass. My knees are digging into my stomach, my cock trapped between my thighs. We did this position at the yoga class, but I didn't realize I'd be revisiting it so soon. I can't get off this way, but I'm okay with that for now. Brady's hips slap against me, his balls against my taint. He's breathing hard, and his strong hands have my hips held tight, so the only thing I can do is take what he's giving me. I've asked for it, so I should be grateful.

"Yes. Yes, yes."

"Fuck. Nash, fuck. You're so—" He plants a hand between my shoulder blades, driving me down. I can barely breathe, my whole torso crushed between him and the mattress, but he doesn't seem to care about my comfort anymore, and I'm so grateful. I don't want to be protected. I want to be held open and used up and—

He groans above me. The sound is a long, strangled thing, while his hips buck and his hand slides off my back. At the last second, he pulls himself out, and I hear the snap of the condom before stripes of hot come spurt over the length of my spine. He's panting and shouting above me, and I wish I could see him, but the sticky wetness on my skin is enough. I spread my knees, finding room for my hands. My cock throbs at my touch, and I'm so close. I can't get the grip I want, though. Can't find the speed. Not without moving, but my whole body is a mess of aching muscles that I can't figure out how to unwind.

A new wetness slides over my back, and the brush of his hot breath grounds me as Brady licks the come off my back.

"Jesus Christ," I moan, but the image of it, the flat stripe of saliva, the slow swipe of his tongue, it's enough. I curl up on myself, cheek pressed to the pillow, and finally my orgasm erupts in a snap that steals my breath while my body spasms and empties itself onto his bed.

He flops on one side, landing next to me while I twitch. I'm relearning how to move my limbs as he laughs.

"Holy shit. That was so hot."

My ass throbs, used and sore. It's been years since I've had this feeling. Dominic was never rough, even on the nights I asked him to be.

Slowly, we spread out. My legs finally shoot out from under me, and my stomach lands in an unpleasant wet spot. More laundry. I'd apologize, but he did this to me, so he can clean it up. I stretch my arms overhead, grimacing as one shoulder pops.

He smooths a hand over my back, still damp and sticky.

"That was good, right?" he says, and the question makes him seem so young again, looking for reassurance when he has practically fucked my grasp of language out of me.

"Uh-huh."

He snuggles up, rooting his nose into my armpit where he inhales deeply.

"We should do that again."

I groan. "Give an old man a break."

His hand comes down on my ass in a smack. "Not right now, asshole. But, like, some other time." I lift my head, and he's turned to stare at the ceiling. "We could make it a regular thing." He glances at me, dark eyes sparkling. "If you wanted to?"

I'm not sure I'll survive another round with him, but at the same time, he's here and he's willing, and he seems to know what I need. I don't want a boyfriend. A good hard fuck, that's all I want right now.

"It wouldn't be serious," I say. "I'm not looking for anything serious."

His smile glows. "Neither am I. My life is too busy for anything more than a hookup." He squeezes my ass. "But if I know it's you, it makes it easier to plan for."

I don't want to be someone he plans for. Dominic tried to plan for me, and too many nights I wasn't there when the festival needed my attention. I open my mouth to tell Brady, but an ominous musical trilling sounds from somewhere far away. It's vaguely familiar, but before I can place it, Brady leaps off the bed.

"Shit!" His feet pound up the hall.

The Good, the Bad, and the Ugly. That's what the sound is.

The music cuts out as Brady answers the call. "Hello? Brady speaking."

Gingerly, I push myself up to my hands and knees. I need a shower, but doing it here feels presumptuous. I'm surprised when my legs actually hold me as I step onto the floor. I'll hurt for days, but I'm already thinking about when we can do this again.

My clothes are in a heap, and I put them on carefully, feeling the places where muscles pull. Brady is down the hall, speaking quickly, and when I wander into parts of the apartment I haven't seen before, he is leaning against a worn dining room table. His phone is crooked between his shoulder and chin while he pokes at a laptop with one finger. His other hand is held out to one side, and I realize a used and wrinkled condom is pinched between his fingers.

"Yeah. Yeah," he says. "How long?"

He's naked, and apparently unashamed, so I take a moment to look him over. Broad shoulders, tanned skin, barbells in both nipples. His stomach is flat and has a hint of definition, dark hair swirls from his belly button down to where it thickens at his groin, and his cock, limp and resting, hangs against his balls. He's perfect and young, his body still resisting age and gravity.

"Yeah, no problem. No, not at all. I'll be right there."

My heart drops, and I don't know why. We weren't going to cuddle or order takeout and tell each other about our weekend.

I smooth my shirt over my stomach, ignoring the way the material is still finding places to stick to my back.

"You have to go," I say as he hangs up.

"Yeah. A client needs me. Football phone," he wiggles it toward me, like I should know what that means.

"No problem." Something stings in my chest, though, that someone else wants his attention when I wasn't done with him. But I have no right to expect anything else.

He strolls to the small apartment kitchen, and I can't help but stare at his ass as he opens a cupboard and bends over to throw away the condom. He glances over his shoulder as he straightens, and his smile is wicked as his eyes connect with mine.

"We'll do this again, though. Right?"

"Yeah," I say before I can think too much about it.

His grin is soft as he presses his lips to mine. We kiss for a second, the heat between us banked and sated.

"I'll talk to you soon," he says, then slides past me, bare feet slapping on the hardwood as he disappears back up the hall.

I've been dismissed, and the idea hurts more than it has any right to.

"See you soon," I say.

13

BRADY

*R*amona is back from her long weekend on Monday, and I don't do a very good job of hiding my blush when she asks if anything out of the ordinary happened over the weekend.

"What's that look for?" she says with a smile as I scrunch down in my chair and suddenly become very interested in my inbox.

"Nothing. DiNardo had a printer crisis yesterday evening."

"DiNardooo!" she shouts, trailing out the last syllable. He's a personal injury lawyer with a series of particularly obnoxious radio ads that everyone in the city knows. "And he couldn't wait until this morning to call you?"

"He was due in court at nine." No time to wait for normal business hours. I could have killed him, though. Way to spoil a guy's afterglow.

Nash. Holy fuck. I was not prepared for him in my bed. The way he fought himself and me and been so needy at the same time . . . He looked completely and utterly wrecked when we were done, and I would have loved to have a few minutes to revel in the mess I had made of him. Instead, the damn football phone ruined it all.

Also, my quilt and pillowcase were crusty and disgusting by the time I got back, which resulted in late night laundry that I would have preferred to tackle before my eyelids were like weights and my whole body was trembling with fatigue. Printers are such a pain in the ass, and it took a dozen tries to find the drivers that would get the damn thing to print. DiNardo's firewalls are brutal, even if I installed them.

"And that's all?" Ramona says.

"That's all what?" I say.

"DiNardo had a printer crisis, but otherwise you spent the weekend with your hands in your pants watching *Drag Race* on Netflix?"

I mean, basically, except for the part where I invited my favourite customer over for a booty call that turned into a truly pornographic fuck fest, and then I offered to make it a standing agreement.

His skin, though. The sounds he made. The way his body coiled tight as he reached for his orgasm before letting me drive the tempo and rhythm completely. I have never met anyone willing to wait so long to get off, even if he sniped and snarled the whole time.

Totally worth a crusty pillow.

"So, listen," Ramona says. "I'm leaving."

"Oh, okay." I don't remember her having any service calls on the calendar, but to be honest, I don't check her schedule too closely. Finding Ramona has been the best thing to happen to me in the last year. "Will you be back before lunch? Wanna go get veal sandwiches?" I've had the worst craving for one since Friday afternoon but spent most of the weekend too strung out waiting to hear from Nash to follow up on it.

"No," Ramona says, and her voice is strained in a way I don't know. Tension frames her mouth and her eyes, and the expression makes my heart stop. We've been stressed before. I've seen her gut it out while dealing with an angry customer. I've listened to her pull herself together while she tells a delinquent payer she can't help him until he coughs up some cash. But the look on her face right now is . . .

"When will you be back?" I say, but then I spot the plain white envelope in her hands and I know.

She's taken a corporate job. Systems manager. No more network setups, no more panicky calls when someone deletes an important email or can't find their contacts. I bite back the angry words that want to tell her she's kidding herself. Instead of all that, she'll spend her time clearing duplicate entries and trying to get people to buy into software they don't understand and that should make their lives easier, but only if they use them the way the developer intended, when most companies turn it into some weird Franken-system that's doing too many things at once.

I've been that guy. I've seen the glazed looks and received the angry emails when we implement company procedures that log computers out if they're inactive for too long. Everyone wants an exception made for them, but no one wants to take responsibility when someone from marketing decides to play a prank by changing a colleague's screen saver and instead accidentally emails porn to the whole management committee.

She'd laugh, but it's happened, and I was the one to catch the fallout for not predicting how dumb other people can truly be.

"I'm really sorry," Ramona says, voice wobbly. We've gone down to the office's shared kitchen to get a coffee. It seemed necessary to fortify ourselves for this conversation.

"I know," I say, blowing over my mug. And I do. Because we've been great together. She was the first person I hired, and we have been a good fit. She's patient with the customers and brings ideas I would never have thought of when we talk about how we can grow. But the new place is offering her fifteen grand more than I'm paying her, along with benefits I won't be able to afford for another five years at least, and I can't compete with that.

Still, I'm pretty much fucked. Next Friday is her last day, which means I get to take back her entire client roster over the next two weeks. Some of them I haven't even spoken to since they signed their initial contract. They're Ramona's people, and I'm going to have to build a relationship with them all over again. And just as I was starting to consider hiring a third person for our little team. I may not be able to give Ramona a raise, but I was thinking about finding a way to bring on someone fresh out of school to handle the simplest accounts and do the admin work. We could have afforded that, with the extra business I'd have time to go out and find, once I'm not the one writing all the quotes and sending the invoices.

But now I need a new Ramona. And finding someone as great as she's been is a tall order. I interviewed for three months before the day she walked into my home office and told me she was the answer to my problems.

"I'll be okay," I say. Because I have to be. Because the alternative is what? Closing up shop and seeing if Ramona's new boss wants to hire me too?

"We can still get together. As friends. Hang out." Her eyes are pleading, and somehow this feels more like a breakup than a resignation. She's not just my only employee, she's basically been my only friend for months.

"Of course," I say, but we both know I'm lying. If I don't have time for friends now, when will I make time to see her now that I have that much more to do at work?

"Brady." She puts a hand over mine. "I'm worried about you. I can't pass up this opportunity, but I need to know you're going to be okay."

Well, she should have thought of that before she quit, shouldn't she? But I don't get to say that. My work-life balance has never been her problem, and especially not now.

"I'll be fine. People are always looking for work. I'll have someone new hired before your last day." Please, God, let me find someone fast. The anxiety is already knotting my stomach, and I'm going to need a mountain of meditation if I have a hope in hell of sleeping tonight.

There's a message from Bill Immerchuk when I get back to my desk. His landlord at one of the new tutoring centres is available to do a walkthrough so we can discuss his setup. I want to tell them today isn't a good day. That I've lost my best and only employee and need a few days to make a game plan, but Bill's payments will take the sting out of the late nights and busy weekends I will to have to work until I can get someone else up and running.

The tutoring centre is big. Bigger than I envisioned when we'd talked about it. Bill is planning for a dozen work stations, as well as two multimedia rooms. I wonder how he's going to drum up the business he'll need to pay for the equipment and the square footage, but that's not my problem. He needs a dozen computers, a raft of tablets, and a color printer. He wants smart boards and wall-mounted TV screens.

"It's the parents," he says to me with an easy smile. It's about a thousand degrees outside—a million if you count the humidity—and he's dressed like a summer version of Mr. Rogers. Khakis, golf shirt, some kind of light cardigan that would be sticking to my skin. "So many millennial parents these days, and they want the technology. We can't just do paper handouts and worksheets anymore."

"And when do you want to do the install?" I ask, making notes on my tablet. The stylus shakes in my hand as I write.

"The sooner the better," he says. "School starts in six weeks, and the parents will start calling the week after that. So you work up the cost of the equipment, and we'll get started as soon as you can have it delivered."

My stomach rolls. As soon as possible. I can't manage an install this big on my own.

"No problem." I shake Bill's hand with the firm grip my dad taught me. "I'll get some costs over to you by tomorrow afternoon." I sound like the confident kind of partner you want to be doing business with. I'm sure as hell not feeling it today.

The panic attack starts on the streetcar. I haven't had one of these in a few months, and I'm almost relieved that my stress levels are somehow low enough that my body can still reach for this response when I need it. My vision goes blotchy, and my skin is too hot. My lungs fill with static, and I drop my phone as I try to flip through my apps to find the meditation one. I can barely get my earbuds in, my fingers shake so badly. I'm fucked, I'm fucked.

The soothing voice of the rescue meditation tells me to close my eyes. Behind my eyelids, sparks of red and blue and bright green burst like fireworks. It takes long minutes of breathing and visualization before my heart finally drops out of my throat and back down into my chest again. The vise that makes it hard to inhale relaxes. Goddamn lizard brain. Sometimes I wish we still had saber-tooth tigers so I didn't feel so ridiculous when my nervous system goes on alert.

I've missed the stop for the office. I text Ramona and tell her I'll be working at home for the rest of the afternoon. She probably thinks I'm pissed at her, when really I'm overwhelmed by my own choices. I would never go back to an office job again, but being the master of my own destiny means I have no one to blame for my erratic mental health but me.

Plus, I'm going to need a nap once the adrenaline finishes crashing. There's nothing quite like forced self-care after a panic attack.

The nap helps. The mountain of emails in my inbox when I wake up does not. Requests for quotes, random offers from sketchy freelancers who want to help me optimize my website and SEO but somehow can't even spell my company name right. Optimizing my website has suddenly fallen so far down my priority list it probably won't dig itself out for a decade. Who needs an optimized website when you can't keep up with the work you already have?

There are a few forwarded messages from Ramona that start with "Hi there! Unfortunately, next Friday is my last day. I'm cc'ing Brady, the company president. He'll be taking care of you."

My dad texts, asking how my weekend was and if I've still got time for lunch this week. I can't decide if it's worse to tell him I can't or to ignore him, so I lie and say I need to check my calendar and will get back to him.

On social media, I get invited to a Stag and Stag for a couple I used to hang out with but haven't seen in a year. I've already declined their wedding invite, so this invitation to a party that's basically about giving them money is a giant fuck you, or they've spammed everyone on their Facebook accounts, which doesn't leave me feeling all very special either. Even if I wanted to go for the sake of getting out and seeing people, it's the Saturday two weeks from now, which is the day after Ramona's last day. No doubt every single one of my clients' systems will be suddenly overcome with gremlins, so I'd have to leave the party early anyway.

Minutes from throwing myself the deepest pity party I can— okay, I basically kicked off the festivities this morning when Ramona handed me her resignation letter, but at the rate I'm going, I'll be at the "tequila for dinner" phase of things very shortly—I grab the only option that remains to me.

I pick up my phone and draft a text to Nash.

Wanna get laid?

Fuck, Jesus, no, that has to be the cheesiest thing I have ever written. I might as well send him an eggplant emoji and a gif with waggly eyebrows.

I delete it and try another.

Can I see you again?

Mmm . . . nope. No, that sounds like a date, and what I need right now is very un-date-like.

You were so hot last night.

True, at least, but also right out of bad porn.

I close my eyes and accept my fate.

Eggplant emoji, peach emoji, raindrops emoji, Send.

I skip the waggly eyebrows.

Fuck. Fuck fuck fuck. I may succumb to tequila yet.

Except the reply is almost immediate.

I don't understand. Are you cooking?

"Oh my God." I facepalm in real life but hold off on sending the corresponding emoji, because I *would* happen to hook up with a forty-something who has the technological wherewithal of my grandfather. If I sent the facepalm, he'd probably think I was trying to play some kind of digital peekaboo.

Finally, in desperation, I call him.

"Hello?" He sounds like he isn't expecting my call.

"Hey. It's Brady."

"Oh." Still distracted. "Hi." Nash's voice is clear, but I can also hear a lot of background noise. People cheering, a whistle blowing.

"Is . . . is this a bad time?"

"No. Uh. Not— What's up?"

I tried to be slick via text and wound up crossing all the signals, so I go for the direct approach. "Wanna come over tonight? Go for round two?"

"Oh." The word is surprised, but he follows it up with a low laugh that I can feel in my gut, even over the phone. "I can't tonight."

Of course he can't. Two in a row is too much to hope for. Too fast, too soon. Patrón, pull up a chair. I'll provide the salt and limes, you provide the oblivion.

"No problem," I say, trying to sound casual. "I just thought I'd—"

"Tomorrow?"

"Oh. Oh yeah. Tomorrow's good."

Somehow, even the knowledge that he wants to get together again is enough to stave off the call of Cuervo.

14

NASH

I haven't had so much sex in a very long time. Brady is . . . I'm not even sure I'd have been able to keep up with him when I was his age.

When he calls the first time, I'm at a soccer game, watching small people kick each other in the shins instead of learning the proper passing technique their coach keeps trying to yell at them from the sidelines. Brady's texts are a welcome distraction, because not only is Dominic here to watch the boys play, but so is his mother, his sister—Miranda—and her two sons.

"Didn't I mention it was a family thing?" Dominic says sweetly as I stop short when I see everyone all set up with their folding chairs and cooler of drinks and snacks.

"Yes, you did." But I, who somehow lost the ability to take a hint, thought he meant the four of us—him and me and the boys. That family. Except I guess that doesn't count anymore.

"Is Karim coming?" Miranda asks, watching me, and I have to clench my jaw to keep from reacting.

Dominic gives me a smug smile, but says, "Not yet." And I can't tell if that means he'll be around later or if he's not ready to meet the kids. Either way, I glare at Dominic, but he opens a can of mineral water and turns back to the game, leaving me to stew.

So Brady's text is great, even if I only sort of know what it means. His name on the screen, though, as the call rings, sits a little more uneasily, but the call is brief and to the point, shall we say, and I get off the phone relatively easily.

Dominic is watching me as I hang up. "Who was that?"

I say, "Just someone from work." Dominic scowls, and it brings old memories of the times I took phone calls in the middle of dinner or while we were waiting to meet with the social worker about the adoption, but if I can't comment on his love life anymore, he has no room to lecture me about my work-life balance, particularly not as Jacob gets the ball and hustles it up the sideline. We all turn and cheer, even though Miranda and Rosa haven't said five words to me since I arrived.

One big happy family.

By the end of Tuesday, though, I'm practically itching to get out. Of everything. My office. My clothes. Doug is trying to walk me through early submissions for the short film program, and I can't help myself from tapping at my phone screen. Even I don't know what I'm expecting to find there, other than a very slow countdown until the minute I can leave and rush over to Brady's.

"Are you expecting a call?" Doug says, lifting one bushy eyebrow.

"Sorry." I slide the phone back into my pants pocket.

Doug frowns. "I know the field's not great this year."

"No, no!" I try to smile. Doug takes a lot of pride in the slates he puts together for us. "I'm sure they'll be great. Except maybe the one about the woman learning to fist herself. We always get sexual awakening submissions, but that one . . . Are we really sure we need it? It's hardly even cinema. Just fetish."

He shrugs, and I have to smile. Doug is unflappable. He has seen it all in his years here. Everything from Oscar-calibre submissions to home video that is practically porn with a voiceover.

"We needed one more European submission. I don't know."

He rolls his eyes. "So many pieces were the same this year. Lots of staring at bridges after heartbreak and wondering if it all means anything."

I get it. But we have a reputation to maintain, and I'm not feeling that one.

I check my phone again.

Doug shuffles anxiously. "I'll see what I can do about the fisting film."

"Let me know what the other options are. We can go through them together if you want."

His smile is tight. I know he doesn't like me seeing the submissions he doesn't pick. I'm not trying to stick my nose where I'm not wanted. Just trying to be helpful.

But I'll be helpful tomorrow. For now, someone else needs my attention.

As I head toward the office door, Harpreet gasps. "Did someone die?"

"What?" I say.

"Is one of your kids in the hospital?"

"Why would you say that?" I ignore the thump of my heart at the very suggestion.

"Because you're leaving before five o'clock. I assumed you had some kind of personal emergency." She's smiling, but her eyes hold a hint of worry, as though she'd leap into action if I said either of the boys really was hurt.

"I'm fine," I say. "Just have an appointment."

Let her assume I'm having my eyes checked.

Brady lives in one of the ubiquitous towers that seem to endlessly pop up in Toronto, slowly swallowing old strip malls and factories, replacing them with perpetually looming chrome and glass. They all feel the same to me, but I can't help the way my heart starts to beat and my skin heats with anticipation as I walk down the hall from the elevator to Brady's front door.

His hand is up my shirt before I even have a chance to say hi. "Get in here."

"Hi yourself," I laugh.

"Too many clothes." He fumbles with the buttons, then flat out curses as he tries to navigate my cufflinks. I take them out myself, because I'm wearing the ones my grandfather gave me when I finished university, and I'd hate to lose one.

Finally, though, I'm naked.

Brady's mouth on my cock is the thing I've been needing all day. Wet and slick. Determined. No. Confident. He doesn't flinch when I put my hand on the back of his neck to hold him in place, and my orgasm boils out with a force that makes my knees shake.

He grins up at me, white smear on his lip. "Nice to see you."

I'm still gasping, but suddenly I'm unsure of what happens next.

Should I go? If I'm only here for sex, does that mean our time together is done already?

He somehow knows what I'm thinking, because he rises to his feet and presses his lips against mine. I can taste myself on his tongue, faint and salty.

"Don't think you can leave yet," he says. His clothes are rough on my too sensitive skin. "We're just getting started."

At my age, a second orgasm so close to the first one seems unlikely, and yet, less than a half hour later, I'm whining his name while my knees clench against his sides and my heels dig into the small of his back. My cock throbs as he thrusts into me.

"Yeah. Yeah, you want that," he chants while a drop of sweat drips off his nose and onto my chest.

The second time, we come together. He spreads himself over my body as his hips rock and spasm and he fills the condom. His groan is a deep, primitive thing, and the sound fills me with pride at the thought he wants me as much as I want him. I'd forgotten this feeling, the heady rush of need and power.

He slides out of me, and my whole body goes limp. I lie, naked and so blissfully done with everything, while he scoots off the bed and disappears up the hall to the bathroom, where I hear running water for a moment before he returns. He pulls a pair of lavender briefs off the floor, slips them on, and then flops himself down next to me with a contented sigh.

"Why didn't we do this sooner? I've been working with you for more than a year," he says as he drums a quick rhythm on his chest.

"I was married."

His smile fades, and I'm sorry for that, but he did ask.

"Divorced?" he says.

"Yeah."

"Good."

I lift my head to stare at him. "Good?" The divorce is the most disruptive thing to ever happen to me.

He shrugs. "I mean, better than if he died." He lifts his head too, so we're eye to eye. "It was a guy, right?"

I lie back down, uneasy at the confrontation in his gaze. "Yeah. Dominic and I were together for almost seventeen years."

Brady laughs and arches an eyebrow. "Should I tell you what I was doing seventeen years ago?"

"Don't you fucking dare." Christ, I can't picture him then, not while we're naked. Still a boy, like my boys.

He chuckles as he stretches, sighing contentedly. "But still, better to be divorced than him being crushed to death in a tragic garbage truck accident or something, right?"

I'd never thought about it in so many words, but I guess he has a point. "Sure."

He keeps talking. "Divorce isn't so bad. My parents split up when I was ten. Best thing that ever happened to the three of us."

I laugh bitterly. "You can't mean that."

"Of course I can." He rolls, pillowing his head on his elbow.

Brady's dark eyes are bright, and nothing about his face says he's making fun of me. "My mom was a flower child born in the wrong decade. She wanted to talk about auras and energy healing and silent meditation retreats. My dad has a chemistry degree and teaches junior high with the authority of a drill sergeant. I don't even know what they saw in each other in the first place. Mom must have been amazing in the sack in her youth. All that tantra."

"That's your mom you're talking about!"

"She's always been really bad at boundaries. Probably where I get it from." His hand runs over my stomach, raising goose bumps. "We had the birds and bees talk when I was six. And seven. And then when I came out to her, she had a whole other talk prepared."

"She sounds great." My parents are your average upper-class WASPs. I got shipped off to private school as soon as I was old enough to sleep over. I've never seen my mother look more uncomfortable than when she showed up at our big gay wedding and the chamber quartet Dominic hired played "*White Wedding*" while he walked up the aisle.

"She's a lot of fun. But she and my dad were awful together. I was young, but those last few years before they split up, we were all miserable. They fought all the time. Mom wanted to quit her job—well, her jobs. She always seemed to be working part-time at three different places—and take us all to Nepal, and Dad was trying to do grown-up things like pay the mortgage and make sure I got to soccer practice on time."

"My boys play soccer," I say absently.

"Mom thinks organized sports are barbaric and an instrument of toxic masculinity. Which . . . " He stretches his arms overhead. The hair at his armpits is black and looks so soft. I want to stroke it. "They probably are."

Is it? The boys always seem to have a good time, and the league they're enrolled in doesn't even keep score. We cheer for every goal like it's the World Cup, and then at the end of the game, everyone does a group song while juice boxes are passed out.

"And after?" I know the research says children of divorce can thrive just as well as those where parents stay together, but the guilt that I've disadvantaged my kids when they had so much stacked against them from the start eats at me.

"Hmm?" He blinks at me sleepily even though the sun's still out and will be for hours. "Oh. After, it was way better. I lived with my mom. She took me to yoga retreats and taught me about healing herbs."

I snort. "You don't honestly believe in that shit."

"Turmeric's awesome," he says seriously. "But sometimes you need penicillin, you know?"

We stare at the ceiling. I have a question I desperately want to ask, but I'm so afraid to know the answer.

"And your dad?" I finally say.

Brady shakes his head, and my heart drops.

"Nah," he says. "He's a duct tape and Tylenol kind of guy."

If it were my bed, I'd whack him with a pillow. "I don't care if he believes in traditional medicine, jackass. I meant, are you still close to him?"

"Oh, totally," Brady says immediately, but his brows wrinkle. "Well, I should probably see him more than I do. But we talk a lot. He bought into my business when I was trying to get it off the ground and no one was willing to give a twenty-five-year-old kid with a spotty employment history and no customers a loan."

My post-coital buzz is almost completely gone. I didn't realize we'd be having conversations like these. A plan where Brady fucked me senseless and we made small talk between orgasms seemed far more plausible. But the more he speaks, the more I want to know.

"But what about when you were a kid?"

"It felt okay to me. I mean, my dad's a teacher and I sucked at school, but he never made me feel bad about it."

"You had trouble at school?"

He gives me a wry smile. "Let's just say I did best in non-traditional learning environments. Sitting still, raising my hand, and being patient when the other kids didn't catch on as fast as I did were not my strong suits."

I can see that. Brady's confidence, even the way he handles me in bed, speaks of someone who likes to set his own pace.

He groans. "And don't get me started on math. Math is my nemesis. I basically spent all my teen years in summer school, but it got me to graduation."

I'm less worried about whether he can do long division and more worried about how his father managed to maintain a relationship. "If you lived with your mom, how often did you see your dad?"

He shrugs, like the question is no big deal. "I think officially I was supposed to spend every second weekend with him, maybe one or two nights a week. But it was sort of whenever it made sense, you know? Like if my mom was teaching at a retreat, then I'd go stay with him. And if he was buried in report cards, then maybe I didn't see him for a month until the term wrapped up." He laughs. "I don't know. It wasn't a big deal then. We saw each other when we did, and sometimes I think he felt guilty and would try to do these fancy things with me, like we'd go to the zoo or maybe a Blue Jays game in the summer. But most of the time, it was totally cool to just hang out at his house. He'd make his special hamburgers, and we'd play a board game or watch wrestling on TV."

"Wrestling?" I can't help myself. "Tell me you didn't watch that crap. It's all fake."

"It's performance art," he says indignantly. He shoves at my shoulder, and I shove back. We grapple for a few minutes, the bedroom filling with the sound of laughter and playful cursing.

We wind up with him on top, settled between my hips. He's got my hands pinned over my head, and when he bends down to kiss me, I open my mouth for him. God, I want him.

"How old are your kids again?" he says as he lifts his head. He's grinning, but my whole body goes cold at the question. Protectiveness swirls around me. My kids don't belong here. This space smells of sweat and sex, and it's not for them. They'll never know about Brady.

"They're seven," I hear myself say.

His grin spreads. "Both of them?"

"Twins. We adopted them through Children's Aid when they were two."

He flops over on to his back again, humming to himself. "Twins. That's a lot of work."

"It was," I say. Less when you only get them for five or six days out of every fourteen.

"Bet you're a great dad," he says.

What made him think that? I push up on my elbows, suddenly uncomfortable. I should go. Orgasms have been had. Time to hit the road.

"You ready?" Brady says, sitting up as well.

"Yeah." I say, but before I can get to the edge of the bed, he's crawling onto his hands and knees and straddling my lap. His kiss is hungry, and he pulls my palm down to the erection swelling in his briefs.

"Good. I wasn't sure you'd be able to do another round."

"What?" I can't help the way I squawk.

He pouts like the smug bastard he is. "Well . . . someone your age. If you were—"

I grab his lip between my teeth. "Don't be a know-it-all, Brady."

He swallows my growl in a laugh.

15

BRADY

*D*ear Sir,
      I am not nearly old enough to be a sir.

Dear Mr. Jensen,

Technically—no, wait, what's bigger than technically? Literally? What word means *in every sense*? Omnisciently?—my last name is Jansen, not Jensen, but you get half points for trying.

Dear Hiring Manager,

Oh, man. If you think this is the kind of company big enough to have a hiring manager, you are going to be sorely disappointed on your first day when you show up and find out it's only me.

To whom it may concern,

Oh, come on, now you're not even trying.

Hiring people is the literal—technical, metaphorical and every other *-al* you can think of—worst. From the new graduates who don't know the difference between a printer driver and a screwdriver, to the laid off corporate IT managers who want me to pay them—and rightly so, given their qualifications—50 percent more than I am capable of shelling out, the pool of applicants is both overwhelmingly large and dismally small.

How can the largest city in the whole country yield not a single person I actually want to meet?

The week has been busy. I've been out on calls almost every day with Ramona, reacquainting myself with clients that she took off my plate and I have not had to worry about in ages.

"We're sure going to miss her," one client says.

"You and me both," I say. He doesn't even know.

Nash is over almost every other night. He's insatiable. I've slept with my fair share of guys in my tender young life, but never anyone who responds the way Nash does. He arches into my touch like he craves it and begs shamelessly as I tease him with my cock. So much of my life is spiraling out of control, but with Nash, when he's naked and needs me, everything makes sense, at least for a little while.

He's late too. It's Friday night. He said he'd come by after work, but now it's closer to eight o'clock. I can't exactly text him and ask him if he's still coming. I don't know what this is between us, but it's too casual for me to be sending needy "where are you?" messages. Not like I haven't had enough orgasms already this week. If something came up—maybe with one of his kids—I'm not really in a position to complain.

Instead, I pour my frustration over the poor souls who had the audacity to think they might want to work for me— hundreds of them, and each one leaves me more certain that I'm going to wind up running this company alone. For the amount of time it would take me to hire and train up some of these people, I could be making client calls myself.

"Hey." Nash's voice in my ear makes me jump, but his mouth against my neck, pressing slow kisses into my skin, has me sinking back into my couch again.

"Did you knock?" I say.

"Mm-hmm." His hands glide over my shoulders, thumbs digging into knots that radiate pain all the up to my forehead and make me groan. "But the door was unlocked." He finds my nipples, fingering the piercings through my shirt.

"I was starting to think you weren't coming," I say as I arch up toward him.

"Sorry. Doug invited me out for dinner with his fiancé."

I pout, because I know he likes it. "And you'd rather go be their third wheel than come hang out with me?"

He undoes my shirt snaps, one at a time. "Calvin works for our largest donor. And he and Doug are my friends. I didn't think you'd mind."

Do I mind? A week of fucks and blow jobs doesn't give me much claim on him. But his words leave a sour sensation in my chest. Maybe jealousy that he has any kind of social life. I'd have gladly been their fourth wheel tonight, with Nash and his friends, if it meant not staring at this giant list of applicants I am not going to hire.

I rise and find the buttons of his shirt and work them open one at a time, drowning myself in the taste of his mouth and the scrape of his late-day stubble on my skin. His cufflinks are more difficult to deal with, unfamiliar when my fingers are used to buttons.

"Why do you wear these?" I ask, fumbling with the first one.

"They're distinguished."

"They're a pain in the ass when I want to take your shirt off."

He laughs and pulls his sleeve from my grasp. Of course, he undoes the cufflinks like they're no big thing and sets them on my table with a soft clack before holding his arms out wide so I can go back to my task of peeling him out of his shirt.

"So obliging when you want something specific," I say, sucking at his throat.

"Is that a résumé?" Nash says. His eyes are on my laptop even while his fingers slide lower to my waistband. "Looking for a job? You better not be thinking of leaving me." His voice turns to a growl, and his hands on my fly are making it hard to think.

"Nash." I might actually whine as he leaves the front of my jeans open and untended, but he kneels in front of me, and the sight of him licking his lips hungrily obliterates what's left of my Friday blues.

Nash does this thing with his tongue . . . I don't even know if I can describe it, but I already know I'll never get tired of it. He knows exactly how to tease the crown of my dick, finding the sensitive places under the ridge. And his tongue in my slit . . . the walls in my apartment are not exactly thick, and I have to bite my hand to stifle the noises that come out of my throat when he does that.

As I come, heat rushes over me. I bury my fingers in his hair. He doesn't fight me. For a guy who I used to think got his rocks off by being condescending every time he called me, turns out Nash actually gets his rocks off by letting me do literally anything I want to him. Right now, I want to watch my come drip down his chin and onto my thighs.

The football phone goes off.

"Motherfucker."

Nash looks up at me with surprise. He wipes his chin with my shirt, which came off a while ago, instead of on my skin, and I am now doubly annoyed.

"Do you need to answer that?" he says.

No. No, no, fucking no. I don't want to. Nash is still at my feet, and I know he's sporting a rock-hard erection in his pants. I can't leave him hanging. And fuck, it's Friday.

"I'm sorry," I say, skirting around him, pants around my ankles. I shuffle to where the football phone is vibrating on my breakfast bar, my ass hanging out for anyone to see. "Hello, Brady speaking."

"Oh, thank God you're there," the voice on the other line says breathlessly. I sort of recognize it.

"Yes, I'm here." I glance at Nash, who is lifting himself to the couch. He sprawls on it like a king, torso bare, arms spread over the back. The outline of his erection is plainly visible, pressed against the front of his pants, and I want to cry.

"My printer is dead."

Fucking printers. Whenever the football phone rings, ninety percent of the time it's about a printer.

"Okay," I say, trying to think in the post-orgasm haze. "Have you tried turning it off and turning it on again?"

Behind me, Nash snorts, and I give him the finger. His chuckle is dark and satisfied.

"Yes. It didn't help."

"When was the last time you used it?" Oh my God, I don't want to be having this conversation right now. Why couldn't the goddamn thing have waited until Monday to break down?

"A couple months ago."

"A couple months?" I say, frustration mounting. Who goes to the expense of a printer they only use every few months?

"We're paperless."

The thing is, if no one even turns the damn thing on for that long, the problem could be anything.

"Are you getting any error messages?"

Behind me Nash shifts. I glance over my shoulder. He's pulling himself to his feet. The front of his pants is smooth. He picks his shirt up off the floor, collects his cufflinks from the table, and points up the hall toward the door.

"No. It just won't print."

My heart picks up, and a roar fills my ears. He's leaving. I'm helping this poor sucker on the phone when I really want to be sucking Nash.

He gives me the universal signal for *I'll call you.* I grip my phone so tightly I'm surprised it doesn't crack. Thank God for a decent case.

"Hello? Brady? Are you still there?"

"Yeah. Yeah, I'm here." I close my eyes as Nash kisses my cheek and squeezes my free hand.

"So, can you come look at it?"

Yes. No problem. I'm on my way.

Nash's fingers drag out of mine, and my heart kicks up another notch. I don't want him to go. I don't want to be this person who leaves home on a Friday night to run diagnostics on a printer because someone thinks they have an emergency.

"Actually," I say, snapping my fingers. Nash doesn't turn, so I snap them again. He glances back, and I make sure I catch his eye, putting all my intention on it. He freezes.

"Actually what?" the client says.

I lick my lips as I point at Nash and then back on the couch. I keep my gaze on him the entire time. When he doesn't move right away, I snap and point again. A lazy smile spreads over his lips, but his whole body seems to roll as he makes his deliberate way back to the living room. He wants me to know that he's making the choice to stay, and my blood goes hot at the idea.

"I'm sorry." The words sound far away, even though I can feel the vibrations in my throat. "I'm already with another client right now."

Nash's smile goes devilish as he folds himself back down onto the couch, slowly undoing his belt.

"So you're not coming?" the client says.

Oh, I'm definitely coming. Nash first, but I'm patient and willing to keep us both busy for a very long time tonight. Way beyond how long the person on the phone is going to want to stay at the office waiting for me. I'll make sure of that.

"I'm really sorry. I think I'm going to be a while. I can be there first thing tomorrow." No yoga, but Nash's expression as he slides his hand into his underwear and slowly pulls out his cock says we'll both be lucky to be able to walk in the morning. Sun salutations may be ambitious.

"No. Don't bother. I'll just send the report to the print shop and pay them to take care of it." He sounds pissed, and my conscience bucks hard against my libido. I have built my client base by being available. I am the person you want to go to in a crisis. I have never, in the last three years, turned a client down when they called with an emergency.

"I can prioritize it for next week. No sense letting the printer sit there. Can we set up a time for Monday?"

"Just send me an email." His tone is flat. Fuck. I've fucked this up.

"I could—"

"That's fine. Sorry to bother you."

The line goes dead.

Nash leans back against the couch, one arm behind his head while he works his cock with the other hand. "Does this count as overtime?" he says with a smile.

I'd tell him the joke is inappropriate, but my heart won't stop pounding, even after I set the phone down. My fingers are numb, and my brain goes stretched inside. My feet don't feel like mine as I turn to face him.

I must go pale or something, because Nash's smile disappears in an instant, and his hand stills.

"What's wrong?"

"Nothing." Even I know my smile is wooden. "Just need a glass of water." Except, I stumble toward the couch instead, feeling my whole world start to crumble as Nash discreetly tucks himself back into his pants.

"Should you go deal with it after all?"

Fuck. I'm making a mess of everything.

"No. I—" I more or less collapse down next to him in a heap. "I need to sit down for a second."

The fluttery stretchy feeling always takes longer to pass than I want it to. Somewhere along the way, Nash puts one arm around my shoulder. I should tell him I'm fine. Remind him he's here for sex, not to cuddle and keep me from flying to pieces as my brain crashes through a million what-if scenarios that all start with me turning down a client request and end with me unemployed and slowly eating into my dad's pension because the failure of my venture has somehow made me both unemployable and unfinanceable. My only option is to go back to setting up lemonade stands on Dad's front porch in a sketchy attempt to earn a living.

Somewhere along my slow return to a normally functioning nervous system, Nash goes to the kitchen and comes back with a couple beers. The hiss as he cracks open each can seems overly loud, but the smooth citrus taste of the local craft brew is good, a chilling relief that grounds me as it slides down my throat and settles in the bottom of my stomach.

"Does that happen a lot?" Nash asks softly.

"Panic attacks?" I give him a rueful smile. "Less than the first couple years. Probably only a few a month. The joys of working for yourself, right?"

His jaw is tight as he nods. "I meant the after-hours phone calls."

"Oh, the football phone." I shrug like it's no big deal. "Catch-22. The more clients I bring in, the better the odds that at least one of them will have an IT-related emergency at any given time of the day or night, you know? But it pays the bills."

"But don't you have— Isn't there someone else who—" His hand on my shoulder is gentle, and I lean into it.

"She quit." Technically I could have made her take the phone for one last weekend, but why delay the inevitable? All those people have to get used to calling me. I shudder at the thought. Fuck. All those résumés on my laptop. Someone in there has to work out.

He pulls me against him, and I turn into his warmth. We don't talk about it much after that. The silver and brown hairs over his sternum tickle my cheek. I run my fingers over the softer hair on his stomach and look up at him. His mouth is incredibly close, and his lips look so soft and inviting, even when I know how rough and demanding they can be.

I've never met anyone I wanted as much as I've wanted Nash O'Hara.

When I stretch up to kiss him, he hesitates for a minute. "We don't have to," he says.

"But I want to." I slide a hand down over the front of his underwear, and we're only kissing a few seconds before I can feel his dick start to perk up again. Poor neglected boy. He was all set to go until I had a professional crisis.

I'm going to make it up to him all night.

16

NASH

We don't talk about the night with the phone call again, but that doesn't mean I don't think about it.

Brady and I have always had a certain kind of banter. The edge to his voice when I would call him from the office said he knew he was pushing my limits and liked it. I liked it too. And everything, from the firmness of his handshake to the light in his eyes said he was someone who could take me at my worst and give it all right back.

I didn't know how much strain it put on him to be that person, not just with me but with everyone. Selfishly, although maybe not unexpectedly, I never thought about who he was when he wasn't with me.

Now I've seen it, and I'm left unsettled.

I'm with him every night I can manage, some protective instinct kicking in that says if he's with me, he'll be okay.

Some nights we barely even get the door closed before the clothes come off. Others, he's already on the phone solving a crisis or taking down details, and then he has to leave. He apologizes on those nights, and I tell him it's okay, and I mean it. I'm not his husband, and the stab of disappointment as he walks me to his door isn't his fault. Nothing we've promised each other can't wait until another day.

He's at his laptop one night when I arrive, absorbed in something, but when I go to kiss him this time, he flinches away then realizes what he's done.

"Sorry," he scrubs his hands through his hair. "I'm so behind on invoicing, and they're upping the membership at the co-working space."

"Well, nothing gets my heart going like invoicing and lease rates," I say with a smile, but he doesn't laugh. When he pushes up from his chair and starts undoing the snaps of his shirt, the motion is mechanical, and his gaze is still on the laptop screen instead of my face. Not that I'm here to be wooed, but his heart's clearly not in it.

He stills when I put a hand on his. "What?"

I've come straight from a late meeting with the Ontario Arts Council. I left my laptop bag by the door and retrieve it now, pulling the computer out and setting it opposite his on the dining room table. I suppose I could just leave if we're not having sex, but I'm not that much of a dick, and I was genuinely looking forward to seeing him.

He stays standing, hands on his hips, while I sit and turn my laptop on. I undo the top two buttons of my shirt, but only to be comfortable, not because I want anything else from him.

Brady watches me for a long time without moving, like he's waiting for the punchline, so finally I say, "Don't worry. It's fully charged."

He settles back down, and I know he's keeping an eye on me. I don't want to make a big deal about this, but I need him to know I don't care if he chooses work over me some nights. Plus, I've got a funding application to update, and it's due by Labour Day.

Eventually, the keys of his keyboard start tapping, and we

both work through our to-do lists in silence for a few hours before his stomach rumbles.

"Takeout?"

"Hmm?" Brady's eyes don't leave his screen, almost like he's forgotten I'm here at all. I order us some pad Thai and spring rolls, which he eats without closing his laptop.

I don't intend to, but I worry about him. And in turn, I worry about me. Is this what living with me was like all those years? Brady is only a few years older than I was when Dominic and I met, and a year younger than when I started the festival. The look on his face, after he'd told his client he couldn't fix his printer issue right away, is a feeling I know too well. Too many times I'd be at a parent-teacher conference or on a family trip, and think that I'd check my email quickly, only to find that a funding source was pulling out, or an overseas filmmaker was being barred from traveling to his premiere, or that some idiot journalist had decided to write a think piece titled "Do we really need distinct queer cinema spaces now that *Call Me By Your Name* is in the mainstream?"

In case you're wondering, the answer to that last one is an unequivocal yes. I don't have time to go into all the reasons why, and many people have expressed it better than I have. All you need to do is google.

But every time one of those emails came through, I'd lose an hour or more. Even if the message didn't need urgent action, it would lodge in my brain like a sliver, and I'd have to mull it over while the teacher's voice became a blur or while Lightning McQueen skated by at Disney on Ice, until I finally tweezed out a solution.

"You're thinking about work again, aren't you?" Dominic would say, and I always felt guilty, but how was I supposed to not solve problems for the baby I had been shepherding into the world even longer than we'd had the boys?

Eventually, I learned to stop checking my email, but by then it was already too late.

So yeah, I know that frightened look on Brady's face, that panicked voice in his head that tells him he's the only one who can solve this problem, because I've been there too.

And I'm worried what it will mean for him if he doesn't get it under control. I don't want him to be like me when he's my age. I care too much about him to let that happen.

Except, of course, what am I supposed to do? I'm the customer who's broken all the rules and currently thinks Brady's dick is magic. Our arrangement doesn't have the longevity needed to make sure Brady hasn't descended to full-blown workaholism by his fortieth birthday.

The question nags at me while I'm in a meeting. Harpreet and Patrick, the intern, are pitching a podcast. I should be paying closer attention, but I can't stop thinking about how I can help Brady instead.

"A podcast will help us maintain some visibility throughout the year," Harpreet says.

"We can interview queer creators, filmmakers, and actors." Patrick pushes his glasses up his nose as his head bobbles excitedly.

"And some of the participants in the screenwriter mentorship program," Harpreet says.

"The who?" I say.

Her eyes widen. "The screenwriters? The mentoring program? The one you're arranging."

"Oh. Right. Right." I tap at my phone screen, watching the seconds tick away. Most nights these days, I don't even bother going home before I go to Brady's. He likes peeling my clothes off me and finally stopped harassing me about my cufflinks. We put them in a little dish on his dresser, and he helps me put them back on when I leave.

And tonight I'm on a bit of a crunch. I have a phone call with those same screenwriters this evening, so my time with Brady will be limited.

Harpreet eyes me, while Patrick's gaze ping-pongs nervously between us.

"Are you okay?" she says.

"Yeah, fine. Why?"

They continue on with their presentation. Patrick does most of the talking, and I know she's set up this pitch in part to give him some public speaking experience. He's young and earnest as he talks, as if this podcast could change the world, and he does that upspeak thing that millennials do that drives me nuts. Is he even a millennial? What comes after them? Gen Z? Something about that always makes me think of zombies. I really am that old.

"Do you want me to send them to you?" Patrick says, throat bobbing anxiously on the question.

"Send me what?"

"Nash," Harpreet hisses, and I glance at her then back at the screen Patrick is standing next to. On it are four different mock-ups with the Out & About logo.

"The ideas for the official podcast logo," Patrick says. "Should I email them to you?"

"Nash doesn't check his email," Harpreet says at the same time I say, "Which one do you like?"

The room gets quiet. Harpreet and Patrick have some kind of silent conversation before Patrick licks his lips and says, "This one. It has the festival logo, and the headphones and aux cable make it clear it's a podcast."

"Fine," I say. "Let's go with that one."

"Doug!" Harpreet's voice rises in alarm.

"What?" I say, annoyed that she's making a big deal about this when the decision should be simple.

Doug's head pops through the meeting room door, like he's been waiting to be summoned. "What's wrong?"

"Nash just made a decision in less than a minute." Harpreet points at me like I might be carrying the plague.

I roll my eyes. "Oh, shut up."

Doug shrugs. "Must be a glitch in the Matrix."

"Well, which one do you like?" I ask.

He squints at the screen, then says, "The second one, with the headphones. It differentiates the podcast from the rest of the festival."

"See? Why does this need to be a big deal?"

"Because you make a big deal about everything? Have you picked a web designer yet?" Harpreet says.

I scowl at her, but Doug is nodding beside her. I glance toward Patrick, and he looks ready to step in front of the projector beam to be incinerated rather than say anything. The way his head is tilted, a faint shine of something sparkly, like the craft glitter the boys use sometimes, is visible in his hair. It distracts me for a second before I remember I'm trying to leave.

"Is there anything else?" I ask Harpreet.

"Patrick is going to be talking to a few freelance sound editors about production. Do you want to see his shortlist when he's done?"

That sounds tedious. I check my phone again. 4:42. So close to getting out of here.

"Just let me know if your preferred editor is more than 10 percent more expensive than the others. If they are, put together a case for why we should hire them or go with the runner up."

"Are you going to want to talk to them?" Harpreet says.

"No." I go to stand. "Is there anything else?"

"What about the web designer?"

I wave my hand in annoyance. "Whichever you like is fine, I trust you."

"What is with you lately?"

I scowl. "Nothing."

But she persists. "You're leaving work early; you don't want to be in charge of making every single decision. Something's changed."

"Nothing's changed." My toes are tapping impatiently, and I have to clench them in my shoes. "You guys could run this place without me. I'm trying to give you more room to do what you're good at."

Harpreet is gaping at me, so I take advantage of her shocked silence to flee. I'm halfway to the door before she says, "Patrick's computer keeps crashing when we run PowerPoint."

"What?"

"It . . . as soon as we turn it on in presentation mode, it freezes and—" She shakes her head. "You know what, never mind. I'll call Brady."

My skin prickles at his name. "What for?"

Harpreet and Doug exchange a look.

"Because he's our IT guy?" Harpreet sounds unsure.

I shrug. "We shouldn't bother him with things like that."

"With IT problems?" Doug says slowly.

"Have you tried Google? There has to be a forum somewhere with the answer."

"Well, we *could*," Harpreet says. "But Brady would be—"

"Just try online first." I glance at Patrick. Using the intern is a low blow, but I am not above it. "Check and see if you can find the answer online, okay?"

Patrick nods eagerly, but Harpreet scoffs. "What, did you guys have a fight or something?"

I spin back to her so fast I risk whiplash. "What? No. We . . . we shouldn't take advantage of him because he's available." I resist the urge to check the time again, but I can feel the seconds ticking away. My hours with Brady are too short tonight already.

"But we pay him?" Harpreet says.

We do, but not enough. Not for the sleepless nights and the

acid stomach and the disappointed look in your son's eyes when you—

Fuck, no. That's me.

"I have to go." I do my best to save face by giving Patrick one last smile. "Thanks for the presentation. The podcast sounds great."

"Oh, Nash—" Doug says, but I push past as if I don't hear him.

My laptop is still in my office; otherwise I'd make a beeline for the door. But I don't need to stay here any longer than absolutely necessary. Grab the computer, get the hell out.

Except the second I'm through my office door, my heart screeches to a halt as Brady swings around in my desk chair to face me, grinning like a silver-screen villain.

"Well, hello, Mr. O'Hara," he says, twirling an invisible moustache. "So good of you to join us."

Carefully, I close the office door. "What are you doing here?"

He's still twirling. "I want to make you an offer. Trust me when I say you won't refuse it."

"Brady," I growl. His spinning and twirling stop, but he gives me an unrepentant smile, instead.

"Thought I'd pop by."

"What for?"

His eyebrows arch, and his voice drops to a rough purr. "I think you know."

"Brady," I sigh, sagging against the door.

He's out of the chair in a second, but the playfulness has gone out of his face and his body. "Is everything okay? What's wrong? Should I not have come?"

"I—"

A knock frays the last of my nerves.

"Yes?" I say, voice cracking like I'm Patrick's younger brother instead of his boss.

Doug's voice comes through muffled. "Is Brady in there with you?"

Brady's eyes widen, and we are going to have words later, but I yank the door open. Doug takes a step back.

"Yes, he is. Why?"

"Oh." Doug looks apologetic. "Well, he showed up a few minutes ago. I told him he could wait in your office, but then you left the podcast meeting too fast for me to tell you he was there so . . . " His gaze shifts over my shoulder to where Brady must be and back again. "Anyway." He jerks a thumb over one shoulder. "I'm going to go. Calvin and I have a suit fitting tonight."

"Yeah, sure. Thanks, Doug."

"No problem." He gives a quick wave. "Good night. Night, Brady!"

"Bye, Doug," Brady says.

I watch as he disappears into his office and can't help myself when I wait to make sure he's really leaving before I shut the door.

"You are in so much—" My threat gets cut off by Brady's mouth on mine. I sigh. No matter how many times we do this, no matter which sentences get stopped short or where we might be, this moment of collision, the need that sparks low in my belly and spreads all over me as Brady's hands and mouth take control of me . . . I can't deny how much I want this, even if it feels risky after Harpreet's questions.

But I brought that on myself, trying to make things easier for Brady. She can't possibly guess what was motivating it, other than maybe she thinks I'm looking to save us some cash on Brady's monthly invoice.

Letting go of my worries, I tangle my fingers in Brady's hair. The curly strands catch in my grip. He puts something in them that makes them smell of vanilla. Since I've never stayed the night as his place, I don't know what kind of shampoo he uses, but my brain has very quickly learned to associate the scent with the overwhelming hunger that takes me over whenever he's close by. If the boys ever want to learn to bake, I'm fucked.

Adjusting based on last time, I take a few steps forward, propelling us away from the door. I don't know what he has in mind, but we are going to be more discreet.

"Brady," I say between kisses.

"Want you," he says.

"Yeah. Yeah, let me get my stuff and we can go."

"No." He pulls me toward him. "Here."

My pulse thunders beneath my jaw as he presses himself against me. His fingers are working quickly on my belt, and even if I'm still catching up, my dick is not. It is fully on board.

"Here?" I say.

"Been thinking about it for weeks." He's pulling open my shirt now.

"Have you?" Since the first time? Since before that?

Maybe I'm overthinking things. Maybe this protective streak I've suddenly developed is going too far. We always said just sex. I'm not here to look out for him. I'm here to be a—very willing—participant as he slowly takes me apart.

"Nash?" He spreads his hands across my chest, following with his tongue over my nipples. "Can we?" He looks up at me with his endless dark eyes.

I pull one of his hands down to my aching cock, showing him exactly how willing I am. "Whatever you want."

17

BRADY

*T*urns out sex in a wheeled office chair is trickier than I thought it would be.

At least everything starts well. Makes up for the shit show that has been my day so far.

I had three interviews this afternoon. Well, I was supposed to have three interviews. One didn't show up. The second did but was twenty minutes late and didn't so much as apologize or blame transit or anything. The third one, he had clearly either bought his resume online or stolen it from a friend, because he looked completely confused every time I asked him about his past job experience. When I finally threw him a softball question and asked what part of his education or career history he was most proud of, he gave me a shy smile and said, "Well, everyone I've ever worked with really likes me."

Wow. Is that what counts for qualifications these days?

I need Nash. I'm starting to think I might be addicted to him. Not just his body and his needy sounds as I slide into him. Lately there are nights where we don't even have sex at all. He just comes over and we hang out. Having him in my apartment, eating with him, and talking about the things that keep me up at night . . . I know that's not what we agreed to, but sometimes I want it almost as much as I want his fingers in my hair while he begs me to come.

We talked about the candidates last night. He went through their resumes with me and shared some of the questions he likes to ask when he's interviewing people. I felt prepared when I left for work this morning, and then it all went wrong. I need to talk to him about it and figure out what I'm going to do now before hopelessness swallows me completely.

So I hoof it to the festival office as early as I can and, as I go, a very specific fantasy plays over and over in my head. We can talk once I've worked some frustration out.

He's stiff, at first, and I'm probably not much better. The last time, the day I came for the broken extender, we had no plan. We'd been caught up in this thunderstorm of sex and need, never mind that we were in Nash's office and people might hear us.

Today, I've come with a plan—or an idea anyway. And Doug's polite check-in to make sure we'd found each other is a reminder that we're not alone.

So we take it slow, once Nash agrees. We kiss and touch for a long time. Every second, every sweep of his lips on mine, blows the frustration of people who don't know the first thing about job hunting away, scattering it out over the Toronto skyline.

I undo his cufflinks, slipping them into a pocket so we know they won't get lost. I'm getting better at undoing them without dropping one, which is good, because while we both like having the other one on his knees, being there so I can hunt under his desk for a missing cufflink is not on today's agenda.

I push his sleeves up. He has strong arms. He likes to lock one around my hips while he sucks me off, holding me in place while he takes me all the way to the back of his throat. I kiss the inside of his wrist, running my tongue over the thin skin and fine blue veins there.

"Brady," he says, threading his fingers into my hair.

I drop to my knees, nosing at him through the fine material of his pants. I used to think his wardrobe was so fussy, but now I think he wears it like armour or a second skin to stake his place in the world.

Everything makes sense when I'm with him. When our eyes meet and I pull down his fly, I don't have to think about anything else, and that's all that I need.

He's heavy on my tongue. Smooth skin, warm blood beneath, salty fluid at the tip. I love the taste of him.

"Yeah." He leans back against the desk, arching his hips toward me. His voice is barely a soft whisper, but after so many nights together, I know the noises he makes.

My goal isn't to get him off, just to make sure he enjoys himself while I get organized. I grab the lube I stashed in his desk drawer while I was waiting—thank goodness my plan worked and no one else found that unexpectedly while they were looking for Post-It notes or pens or whatever—and pop open the cap.

"Turn around," I say, and he grins while I slick up my hands. One, I use to keep jacking him slowly. Each tug makes his thighs shake and his spine bow. The curve of his back ends in his perfect ass that I know so well. With the other slippery hand, I slowly work him open while he punches out smothered curses between his teeth.

"Jesus. Yeah, Brady. Shit. Good, so good." For a guy who was such a jerk for so long, he really is liberal with his praise once you get him going.

"I have this idea," I say, trying to keep my tone conversational, even as my fingers sink deeper and deeper into his ass.

"You're going to fuck me?" he asks.

"Mm-hmm." I love the way he softens under my hands and opens up for me.

"Against my desk?"

I dig my teeth into the thick muscle of his buttock. "No."

"At the window?"

The mental image that suggestion paints has me working my fingers faster. Not here. Even I'm not that much of an exhibitionist. But later, at my place. The windows on the north side of my apartment face the train tracks. No one would see us there, but I like the idea of Nash, willing and exposed, begging for me as commuters and freights zip by below us.

But for now: "In the chair," I say, sliding my fingers out one more time. He's open and flexes eagerly for me. The glance he throws over his shoulder is nervous, though.

"The chair?"

I rise, shucking my pants and getting myself ready with a condom and lube. Nash is back to bracing himself on the desk, shirt open, cock out, and his smile goes crooked as I settle myself in his black leather chair, sinking low and letting my thighs sprawl wide.

"Come on," I say, crooking a finger toward him. He does as he's told, but he hesitates when our knees knock together.

"I don't—" He braces his palms on the chair's arms. "I could—" But the chair tilts and creaks ominously as he lifts a knee.

"Other way." I turn him, then guide him back toward me. Positioning ourselves still takes a little more work than I expected. Every time he leans back, the chair scoots backward too. We finally have to let it glide all the way to the wall to keep it still.

He shakes as I brush a hand over his spine.

"Are you laughing?" I ask, annoyed that my plan has not been quite as effortlessly pornographic as I'd hoped.

"Aren't you?" He throws an arch glance over his shoulder.

More like pouting, but now that we have some support, I pull him backward, and this time, he slides down onto me with a long, low groan.

The chair squeaks as I start to thrust. He's heavy on top of me, and even with the wall behind us, we shift awkwardly as I try to set the kind of pace I know he likes.

"Should I—" He shifts and squirms.

"Just a second, I—"

"Are you—"

"Hold still while I—"

"Could you just—"

We both shout as the chair tips to one side. Nash puts a foot out, saving us from tumbling to the floor.

The room is silent before he shakes with muffled laughter again. I bite at his shoulder. "Shut up."

"Sorry. I can't help it." His voice is louder now, even though *now* is the time for secrecy. Anyone who walked in right this second would get an eyeful we'd all regret. I pinch him. Nash O'Hara, terror of the queer film festival circuit, is flat-out giggling in my lap. I growl and force him up. Somehow, despite all the contortions, I've managed to stay inside him, and slipping out now is a loss, but before I can even begin to reorganize, Nash drops to the carpet, spreading his shirt out like a blanket before he lies down on his back, knees wide.

"You're overthinking this, Brady," he says.

I mourn my chair vision a moment longer, but really, what's there to overthink? He's willing, I know what he likes. No need to make this harder than it needs to be.

His satisfied groan as I slide back into him warms me to my toes. How did this happen? Every snipe, every name he's called me, every time he's told me not to be a smart-ass. Was it always going to lead to this?

And what do we do now?

The air conditioning cools my skin as I thrust, watching his face intently for all the things he loves. When we hit our rhythm, the point where pleasure takes over and we're moving with each other, his lips always turn up in the corners. I don't even know if he knows he does it. Just this sleepy, happy, contented smile that says he has nowhere else he wants to be right now. I do that to him.

"You feel so—" I hesitate because I want to say *right,* but the word feels too big somehow. "So good."

He brushes a hand over my cheek and slips a thumb in my mouth. I run my tongue over soft skin and small calluses before I let him draw me down for a kiss.

"Brady." His soft voice is rough. "I'm ready. Fuck me."

The rhythm changes, moving from the easy flow to sharp thrusts as I pick up my pace. I want to wrap myself all the way around him so he can feel me, inside and out. I want him.

I love him.

The thought is so sudden and loud in my head that my hips falter, and Nash digs his nails into the small of my back, urging me on.

"Come on," he says between clenched teeth. "Come on."

He doesn't know I'm suddenly living in a new reality where I'm in love with Nash O'Hara.

"Fuck me, Brady," he grits out.

Right. First things first. Orgasms now, paradigm shifts later.

He shouts when my cock hits his prostate, and I press a hand to his mouth, trying to smother his sounds.

"You're mine," I say, biting at his earlobe. His hands skitter over my back as I piston into him, over and over, driving him to the edge.

"Don't stop. Don't stop. Fuck. Jesus. Brady. Don't stop."

Sometimes I stop. Sometimes I like to listen to him howl as I back off and his orgasm recedes, leaving him begging and frustrated. He knows I'll never leave him hanging completely, but those moments, when he's angry and understands that his pleasure is entirely under my control, are pretty heady.

Not as heady as the certainty that floods me now, though. I love him. His moods, his snark. I can see how much he cares, underneath it all.

So I don't make him wait.

"Touch yourself," I say, pulling up onto my knees. "Show me."

He makes this heavy whine in his chest as he starts to jack himself. The head of his dick is nearly purple, and he works it relentlessly as I pull his legs wide and rock into him, looking for the spot that drives him wild. My own orgasm is building, tingling in my back and in the tightening of my balls. I'm ready when he is, and the flush spreading over his cheeks and chest says he's close.

I love you.

I love you.

The words are there, on the tip of my tongue, and part of me thinks saying them will be the thing that pushes us both over the edge. But, in the end, Nash's jaw clamps shut and the cords in his neck strain, and he doesn't need anything so kind from me before he's splashing come all over his belly and his ass spasms around me like the best kind of fist, holding me tight as I spill deep into the condom.

He lets me collapse on top of him. I feel like jelly, but somehow Nash still has enough control to run his hands restlessly over my body, raising goose bumps as I shiver in the cool air.

"Your office is cold," I say, amazed I can string that simple sentence together.

He rumbles contentedly under me. "We didn't set the thermostat with nudity in mind."

Nash grunts as I slide out of him. I grab a few tissues off his desk and wrap the condom in them. We're a mess, sticky with lube and Nash's come, but I came prepared for that too. In the drawer where I'd stashed the lube and condoms, I also left a pack of disposable wipes. I grab it, the plastic crinkling, take a couple for myself, and toss it to Nash. He catches it but gives me a wry look.

"What?" I shrug. "You'd rather try to deal with tissues?"

He shakes his head and dabs at his skin. "I'm going to need a shower anyway, even with these."

"You can shower at my place," I say. As the fuzzy buzz of orgasm recedes, the day's events—the missed interview and the poser who is barely qualified to tie my shoelaces—come back. Right. I need to talk about some of this. Maybe we can grab a pizza and he'll let me talk through my new plan.

My heart drops when he shakes his head. "I've got a call with the screenwriters at seven. I was going to try to grab a quickie at your apartment before I rushed home. But now . . . " He trails off as he wads the wipe up and tosses it to the trash with all the style of an NBA superstar.

I open my mouth to say he could come by anyway or even do his call at my place. I have to go through another tranche of resumes. I'll be quiet as a mouse while he inspires future movie-making icons. The idea of going home alone makes me queasy.

But he's already on his feet, pulling his pants back up. He won't quite meet my gaze, and for once, my courage fails me.

"Yeah, no problem," I say. "I've got a bunch to do tonight anyway. Better if you're not there to distract me."

He huffs a laugh as he lifts his shirt off the floor. We've wrinkled the hell out of it, but it slides over his skin with a hiss that makes me want to wrap myself around him all over again.

"Where'd you go?" he says.

"Hmm?" My own shirt is not nearly as accommodating. I've done it up but somehow missed a button, and now I have to start over.

"You got this look on your face for a second. In the middle of it. Like you were thinking about something else."

"No." I give him a smile that feels too tight at the edges. "Just thinking about you."

About how I don't feel about him the way I've ever felt about anyone else. About how it's more than hormones and sex, and maybe always has been. Nash challenges me more than anyone else, but he gets me better than anyone else too. And I don't know what to do with this information.

"If anyone asks," I say as we head to the office door, "I was helping you sync your contacts."

He snorts. "Is that what you kids are calling it now?"

I laugh and shove at him. His whole face creases in his answering grin.

"You know what I mean."

Nash shakes his head. "They'll have all gone home anyway."

Except, when we open the door, we're greeted by a set of wide eyes behind thick glasses.

"Oh." Patrick pushes his specs farther up his nose. I can only sort of see him over Nash's shoulder. "I thought you must have left."

"Cell phone problems," Nash says. "You're here late."

"Yeah." Patrick shrugs. "I'm meeting someone downtown in a little bit. Didn't make sense to ride transit all the way back out to my apartment."

"Where do you live?" I ask, clinging to the *keep it casual* mantra echoing in my head.

"North Etobicoke? Near the airport."

Makes sense. He's glancing nervously between us, but every time I've met Patrick, he always seems nervous, so his expression now doesn't mean he heard anything untoward coming from Nash's office.

But we weren't exactly quiet. Not at the end anyway. Not the way I would have been if I'd known the intern was still out here listening to us. At least we got off the chair before we wrecked the place completely.

"Well," Nash says, "make sure you turn the lights out when you go."

"Oh, yeah. Yeah, of course." Patrick gives us a smile and a goofy thumbs-up.

We don't exactly hurry out of the festival office, but I'm not sure we manage to be convincingly low-key as we go.

"I'll see you later?" Nash says as we step out onto the street.

"Yeah. Yeah, sure," I say, sounding about as confident as Patrick did. For a second, I almost rise up on my toes to kiss him goodbye, but I catch myself before I can give us away.

I can't tell him I'm in love with him in the middle of rush hour on Sherbourne Street, can I?

Whether he knows it or not, Nash answers my question as he turns and walks away.

18

NASH

*S*omething's changed, and I don't know what.

On the one hand, suddenly everything at work becomes a whole lot easier. I let Harpreet and Doug run things, leaving me to handle only the highest level administration. I have time to review mentorship applications and still get to leave most days by five or five thirty.

Or maybe I'm making sure to leave early because I'm worried about Brady.

Don't get me wrong. On the face of it, everything is still good. He meets me at his apartment door with hungry anticipation on his face and desperate hands that pull at my shirt. He uses me and cares for me at the same time, leaving me simultaneously fucked out and already counting down until we can go all over again.

But he's different. I'm not an idiot. I notice the moments he goes to say something and changes his mind. Or the look he gets when we're face-to-face and he's deep inside me and moving with the confidence and control that has pulled me toward him for what feels like forever. The look says he's not really there, that he's already thinking about something else. Every time, I try to bring him back, remind him that I'm here and I want him.

"Brady. Come on. Please."

And every time, he comes back to me, gathering himself to drive us both over the edge, his mouth and body and great big brain knowing exactly what we need.

Inside, though, I'm afraid, because Dominic must have gotten that look—already planning his speech that we were over and I needed to leave— and I didn't notice, not until it was too late.

We tried, of course. We went to counselling for a year. I tried to shorten my work week, but he'd literally caught me at the worst moment, just as we announced the festival lineup and everyone went into hyperdrive for two months. By the time it was over, I was at such a deficit I never got it back.

How many signs did I miss with Dominic?

I won't miss them with Brady. Whatever is going on, whether it's us or something at work, we're going to deal with it before he tells me he doesn't want me anymore.

Except, of course, I have the kids this weekend, and so any and all discussions need to be postponed until they're gone. I feel guilty, anticipating their departure, but finding the balance point between work and family has always been my weakness, and adding Brady to that mix has only complicated things. I don't mind leaving work early to see him, but my kids deserve my attention too.

We take a page out of Brady's "child of divorced parents" handbook, though, and I don't try so hard this weekend. We sleep in—which, when you're seven means no one gets up before six-thirty for a change—and, instead of trips to the zoo or science centre, spend most of the time in my apartment, where we play games and watch movies. The approach is moderately successful. I try to teach them to play Clue, but Jacob can't keep track of the rooms, and Karter keeps trying to peek at his brother's cards. Operation is better, in that they're both equally terrible, and because who ever follows the rules for Operation anyway?

On Sunday morning, we go to the community pool, which is down the block from my building, but which I have never been to before. I make them put on their swim shirts, because Dominic will scream bloody murder if either of them come back with anything remotely like a sunburn. Karter puts his on without protest and hops straight into the water. Jacob howls like I've told him Santa doesn't exist.

"It's not fair!" he says. "These are for babies."

"They're for boys who want to go in the pool. The other choice is to not put it on and sit here in the shade next to me, and we can watch your brother swim together."

He glares at me, letting me know I am the source of everything wrong in the world. His eyes are flat and steely, and his thin shoulders square as he spoils for a fight. If I could show fear in front of my children, I would acknowledge that Jacob will be a huge handful as he hits his teen years.

"I don't have to wear one at the cottage," he says.

"Yes, you do."

"No. Not this summer. Papa says I only have to put sunscreen on."

Oh, he does, does he? Well, my house, my rules. I'm not even sure how I'm going to keep track of them, amidst the hundred bobbing heads in the water and the six competing games of Marco Polo that seem to be going on at any time. The brightly coloured shirts help tell them apart.

"You can put the shirt on and swim, or you can sit and pout. These are your options."

He glares. We're in so much trouble. We'll be lucky to make it to twelve without some serious behavioural issues, but I hold firm. Finally he slides the shirt on before he hurries off to the edge of the pool and promptly cannonballs over the side, splashing his brother as he goes.

"How old is he?"

I glance to my right, and a guy with a silvery buzz cut, a five o'clock shadow—even though it's ten in the morning—in the same color, and a shining ring in one ear smiles from the opposite side of the bench.

"Seven," I say.

The guy nods, then points as a dark-haired boy who waves from the end of the diving board. "Mine's nine."

"Cool." I go back to watching Jacob and Karter. They are racing across the pool. I don't really want to get in there today. Public pools freak me out. But if they crash into someone as they flail through the water, I'll have to intervene.

"You been here before?" Silver Hair says. He could be a biker, or else the drummer in a Bruce Springsteen cover band, but the tough exterior is betrayed by the backpack he's got one hand on, which leaks a variety of water bottles, snacks, towels, and sunscreen. I'm very familiar with this backpack. I have a similar one by my foot.

"No."

Jacob wins the first lap, and Karter immediately challenges him to a rematch.

"Giving your honey the morning off then?" Silver Hair says. Geez, he's chatty.

"No, I'm divorced."

"Me too. Split up with my husband last year," he says. I give him a sympathetic smile. Just because same-sex people have only been able to get married in Canada for the last fifteen years doesn't mean those marriages don't fail like straight people's, I guess.

"Dad! Dad!" Karter's voice echoes from the edge of the pool. "Watch me!" Then he belly flops into the water with a smack that makes me wince.

"You . . . you with anyone?"

I almost say I'm with my kids but stop when I realize what he's asking. Seriously?

He gives me a nervous once-over and a sheepish smile. "Sorry." He runs a hand over the back of his neck. "My ex-husband left the country. More interested in his Instagram career than his family. Hard to meet people when you're parenting all the time, you know?"

I gape. Jesus Christ, is this my life? Picking up guys at the community pool? We've traded in the sweat and booze for chlorine and juice boxes.

"I'm seeing someone, yes," I say. Someone who has a secret he doesn't want to tell me, but that's not the point.

Silver Hair fumbles with the straps on his backpack. "Oh. Yeah. Sure. Can't blame a guy for asking, right?"

I consider him. Despite his hair, he can't be more than forty years old. He clearly works out, and I can see where he'd appeal to a lot of guys.

But he's not Brady. Now, more than ever, I want to see him. I don't want to meet other people. Hang out around pools looking for other lonely gay dads. Whatever is going on with Brady, I need to find a way to fix it.

"Dad." Karter appears out of nowhere, tugging at me with a soggy hand. "Will you come swim with us?"

Public pools are still not my favourite, but Karter's request makes for an easy escape.

We stay at the pool for a few hours, until both boys are wrinkled and shivering. Silver Hair quietly excuses himself, and I see him across the crowd once or twice, but he doesn't approach me again.

After we've dried off and gone home for lunch, I load the boys into my car. It's earlier than I usually take them back, but I text Dominic to say we're on our way, and he replies that he's home. He gives me a look as I carry overnight bags in through the front door.

"What?" I say.

"Something come up at work?" He crosses his arms over his chest.

"No." But I've been sleeping with a guy who is fourteen years younger than me and who technically works for me, and somehow it's gotten complicated, and I need to fix it. "I have things to take care of."

He arches an eyebrow, but he doesn't say anything as I kiss Jacob and Karter goodbye. For their part, they don't seem upset about cutting their weekend with me a few hours short. They're too busy telling Dominic about the trip to the pool and who won each of the twenty-seven cannonball contests they held before the lifeguard told them to stop jumping so close to the other children.

I call Brady as I get back on the highway.

"Good afternoon, Brady speaking." His voice is oddly formal.

"Shit, did I call the football phone?" I say.

He laughs, and it's followed by a smacking sound like he's eating something. "Nah, I'm just screwing with you."

He does it so well, in every sense of the word.

"You busy?" I ask.

Does he pause before he says, "No. You coming over?" Or is it my imagination?

"Yeah. Just dropped the boys off. Be there soon?"

"Whenever. I'm free. And I have something I want to tell you."

Apprehension prickles over my scalp and down my back, but I say, "Great. See you soon."

"We need to talk."

Such a cliché, and yet that's how Dominic started.

"It's not working. The counselling. Everything. It's not enough."

He looked apologetic while he said it, but nothing I said after mattered. No more promises to do better, no offers for more counselling. He didn't want to hear it anymore. Too late.

I can't be too late with Brady.

Except, as I enter his apartment, he greets me with a smile that practically splits his face in half. He takes a running leap, and I have to stumble backward against the closing door to catch him.

"Jesus Christ," I say, as he flings himself at me, wrapping his arms and legs around my shoulders and hips. My hands slide on instinct around his ass, pulling him to me. "Be careful. My back."

He laughs, sucking wet kisses on my throat. "I'll get the Epsom salts when we're done celebrating."

"Celebrating?" I can't help my sigh of relief as he sets his feet back on the ground. "What are we celebrating?"

"I think I found someone. To hire."

"You did? That's great! When?"

"Just now." He tugs me up the hall toward the bedroom.

"Now?" I laugh, stumbling after him. "It's Sunday afternoon."

"I know!" He's pulling off his shirt and hopping on one foot take off a sock. "I emailed to see if she'd be free for a phone call this week, and she replied right away that she was leaving on vacation but could have a call now. Nash." His cheeks are glowing as he slips his thumbs into the waistband of his shorts. "She was amazing. We're going to meet when she gets back next week, but I think I've finally found someone who can do the job!"

"That's great," I say, and it is. The relief is rolling off him in waves. Maybe I've only been sensing his tension lately. The stress of finding a new employee has been weighing on him. "Can we talk first? I have—"

"No." His shorts drop to the floor, and he stands, hands on his hips, dick straight out in front of him. "Sex first. Conversation after. I'm going to bang you like a screen door in a hurricane. Neither one of us will be able to walk when I'm done. Lots of time to talk while we recover."

"Jesus." I laugh as I pull my own shirt over my head. "Don't ever say something like that again. You—" He's on me before I can finish. His kisses are all tongue and teeth, rough and demanding. He pulls on my shorts until they slide off my hips. "Okay, okay," I say when I get the chance.

He's impatient in his movements, spinning me around before I'm totally undressed and pushing me down on the bed. I laugh, relief warming me alongside the desire. He's okay. We're okay.

He licks his lips as he stands over me. "I am going to ruin you," he says, and his voice makes me think that yes, that is exactly what he will do, and I no longer care.

Except then someone knocks on the front door.

19

BRADY

*B*est frigging day of my life. Finally, I find someone who knows the difference between an Ethernet cable and a hard drive cable. And now my hot—well, not boyfriend exactly, not yet anyway—my Nash is lying naked on my bed with the smile that means he's going to let me do *anything* I want to him.

And someone has the motherfucking audacity to knock on my goddamn front door.

"Hello? Brady?" The voice is clear, like they've already let themselves inside.

I know that voice far too well.

"Jesus Christ," I say, echoing Nash's words from just a few minutes ago.

"What?" Nash says, lifting his head from the mattress, and I shush him automatically.

"No. No, no, no." I scramble, sliding back into my shorts commando. I tuck my stiff cock into the elastic of the waistband, but the action is mostly a formality, since my erection is withering with every second that goes by.

"Brady?" The voice is closer now. He wouldn't actually come in here, would he?

"Who is it?" Nash whispers. He's up now too, rummaging for clothes.

"Stay here," I say, pressing him back down to the bed for emphasis, before I rush out, closing the door behind me.

Because standing in my front hall is my father.

"Dad!" Goodbye hard-on, hello awkward. "Hi." I hope I'm not too obvious as I run my hands over my hair and clothes, making sure everything is where it should be. "What are you doing here?"

He shrugs. "You never call, you never write."

"You want me to write?"

"Well, you could text, at least. So I know you're not dead."

I have to fight not to glance up the hall. "Seriously? You're here to guilt-trip me?"

He lifts a six-pack. "And drink. Come on, the Jays are playing. They're up by two in the fourth inning. They snatched defeat from the jaws of victory yesterday, but I'm confident they'll turn it around today." He shoulders past me toward the living room.

"Dad." I trail after him. "Now's really not good."

"Nope." He sets the beer on the kitchen counter and cracks one open. "Try again."

"But—"

"No. You need a break. You can't keep working all the time."

I shove my hands in my pockets, but the movement drags slippery fabric over my naked dick, reminding me—as if I could forget—of the until-very-recently-also-naked man in my bedroom. "Dad. I'm not—"

"No. We're taking the afternoon off." He sits down on the couch, sets his feet on the coffee table, and points at the TV. "Where's your remote?"

Oh. My. God. Why? Why is this happening? And on the best day of my life, no less.

"Um, hello?"

148

I whirl, and Nash is standing there. He's back in all his clothes, and even his hair looks freshly combed.

Oh my God. I have to pull a chair out from the dining room table because my legs no longer hold me up.

"Oh, hello," my dad says, like Nash has been there all along. Then his bushy eyebrows scrunch together, and I can practically hear the brain cells grinding as he looks from Nash to me, then beyond us to the hall—the hall that only leads to my bedroom—and back again.

Kill me now. Problem solved. I will never again have to answer an annoying client phone call or debate whether the cost of sending something to collections is worth what I'm going to have to pay to the bank in interest on my line of credit. I will never again lose a single night's sleep because I will be sleeping forever, buried underground, dead from the embarrassment of the day my dad nearly walked in on me eating out my not-boyfriend.

My much older not-boyfriend.

As Dad and Nash face off, I have the sudden sinking realization of how this looks. Nash, with the silver at his temples and along his jaw. My dad, who started going grey while I was still in high school and whose hair is basically now in a race to see if it will all fall out before the grey manages to take over what's left.

Time has a funny way of slowing down when you freak out, which means I get a chance to do the mental math that reassures me that, in fact, Nash is closer to my age than he is to Dad's. The difference is only a couple years, but those few hundred days are critical for my peace of mind.

"I'm sorry." My dad gets to his feet, nearly spilling his beer. "I'm intruding. I didn't realize you'd have company."

I go to tell him he *is* intruding, but all that comes out of my mouth is this guttural squeaking noise.

"No problem." Nash puts a hand on my shoulder. "Brady and

I were—" He glances at me, and for a second, the panic that thrums through my veins is clear in his grey eyes too.

"Want a beer?" I say helplessly. "Dad brought MGD." My dad has been drinking big label American beer my entire life. We have a million and one amazing local breweries in Toronto, but he likes what he likes.

"I should go. I'm sorry—" My dad looks mortified.

"No! Stay." I put my hands on his shoulders, much the way I did minutes ago with Nash, and guide my dad back to the couch. "I forgot the game was on. We love baseball, don't we?" Do we? I don't know if Nash has any interest in sports at all. He likes movies, yelling at me on the phone, and coming his brains out on my dick. What else do I really know about him? And should I refer to us as *we*? What are we? My dad's going to think we're dating, and I do *not* want to have to explain how we're not dating. We just fuck—a lot—even though I'm still pretty sure I'm in love with a man who could basically be the generational liaison between my baby boomer father and me. Oh, and he's divorced and has kids, but I've never met them and probably never will, because—once again—we're only here for the fucking.

"Yeah." Nash opens two cans and passes one to me with a meaningful glance that I, unfortunately, am incapable of inter-preting. Is he cool? Pissed? Silently trying to tell me that I am going to owe him a week of blow jobs and sexual subservience to make up for this fiasco? "Love the Jays. How are they doing this season? I'm Nash, by the way." He shakes my dad's hand with all the confidence he brings to his persona at the office. I stay where I am, because now I'm thinking about sucking Nash off and lying face down on my bed going, "Please, sir, may I have another?" while he stands over me with a paddle.

Jesus, I am perverse, and my father is here and . . .

The awkwardness lingers in the air for a while longer. Nash puts on a brave face and tries to chat up my dad, while Dad kind of perches on the edge of the couch, ready to steal second at any moment or make a break for the door if Nash or I give any indication that we might start taking our clothes off. I swallow half the can of beer in a single gulp and cheer way too loudly when the Jays score a homer.

"Foul ball," my dad says.

"Oh." I put my arms down. "Well, it looked like it could be fair from here."

My dad gives me this look that says he is not buying a single second of my bullshit and we are going to have a serious conversation before he sends me to the principal's office after class. Then, recognizing the responsible adult in the room, he turns and says, "So, Nash, what do you do?"

If Nash isn't a sports fan today, he has been at some point in the past. He and my dad spend the next few hours talking stats and sharing memories about back in the day when the Jays won back-to-back World Series. I was still in diapers when it happened, so while I know the names, I can't talk about them with the same reverence that my dad always has. Nash can, though. I don't know if that makes the afternoon better or worse.

We drink my dad's beer, and slowly we all relax. The Jays even win, but by then we're all slumped back in our seats, the earlier awful awkwardness mostly forgotten.

"You should have seen this one," my dad laughs, pointing in my direction. "We signed him up for little league when he was seven or eight. No hand-eye coordination. Didn't manage an on-base hit once over the entire summer."

"Hey!" I say indignantly.

Dad's cheeks are pink as he grins at me. "Are you saying you did?"

"How would I know? It was twenty years ago."

"Trust me," Dad laughs. "You remember when your son is a failure in organized sports. Don't worry. You've made me proud in other ways."

I sulk in the corner, but Nash joins the laughter. "We put our boys in T-ball last summer. It was about as successful."

"Your boys?" my dad says curiously.

"Yeah, twins. They're seven now, they—" Nash's smile fades.

My dad is studying him carefully, and something dies slowly in my chest, in part because the discomfort is plain on Nash's face, and in part because the after-school lecture is now going to include such not-at-all-uncomfortable questions as, "Am I a grandfather?"

"Twins," my dad says carefully. "That must be a lot of work."

Nash is fiddling with the hem of his shirt in an uncharacteristically nervous gesture. "It is. They're great, obviously. But two is a lot. They're . . . They live with their dad—their other dad—my ex-husband. In Markham."

"Oh." Dad looks like he doesn't know if he's should say that's too bad or ask another question. Instead, he scrubs his hands over his knees and says, "Well, I should get going."

Nash and I both hop to our feet like the living room is on fire. What am I supposed to say? *Oh no, please stay so we can keep making awkward chit-chat about the "older-man-I'm-sleeping-with-who-has-two-kids-and-you-didn't-know-about-any-of-this" elephant in the room. We'll order pizza.*

"Yeah. Thanks for coming by. I promise I'll check in more often."

Is the *"please leave"* subtext strong enough? I don't want to be rude, but . . .

"Nash." My dad shakes his hand. "Nice to meet you. If I don't hear from my son, I'm calling you."

Oh my God.

"You too. I promise to look out for him." Nash glances quickly over Dad's shoulder at me. The brief silent contact makes me blush.

"He works too hard." Dad's still talking. "I know he thinks

he'll have time for a life someday, but you and I both know it all goes so fast, right?"

Nash's smile is bittersweet. "Absolutely."

My chest hurts. Maybe I hug my dad for longer than strictly necessary, but it offsets the way I hustle him toward the door with more promises to call—hell, maybe I'll even call my mom one of these days, although I think she's somewhere up a mountain in British Columbia right now.

As the door shuts, I sag against it. I'm so twitchy I might as well have drank about a million espressos and topped it off with a Red Bull chaser. If my heart beats any faster, it will burst, and my fingers and toes seem to have become home to colonies of fire ants.

"Oh my God." I bury my face in my hands. "I'm so fucked."

Nash is hanging back, halfway down the hall. He chuckles as he scratches at his throat. "Not the way I thought about meeting your parents."

I gasp. "Oh fuck. What if he tells my mom?" At that point, I might go find a mountain of my own and never climb down again. "I'm doomed."

"Do you want me to leave?" he says.

I spread my hands over the door, blocking the exit. "No."

He runs a hand over the back of his neck. "Do you want to get naked again?"

"No." For once, my dick's not into it, and neither is the rest of me. I'm so tired. Several hours of sustained anxiety is exhausting.

Nash sags with visible relief. "Good. I mean, I would, but after everything, it might—"

"I want to go on a date." The words blunder past my lips like a puppy wearing snow booties for the first time.

Nash stills. "A date."

The part of me that felt trapped under a microscope while my father sat on the couch for the last two hours is still in self-preservation mode, and it says I should retract that last statement. I'm setting myself up for heartbreak.

And yet . . .

"Yes. A date."

His hands go to his hips, and he tips his chin up like he's sniffing the air. "Dinner? A movie?"

"You can take me bowling or to the drive-in. Or we can go to Hanlan's on a weekend when you don't have the kids."

He raises a fine eyebrow. "You want me to take you on a date to the nude beach?"

Do I? "I mean. It's not like I don't already know what you look like naked. It would almost be a good way to ease into it, if you think about it." Oh God, what am I saying? "Sort of halfway between where we're most comfortable now, which is naked and here, and where I want to be with you."

Nash runs his tongue along the edges of his teeth while his eyebrows do this adorable and confused bunching thing. "Which is . . . clothed and in public?"

I want to laugh, but also I want to cry, because he's not saying no, and I hadn't realized until this moment how scared I was that he would. So many times over the last few weeks, I'd gone to ask him, and every time, I told myself to wait, and now he hasn't said no. Relief is like a cool cloth on the back of my neck during the hottest night of the summer.

Which . . . he hasn't exactly said yes, either.

"This isn't about my dad," I say quickly, and his squint deepens, telling me my dad hadn't factored into his thinking yet. "I mean, he thinks we're dating because the alternative would scar all of us permanently. But I'm not telling you I want to go out on a date because I want to make my dad happy or anything like that. I . . . " Okay. Here goes. "I like you." Chicken shit. "A lot." Closer. "And . . . if you like me too, then maybe we could get out of my apartment and stop fooling around in your office and go out and have a night like normal grown-ups."

154

As I talk, Nash walks slowly up the hall. His smile is lazy, and I say "grown-ups" on a long exhale that buffets over him as he wraps his hands around my ass and pulls us together. I rest my forehead on his chest, because if I can't see his face, I won't be quite so disappointed.

Instead he lifts my chin and kisses me softly. "I have something to tell you," he says.

Fuck. Here it comes. "Oh."

"No one ever feels grown-up. It's a myth we all tell ourselves. But the feeling someone else should be in charge never fully goes away."

I sigh. "Nash."

He kisses me again. "You want to go out?"

I bite my lip. It's so rare that I feel our age difference—except when my dad crashes our Sunday afternoon delight—but right now I feel like a kid asking Santa for the one Christmas present he wants most in the world.

He still doesn't know I love him, but one thing at a time, right?

"Okay," he says.

My smile against his lips stretches until it hurts. "Yeah?"

He brushes his nose over my cheek. "Yeah. Anywhere you want to go. Name the place and time, and I'll be there."

I can't help my soft groan as he pulls my earlobe between his teeth. "Anywhere?"

That earns me another bite, harder than the first. My knees go wobbly at the sting.

"Not the nude beach, Brady. Don't be smart."

I bury my face in his neck. "Wouldn't dream of it."

20

NASH

*D*ating is a funny thing. You meet someone, you go on dates. Eventually, you stop, even though you're still together. The relationship hasn't necessarily solidified into something long-term, but you no longer need the guise of a formal event and money spent to see each other.

All this to say, I don't remember when Dominic and I stopped dating and started being just a couple.

But I know it's been a very long time since I stared at myself in the mirror and tried to envision how dinner with a man I'm excited to know better will go.

He *is* a man, too. Brady's embarrassed about his dad showing up unannounced, but despite those small glimpses into Brady's family life and what he must have been like as a kid, all the time we've spent together lately tells me he is very much an adult now. And yes, I've done a lot more living than he has, but fourteen years really haven't made us all that different, except Brady's doing things for the first time, and I'm doing many of them for the second.

But that experience only makes me wiser. I made mistakes with Dominic that I won't make with Brady.

We're going to the Distillery District. In the dead of summer, it's jammed with tourists, but the restaurants—built into old barrel rooms and cellars—are actually pretty good, and the whole area makes for a nice hand-in-hand walk after dinner, if that's something we want to do.

I'm surprised by how much the idea of holding Brady's hand in public appeals to me. I've never been much for PDA— although Dominic always was—but something in the look on Brady's face, the naked hope as he'd asked if I'd go out somewhere with him, makes me want to let him know I'm in. If he wants me to take him out for dinner or hold his hand or anything else, I'll do it.

Although when Harpreet asks, "What are you up to tonight?" I take the easy way out and say, "I'm having dinner with a friend," and leave it at that. Holding Brady's hand in a historic district surrounded by tourists we will never see again is one thing. Looking my best employee in the eye and telling her I'm dating the IT guy is another entirely. I want to talk to Brady first about how we'll tell the team at the festival.

The Distillery isn't far from my apartment, so Brady comes to my place first. His smile as I open the front door is brilliant.

"Hey, you look great!" I say.

"Thanks, so do you." His collared shirt of the day has motorcycles printed in rainbow colours, and he's cuffed his jeans to show off tanned ankles and white sneakers. He looks fitted and pressed, while his hair curls over one eye, and the stud in his ear winks playfully at me.

It occurs to me we've never had sex at my place. I kissed him that one time my computer died, but we've never been naked and sweaty here.

His grin says he knows what I'm thinking. He reaches for me and—despite my earlier contemplations about hand-holding— the way he loops his arm around mine is a surprise. We're always grabbing for each other. Handfuls of shirts, fingers in belt loops. He's always rough and confident with me, so to see him with the grace and manners of someone about to go out in public is new.

"Come on," he says, although he plants a soft kiss at the hinge of my jaw. "We'll do that later."

We're past the hottest days of summer, where the air is a wall of humidity when you step outside. The walk to the Distillery is easy, the streets busy on a Thursday evening.

Brady glances at me nervously as we go. "I had to bring the football phone."

"That's fine."

"If it rings, I'll have to answer it."

"Okay."

"But unless someone's computer is literally on fire, I'll try to—"

"Brady." I put a hand on his shoulder. "It's fine. I understand."

He still looks anxious, but he pats his pocket where the phone must be and squares his shoulders. I love his determination. So many people choose the predictability of a nine-to-five, and I get why. The steady paycheque. Evenings available to drive your kids to hockey or sit around the table together for dinner. But for Brady—and me—that structure is confining. I know the sacrifices he's making to be his own man. I tried to have it both ways, but I failed, and I'm learning to live with that. His dad told me to look out for him, and I will, but the truth is, everyone's balance is different, and if Brady's involves bringing the football phone to dinner, I can deal with that. I've been that guy too.

"I've been trying something new at work," I say, trying to distract him from the weight of the phone in his pocket.

"Oh?" he says.

"Yeah. I don't like the word micromanaging, but it's possible I've been too . . . involved . . . in decisions I didn't need to be part of. So I'm attempting to let Doug and Harpreet run more of the day-to-day."

He gives a short laugh. "Must be nice."

I push on. "Well, I was thinking. If you wind up hiring this new person, and she's as good as you think she might be, then we might have more time to see each other. Like this. Dates. Go out. What do you think?"

The question leaves me feeling strangely vulnerable. With Dominic, when he asked me to be home more often, I tried to move meetings. I tried productivity apps or working in the evenings after the boys went to bed. I never actually tried to do less. There might be something to it.

Brady slides his hand in mine. "If I can hire someone and she's amazing, I will find a way to be with you as much as you want."

The restaurant is a tapas place with high-top tables and brightly coloured walls lined with tiles that look like sketches from Pablo Picasso. The staff is . . . well, to be honest, if you're a gay man, the staff is pretty nice to look at—mostly men with trimmed beards and neat hair, wearing button-downs even tighter than Brady's and shorts that would be a fashion-forward choice out on the street and are definitely quite an ask of your staff.

We take a table by the window, which mostly faces the parking lot, but we get a glimpse of cobblestone sidewalks and tourists gawking at the redeveloped complex that was once a whisky distillery.

The waiter takes our drink order—I ask for a Tempranillo, Brady orders sangria—and we're left alone. Brady's hands are folded in front of him, and we let the buzz of the restaurant wash over us.

Brady gives me a quick grin. "This is the part where we actually have to talk to each other for once."

I cock my head. "We talk all the time."

Brady's lips make a pouty *maybe, maybe not.* "Yeah, but it's always pre- or post-coitus."

"That's only because you can't keep your hands to yourself."

He arches an eyebrow. "You kissed me first."

Fair. I don't regret it for a second. "Because you wouldn't shut up."

The server returns with drinks, pouring my wine with a certain amount of flair that probably impresses the people here on a two-week tour of Canada that includes day trips to Montreal, Niagara Falls, Banff, and Vancouver, but I find it a bit fussy.

Brady's sangria is—

"Oh my God," he says when the server steps away.

"Are you supposed to bathe in it?" I say.

The glass is barely smaller than Brady's head. He has to pick it up with both hands to manage it, and only the striped paper straw in the goblet saves him from spilling it all down the front of his shirt. Bits of fruit roll lazily around the bottom, and maybe they're meant to be dessert, because Brady will need that long to drink the sangria.

He lifts the glass, grip wobbling slightly as he holds it toward me. "Cheers."

I lift my wine. "Cheers."

"To our first date," he says with a smile.

I make sure to hold his gaze as I say, "First of many, I hope."

His smile grows as he sips his drink. My heart patters beneath my collarbone, and I have to take a longer swallow of my wine.

We order too much food, but it all looks too good not to try. Sardines, shrimp, paella, clams, bone marrow.

"You're going to have to roll me home if we eat all that," Brady says, running his hands over his stomach.

I shrug. "You can sleep at my place."

Now his smile sharpens into something mischievous. "Yeah?"

"Why not?"

"You could go to yoga with me tomorrow!"

"No way," I groan. "I will never subject myself to that again."

"Why?" He pouts. "You were really good. I couldn't keep my eyes off you. I got—" His mouth clacks shut, and he lifts his fishbowl glass, tipping it up precariously so it hides half his face.

My lips curl. "You got what?"

He glares at me from behind his sangria before he carefully sets it back down and leans across the table, waiting until I lean in too.

"I got hard just watching you," he says softly, which isn't very soft at all, because the restaurant is busy.

A polite throat is cleared, and we both lurch back to find a server standing there with several plates of food. He sets them down, describing each one down to the parsley emulsion with precision. If he heard what Brady said, he doesn't let on.

But I did. And somehow, the idea of Brady, aroused and with nowhere to go, is so hot I barely taste the first bites of my food. I remember him, the way he was crouched on the floor. Knowing he was hard for me and couldn't do anything about it . . .

"Something wrong?" Brady says, eyebrow arched.

"Eat faster," I say.

He makes a big show of placing a slice of bread slathered in crushed tomato and garlic into his mouth very slowly. He chews with exaggerated deliberation.

"You're a little shit, Brady."

"You love me," he says around a lump of half-chewed toast.

I laugh as I take another sip of wine. "I think I do."

We both freeze at the same time as we realize what I've said. Brady still has half his appetizer squashed into one cheek like a squirrel, and if I didn't actually love him, I'd wonder what I was doing out with someone with those table manners, but . . .

I love him.

"Brady, I—"

He straightens, but his reaction isn't about my declaration or anything I'm about to say. Instead, he pulls the goddamn football phone out of his pocket.

"I'm sorry," he says. "I'll tell them I'll call right back."

"No," I say, and I mean it. "This was the deal. Talk to them. I'm not going anywhere."

I'm not. This life together could be good, I'm increasingly sure of it.

"I'm so sorry." He shakes his head but slides his thumb to accept the call. "Hello, Brady speaking."

He keeps shooting me guilty looks as he asks the same questions I almost know by heart already. "How long has it been like that? Are you getting an error message? Is it plugged in?" He gives me a pointed glance at that last one, and I flip him off over the edge of the table.

I love him. Somehow, the thought doesn't scare me as much as it should. We're good together. I'd have to be completely oblivious not to see that. And I have two kids and an ex-husband, and a festival that I care too much about to ever let other people run fully, so while he thinks the never-ending phone calls are a problem, they're nowhere near the baggage I can fit just in my laptop bag.

"Nash?"

For a second, the whole restaurant seems to go silent. The diners, the servers, the clatter of plates and pans in the kitchen. It all disappears.

Except the sound of my name makes me jerk. I accidentally tip my wine glass over, spilling dark red wine over the tablecloth and drowning the plate of Serrano ham that has just been delivered.

Brady is still on the phone, brow furrowed as he asks questions that sound so basic now to someone who would be helpless without him. So many people seem to need him.

But he's mine.

Except—

"Nash."

Turning my head seems to take forever, but maybe I'm dreading the face I know I'll see, because if I do, the spell will be broken. Reality will set in, along with all the bags and cargo that come with it.

"Oh. Hello." The words are forced, even to my own ears. Tempranillo is dripping onto my lap, and if I stand, I'm going to look more ridiculous than I already feel.

"Fancy meeting you here." His smile is as artificial as mine.

"I—" I glance at Brady, who is still on the phone, but he is watching me carefully.

Screw it. I stand and pretend we can't all see the purple stain on my crotch.

"It's good to see you," I say.

It isn't. Slowly the ambiance of the restaurant comes back. The music overhead on the sound system, the servers moving between tables in their Euro-fit shorts, and the smell of garlic and smoke from the grill.

The polite smile on the face of my ex-husband.

And, based on the way their hands are twined together, my ex-husband's new boyfriend.

21

BRADY

*P*rinters. Fucking printers. One of these days, I'm going to hold a rally where everyone in the city can burn their malfunctioning printer once and for all.

"Please," the woman on the phone says. "I've stayed late to finish this report. My boss will kill me if I don't have it printed and bound by the time he gets in tomorrow morning. But every sheet has this black line in the middle of it. What do I do?"

I'm sort of aware of the two men who walk up to our table, but I really do think this customer is about to have a panic attack right here on the phone.

I'm more aware when the glass hits the table and lets loose a purple tidal wave.

But the thing I really notice is the fear on Nash's face. I'd thought I'd seen almost every expression on him. Frustration, discomfort, amusement, ecstasy. But even that night I went to his place in the rain and he'd thought he'd lost all his presentation slides, I'd never seen fear.

I have now.

He stands until he's eye to eye with the two men who have come up to our table. One is smiling politely at him. The other is speaking and occasionally glancing at me, giving me an up and down look that makes my skin prickle.

"Hello?" the voice on the football phone says.

"Yes, sorry. You're at Church and Gerrard Street, right?" Not that far. I could duck out and still be back in time for dessert.

And what? Leave Nash here to eat by himself? I am such an asshole. Why did I think I could do this?

I glance back up at Nash and the other two guys. Nash still seems distinctly uncomfortable. One of the new arrivals looks amused. The other, who was looking at me before, his smile says he is thoroughly unimpressed with me.

"I'll be right there." I hang up. I'm not even sure she agreed to wait for me. Hell, I'm not confident what she said her name was. Hopefully I've got the address right and we can sort out all those details when I arrive.

But first things first.

"Hi. How's everyone doing?" I say, coming to my feet.

"Brady," Nash says slowly. My name is only five letters long, but the way he says it right now is a warning. And not in a "don't be a smart-ass or I'll make you choke on my dick later" kind of way either. I am legitimately supposed to be on my best behaviour.

The mystery becomes clear when he gestures to the man in the middle and says, "This is Dominic. My ex-husband."

"Oh." Oh shit.

Dominic wraps an arm around the man on his other side and says, "And this is Karim. My boyfriend."

Ohhhh shiiiiit.

Dominic is handsome. Like, he has cheekbones you could cut an entire charcuterie plate on. His eyes are so brown they look bottomless. He's maybe a few years older than Nash, and everything about what he's wearing looks polished. The man beside him also has that professional-chic look, like Bay Street lawyers who don't fully know how to scruff up for a night off. His shirt fits him too perfectly to not be custom, and his silver hair is expertly cut and styled.

I, on the other hand, am wearing one of the fourteen billion shirts I have purchased at H&M sometime in the last decade, and I know I've already got at least one glob of olive oil on my pants. Which is nothing compared to Nash, who is currently wearing most of his wine.

We are at a definite disadvantage here.

"I'm Brady." I reach for their hands to shake. "I'm Nash's—" My gaze wanders to Nash. His eyes are wide, nostrils flared, and I don't know how to finish that sentence without alarming him more. Boyfriend, fuck buddy out on a temporary pass, IT consultant—none of these are going to have the desired effect. "It's nice to meet you."

I realize another man is hovering at the edge of our little group. The restaurant host, clutching a couple menus, looking anxiously at Dominic and Karim, no doubt waiting to show them to their table.

But they seem rooted to the spot. Dominic can't take his eyes off me. I stand as straight as I can, pushing my chest out. I don't know what he sees, but I want him to know that I am to be taken seriously.

"Do you need to go?" Nash says.

"What?" I say.

"Your phone."

My gaze drops to the phone in my hand while my face heats. "Oh. Um. Yeah. Printer malfunction. Senior partner on the war path. You know how it goes."

He gives me a sad smile. "Yeah, of course."

Dominic and Karim seem to break out of their spell. Dominic says, "I guess we'll go sit down."

Karim says, "It was nice to meet you," and his voice is like silk. Somehow I feel very small and scruffy next to him, and I don't even know who he is.

"I'm sorry," I say when they're gone.

"No, it's fine." Nash runs a hand over the front of his pants, like that's going to do anything about the wine. "I didn't really want to spend the next hour sitting here in damp underwear anyway."

"I'll text you when I'm done?"

"Yeah." His hand on my arm is gentle. "Yeah. I'll settle up here for the food they've brought out already."

"I'm really sorry," I say again.

"It's fine. We agreed it would be fine." He leans in and kisses my cheek. I can't help it when, as he pulls back, I glance over his shoulder. Dominic is watching us, eyes narrowed. I feel like I should flip him off or maybe give him a thumbs-up, so I do neither.

But I do hover for a second longer while guilt eats at my insides.

"Hey," Nash says. "Go. We'll have other dates."

We will. I want to kiss him again—really kiss him—so he knows I believe him, but instead, I finally turn and make my way out of the restaurant.

The printer is fucked. I don't even know. We change the toner, check the drums, clean the fuser, turn it off and turn it on again about a hundred times. I spend an hour on the phone—forty-five of it on hold—with the dealer's customer service line and finally we throw in the towel and spend another hour calling all the rush print shops we can find online until we get a hold of someone who is still taking overnight orders and who can have the report ready for her deadline.

"Thank you." The teary woman actually hugs me when it's all said and done. She's been weepy since I arrived. Part of me wants to tell her she needs to find a new job, because whoever her boss is, he can't be worth this kind of stress and heartache, but who am I to give anyone professional life advice tonight? I didn't even make it a half hour into my date.

I text Nash as I leave the office. *Are you home?*

His reply is so fast he must have been waiting for me, and that knowledge makes me feel better. *Yeah. Come by. I have leftovers.*

He's got a spread. Tinned seafood packed in oil. Olives so smooth they taste like butter and smoke. Grilled calamari and charred lemon. Roasted bone marrow—he's been keeping it warm in the oven—that tastes like perfect salty heaven.

"You didn't have to do this," I say, leaning back in my chair. His apartment is still too sterile, but I know him so much better than the last time I saw it. He could build a home here. A life. I want to be part of it. I could help.

He shrugs, licking his fingers. "The restaurant offered. I grabbed a seat at the bar while they cooked up the bone marrow and I had another glass of wine."

I scan the table, but we have picked everything clean. Would it be completely inappropriate if I grabbed the big scraped out cow bone and licked off the last greasy bits?

Instead, I say, "Did Dominic talk to you anymore? After I left?"

His satisfied smile dims a little bit, but he shakes his head. "No."

I nod. "Had you met his boyfriend before?"

He shakes his head again. Yikes. No wonder the whole thing felt awkward.

"Did you know he had a boyfriend?" I ask.

Nash screws up his mouth for a second, before he says, "The kids told me there might be someone."

The kids. I haven't met them. Am I going to? Do I want to? I think of the look my dad gave me when Nash mentioned them. If I'm going to be with Nash, he comes as a package deal. And we don't have to rush it, but someday, the wall between the life I want with Nash and the life he has with his kids will have to come down. I'll be a—

Whoa. That thought is big, and a little scary, and kind of exciting, but let's not get ahead of ourselves.

I come around the table, and Nash pushes back his chair so I can climb into his lap. I straddle him and place my hands on either side of his face to hold him in place and kiss him the way I want to. We both taste like oil and garlic, our tongues slippery against each other. Nash's hands slide around to my ass, pulling me against him.

"I'm sorry I spoiled our date," I say.

"What do you think this was?" He noses at my earlobe and drags his stubble along my neck.

I laugh. "Date part deux?"

He's undoing the snaps on my shirt. "The very same. Now take this shirt off and come to bed."

"I don't know," I say a bit breathlessly, already hardening in my jeans. "That was a lot of food. I might be too full to fuck."

Reader, I was not.

———

Lena comes to the co-working space on Monday at ten, as we'd agreed. She's got purple hair and an entire binder of references from past jobs and volunteer placements. She's from Argentina and, when we spoke on the phone, she hesitantly admitted she didn't have much Canadian work experience.

I don't give a shit where her work experience is from, as long as she knows the difference between an IP address and an email address.

Which, fortunately, she does.

She tells me about the gaming computer she built from scratch using parts she bought on eBay. Before she came to Canada five years ago, she worked in Buenos Aires as the IT manager for a multinational shipping company. Since arrived, she hasn't been able to find another corporate job.

Instead, she's working at a Spanish-language community center helping seniors learn to use the internet.

"They're so sweet," she says. "You've got to take it step by step. Some of them don't even know what I mean when I say double-click. But they've heard about this thing called Facebook and they want to see pictures of their grandson's birthday, and the smile on their faces when I help them get there is totally worth it."

I think she might have been built in a lab, designed exactly to my specifications for what I want an employee to be. And since all the other potential employers passed on her because of her lack of domestic experience, their loss is my gain.

She is also almost certainly overqualified.

"This job is mostly helping people troubleshoot their printers and set up laptops with things like Office and Dropbox."

She shrugs. "I know. You told me that on the phone."

"And it can involve a lot of after-hours work. We carry what I call the football phone. If it rings, you answer it."

She gives me an arch smile. "Because we could be starting a nuclear war with Mississauga?"

I laugh. "You might be the first person to ever get that joke right away."

Lena looks like she's used to exceeding expectations. I'm a monogamous gay, and I'm in love with a forty-something silver fox, but I'm also a little bit in love with Lena.

"I assume I'd have to carry the phone most of the time? You've earned some time off, no?"

I am about to drop to my knees and worship at her altar. Ramona and I had never really discussed what was fair, and since I'd carried the phone by myself for ages, it seemed a lot to ask her to take it on.

But maybe if I set a different tone right off the bat . . .

"We can share," I say. "We'll work out a schedule that fits for both of us."

I'm talking in definites, not hypotheticals, but what's the point in pretending I'm not going to offer her the job? I will pay her almost anything if it means I only have to carry the phone four nights a week instead of seven. Nash said we'd spend more time together if we could find ways to get away from work. Without the football phone, I can spend every free night with him. We will eat at every restaurant in the city and make love on every surface in both our apartments.

Turns out, Nash's bed is way comfier than mine.

I should probably tell Lena I'm sleeping with one of my—our—clients. She has this no-nonsense air about her that says she might not understand the subtleties of what Nash and I have going on. Or at least I should hand the Out & About account over to her. Ethically, that probably makes the most sense. I'd say I was sorry to give it up, but really, what I loved about working for the festival was the rush I felt every time Nash's number came up on my phone, and now he does that even when his printer is working and his extender is sending a clear, uninterrupted signal to his office, so I'm not really giving anything up at all.

I shoot her my best smile. "When can you start?"

"Wednesday," she says with a firm nod.

Seriously. Eternal worship at the Church of Lena.

"Do you like pumpkin spice lattes?" I say.

She wrinkles her nose. "North Americans don't understand good coffee."

No one's perfect. I feel a little less in awe of my new employee, and that's probably for the best.

I text Nash as soon as she's gone. *I found her! She's perfect.*

He sends a smiley emoji in reply.

I can't help myself when I send a couple eggplants and some raindrops.

Brady, I still don't know what that means.

I write, *Call me after work & I'll explain. Bring your glasses so you can read the fine print.*

Nash sends a scowly emoji. *Smart-ass. Going to the boys' soccer game tonight. Will call after.*

I spend the rest of the day in a happy little fog. Nothing can get me down. Not even when the supplier sends an email saying the smart screen I ordered for Bill Immerchuk and his hall of learning is back ordered and will be available in October. Bill is very understanding, and we order a new model that will arrive on Friday. Lena will be here by then. She can help me do the install. Everything is working out.

I spend the evening writing invoices. I wonder if Lena likes to write invoices. She'd probably be insulted if I asked. But if she works out, I can go back to that plan I had of hiring someone junior to take over the office admin. We'll be a team of three then. Three feels big. Legit. A real company, not just me and a laptop and some rented office space in an old jam factory.

As I fall asleep, burrowed down in a cozy nest of quilts and optimism, I realize that Nash never called.

22

NASH

I half expect Dominic to bring an entire entourage to soccer to lecture me about my love life. His mother, his sister, her kids. And Karim.

Having seen him, I'm surprised at how much I'm not upset by his presence in Dominic's life. Maybe it's Brady. If I've moved on, I can hardly blame Dominic for meeting someone new. And it's not like I was still hung up on Dominic himself. I've been grieving the death of my marriage, but only in that I was worried what it would mean for the boys, though they seem to be doing fine. Better than I am, most days. But I'm here for them, and we're finding a rhythm. It's inevitable Dominic and I are going to find people who make better partners for each of us, and who will someday love Jacob and Karter as much as we do.

But still, I'm relieved when I see Dominic sitting on the sidelines by himself. Because we should talk. About Brady and Karim. About what it means for the boys, and when we should tell them. I gather they've already met Karim, and I would have appreciated a heads-up about that, but we're going to be adult about this going forward, starting now. And I appreciate not having an audience for this kind of conversation.

"Hey," I say, setting up my folding chair next to his.

"Hey." He's wearing sunglasses and faces out toward the field where the kids are running drills before the game starts.

"Sorry I'm late. There was an accident on the 404."

"It's fine."

A whistle blows, and the kids fall out of their drills. Chaos reigns for a few moments as pylons are rearranged, and coaches call at the little soccer players, trying to get them into position for the game to start.

"Did Karter get taller since last week?" I say.

Dominic smiles faintly. "Growth spurt. I've had to buy him new shoes twice this summer."

The boys are identical in nearly every way. When they first came to live with us, we could only tell them apart from the mole on the back of Jacob's right calf. Thank God we'd been matched with them in summer. We had a lot of bare feet and ankles, those first few weeks, while we learned their personalities. It's funny that Karter is definitely a few inches taller than his brother. They're their own people now. At two, they'd been an amorphous blob of chaos.

"So," Dominic says.

"So," I say, squaring my shoulders the way Brady did as we'd walked to our date and he'd tried to calm his anxiety over carrying his phone with him.

"You met someone."

"So did you. He seems nice."

"He's a pediatrician. He's the boys' pediatrician, actually. Has been since we moved to Markham."

Of course he is. I thought he'd looked familiar. I did go to a few appointments. But I would have thought of him as Dr. Whatever-His-Last-Name-Is, not Karim, which explains why I couldn't place him.

"He lives close by?"

"Stouffville."

By Toronto standards, he's practically next door.

On the field, Karter may have grown, but he clearly hasn't gotten those extra inches of arms and legs under control. He flails about like a robot with bolts coming loose at every joint. It's hilarious, but the big smile on his face says he's having the time of his life.

"So what does . . . I'm sorry, what was his name again?"

"Who?" I say, dragging my attention away from where Karter trips over his own feet as he tries to kick the ball to his brother.

"Your . . . friend. At the restaurant."

"Brady."

"Yes, Brady." Dominic turns his head toward me. "What does he do?"

"He's an entrepreneur. Runs his own IT consultancy."

"And how did you meet?" For the first time, I hear something under Dominic's voice. It's smooth, but not like silk on skin. More like the way a shark moves through the water. Purposefully. Like he has nothing to think about but his next meal and how to catch it.

"I . . . We hired him at the festival." That sounds better than "he works for me," doesn't it?

"You mean *you* hired him?"

I stiffen. "Why do you say that?"

He looks over the wires of his sunglass frames at me. "Because you've never let someone else hire someone at that place. You're too much of a control freak to let anyone else make a decision."

"I—" I'm trying. But I never did when Dominic and I were still married, and that's the lens he's looking at all this through.

"So you hired him," he says slowly, the venom growing in his voice. "And now you're fucking him."

"Technically, he's fucking me." Wrong move. I know it as soon as the words are out of my mouth. Because Dominic has made some kind of snap judgment and I have confirmed all his assumptions.

"How old is he?" Dominic says.

"What does it matter?" I say, fingers clenching the canvas and metal in the arms of the folding chair.

"You look pretty funny together, you know that, right? Like you're taking your son out for dinner."

"That's uncalled for," I say, trying to hold onto my temper.

"Or else you're going through some kind of midlife crisis. Looking for someone younger to help you recover your lost youth? Can you even keep up without medication? It's pathetic, Nash, really."

"Hey," I say, louder than I mean to. A few heads turn our way. We're sitting a bit removed from the rest of the families here for practice, and now I understand why Dominic set up his chair the way he did. I try to cover with a cheer and a round of loud claps. On the field, nothing particularly special has happened, so I get a few more weird looks.

"What is your problem?" I say in a hoarse whisper. I'm angry, but a deeply insecure voice at the back of my brain wonders if he's right. What did the host at the restaurant see as he sat us at our table? What about the other people around us? Brady was the one who asked to go out, but why would someone like him, with his whole life ahead of him, want to be with me, someone who has already screwed up his pretty badly?

Dominic scoots his chair closer to mine. "What's my problem? Really? You have the gall to ask me that?"

"Yes, because I don't understand. You met someone; I met someone. We're taking it slow. The boys don't even know he exists. What's the big deal?"

"I met someone appropriate. You met—" He flicks a dismissive wrist. "A frat boy."

"Oh, for fuck's sake, D. Who cares how old he is?"

"I do!" The shrillness of his words is muffled partially by the referee's whistle. Dominic drops his voice again. "And you should too."

"What the fuck for?"

I'm so caught up in mounting anger, I don't hear the second whistle blow to call a break or even notice the boys running to us until I have fifty-five pounds of squirming seven-year-old in my lap.

"Daddy!" Jacob says. "You came!"

I squeeze him hard, growling playfully. "Of course I came. It's a big game."

"It is?" he says. "Why?"

"I just mean—" I glance over at Dominic, who is helping Karter fix his shin guards and very pointedly not looking at me. "Every game is important. You have to try your best, every time, right?"

He nods at me seriously before squirming down. "Did you see me? I almost scored!" He then proceeds to reenact his entire glorious—as he tells it—cross-field sprinting, weaving and dodging, nearly taking the ball to victory before he was foiled at the last minute by a pesky goalie.

"I did see that," I say with a big smile. "You're both doing great out there. You and your brother. I'm so glad I get to see it."

The whistle blows, calling them back onto the field, and Karter and Jacob hurry to rejoin their team. When they're gone, they leave a frosty silence, despite the warm summer breeze that swirls across the park.

"Look," I finally say. "Brady is an adult. He has his own place, runs his own business. We're just starting to get serious. We've hardly talked about the boys at all—"

"So you're playing house in the city? Humping like rabbits and pretending we don't exist."

"Jesus Christ, Dominic," I scrub my hands over my face. I'll have to leave if he keeps going and I don't want to disappoint my sons. Not that getting into a screaming match at a soccer game is a great move either. "You didn't want to be married to me anymore. That's your prerogative, and I have moved on. Clearly you have too. I'm here, aren't I? I'm coming to the soccer games, and I'm taking the boys on the planned weekends. What I do in my own time is personal and—"

"Jacob has a learning disorder."

What the fuck? "Excuse me?" I grind out.

"He's been having trouble at school and Karim says—"

"So you're pissed off that I'm dating someone younger, and meanwhile your own boyfriend is suddenly an expert on how my child's brain works?"

"*Our* child," Dominic says. "But he is their doctor."

"He's a pediatrician. His specialty is vaccines and ear infections."

But Dominic keeps talking like I haven't spoken. "Well, he was there. And if you'd ever bothered to listen, I would have told you too." His words make something sick and clammy twist in my stomach. What I remember about the end of the marriage was Dominic telling me how hard it was for *him*, and I finally gave up and let him say it was over, because nothing I did made him happy. I've made my peace with the fact we weren't good for each other. But what if I wasn't there for the boys?

As if to prove my point, Dominic says, "Of course listening would have involved you being home and not glued to your laptop twenty-four seven. It would have involved coming to doctors' visits and teacher conferences and paying attention instead of checking your email every five minutes. It's a goddamn film festival, Nash, not brain surgery."

We've had that argument so many times. He never understood why it was so important to me. But that's not what we're talking about here.

"What do you think is wrong with Jacob?" I say, trying to find level ground again.

Dominic lets out a long breath. "Probably ADHD. Some kind of language disorder."

"Language disorder? He talks fine."

"Not like that. He can't read, Nash."

"He can read," I say, but my mind is already turning. They're only seven. We're just getting into the sort of homework that needs parental assistance and supervision. And it's the summer. I can barely remember what they were working on in school last year.

Dominic looks sad. "Not well. He's still sounding out words like 'cat' and 'ball.' He can write his own name and Karter's, but his spelling on anything else is beyond awful. I tried to help him with it this year, and it just ended in tears and screaming matches. Half the time I don't even know what letter he's writing, much less what word he's trying to spell. I don't think he can do it."

"It doesn't have to be all on you. We'll get him tutors. We'll —" Brady's got a client. He's told me about him. Something about after-school tutoring. I'll have him introduce us. "He's not —" I shake my head, watching as my boy, my smart, funny boy who negotiates like a champ, chases after the other kids, a big smile on his face.

"He's great," Dominic says. "But he's going to need a lot of work to thrive. A lot of time." He throws a glance my way on the last word. "And you're with someone who can't even get off the phone to have dinner with you."

Even as I struggle to understand what Dominic is telling me, I bristle on Brady's behalf. "That's not fair."

"Doesn't make it not true."

I'm fighting to stay calm, and I don't even know what's got me upset anymore. Is it Dominic flinging Brady in my face, like somehow his age and dedication to his job make him unworthy? Or is it the knowledge that Jacob's been struggling and I didn't know?

"I got a psychologist to do an assessment at the end of the school year."

"And you didn't tell me?" My voice rises. Classic Dominic.

I'm not convinced half the recitals and appointments I missed weren't because he wouldn't tell me about them at the last minute. He once threw a fit that I was missing a Christmas pageant because I had a conference call with the Minister of Culture and Tourism, but I'm still sure he only let me know about the pageant the morning it was scheduled.

"I tried to talk about this in the spring, but the festival was on and you were unavailable. And then again once school let out, but you were always distracted." He glances at me out of the corner of his eyes. "Guess we know why now."

"Don't make this about Brady," I growl. We both know this is about Dominic and me.

Dominic sighs. "We got the results last week. We should talk about them." He pops open a can of mineral water. I flinch at the carbonated hiss. "There's a school in Aurora that specializes in helping kids like Jacob."

"You want to split them up? Don't you think that's a bit extreme?" Horror rushes through my veins. They've been the only constant in each other's lives. They were placed with foster parents at birth and came to live with us two years later. We might have been excited, but for them the transition was rough. Whatever our best intentions, suddenly they were living with strangers, taken away from the only parents they had ever known. They've never spent so much as a night apart.

Dominic doesn't seem to care. "I want to help Jacob. We should at least go see it."

"Can't we start smaller? There must be tutors. Brady knows someone. I'll see if that's the sort of thing he does."

"This isn't his problem. This is about what's best for our son," Dominic says, then has the audacity to look apologetic. "I'm sorry to spring all of this on you. I've tried before but—"

"Yeah." The old guilt washes over me. So many missed conversations. Missed signals. The festival isn't brain surgery, but I've treated it like a house of cards that will fall apart without me. In the process, I've handed my family's reins to Dominic, and now he's talking about separating the boys because of a problem I didn't know existed an hour ago.

"And school will be starting soon, so we're already late making decisions," Dominic says.

"It's fine," I say. "Whatever you need. I'll be there." That's what I promised the kids. When I moved out, I looked at them and said, "It'll be okay. I'll be here whenever you need me." And before. We literally chose them. We stared the social workers and even the judge in the eyes and said, "Yes. The twins. They are ours."

And I have never been the father they needed. I did my best, but I failed in so many small ways, until Dominic said I couldn't live with them anymore. But they need me now. The idea of sending them to separate schools doesn't sit well at all, and the set of Dominic's shoulders says he's made up his mind. He never was good at putting in the hard work, instead looking for magic solutions or pulling the plug before all the options have played out.

Whatever they need.

My heart squeezes at the thought, but I promised them, and now, at the very least, I'm going to have to put in the work. I found a way to make all this time to spend with Brady this summer, and now I know I'll have to give that to my kids, because what Dominic is proposing feels incredibly dangerous.

Family has to come first.

23

BRADY

*T*wo days later and I still haven't heard from Nash.

Well, okay, not totally true. I texted on Tuesday when he didn't call after soccer on Monday night. His reply was *Sorry, game ran long.*

But he doesn't call or come over after work. I'm busy getting ready for Lena to start and rounding up the last of the gear and contractors to do Bill's tutoring centre install, so it doesn't seem like an issue.

But Wednesday rolls around and I still don't hear from him. I text a few times but don't get a reply.

After work, I call him.

"Hey. How you been?"

"Good." He doesn't sound good. "You?"

"Great! I hired someone. She started today. I think she's going to be amazing. With any luck, she'll be able to take over the football phone by Thanksgiving."

"That's really good. I'm glad you found someone."

If we're being honest, I was expecting more enthusiasm. "You busy tonight? I could come over."

He's quiet for a while. A weird kernel of worry starts to gnaw at my ribs. "Not tonight. I have—Jacob has an appointment in the morning. I need to be up early."

"Everything okay?"

"Yeah. Nothing serious. I mean—" He makes a weird hiccupping sound. "He's having some problems at school. We're working some things out."

Oh. That doesn't sound so serious. "Okay. Well, let me know how it goes, okay?"

"Yeah. For sure."

Except he doesn't. Thursday comes and goes, and I don't hear from him.

Friday, we're at the learning centre all day. Lena shows up in steel-toed boots and with her own tools. She's definitely overqualified, but Bill seems enchanted by her as she hauls boxes and literally holds up her end while helping the contractors mount the massive flat screen in his multimedia room.

The install runs long, so much so that we have to come back and do a half day on Saturday to finish up. Then Bill insists on taking us all out for lunch as a thank you, which is really nice, but by then the kernel of worry has turned into some kind of lesion that is twisting and spreading over my heart and lungs. I keep checking my phone, and there's never anything from Nash. I send a few eggplants and a question mark but get nothing in reply.

On Sunday, there's a *Sorry. Boys this weekend. We're at the aquarium.*

Am I the asshole for resenting playing second fiddle to a couple children? It's how it's supposed to work. If Nash and I are going to be a thing long-term, I'll have to come to grips with the fact that, no matter how much we love each other, the boys will always come first.

I take a risk and text. *I could join you? Be the friend you "happen" to run into?*

He doesn't reply.

By Monday, the worry lesion is definitely infected. It's telling me all kinds of awful things. Nash is dying. His kids are dying. He's gotten back together with Dominic. He and Dominic are now in some poly relationship with the boyfriend from the restaurant. They've moved away up north so they can all live in the forest and not be judged for their non-monogamous lifestyle.

The last time I saw Nash was at his apartment the night of our failed date. He told me he didn't mind that I had to leave for a work call. He even let me take him to bed and sleep over, but what if he's changed his mind? Maybe the sight of his ex-husband and his perfect boyfriend reminded him what an odd couple we are. Maybe we really only do work well in bed.

On any other week, I'd duck out of my office and go over to the festival, but I'm training Lena, and while she's awesome, she doesn't know all the clients, and a few of them have managed to screw things up so badly even I'm not sure how to solve their problems. I call instead but get Nash's voicemail. I don't leave a message, but he must see the missed call, because he sends another text.

Sorry. Soccer again. Talk tomorrow?

But by lunchtime on Tuesday, I still haven't heard from him properly, and I'm crawling out of my skin. Lena and I are supposed to go to Bill's to make sure everything is up and running to his liking, and all I can think of is Nash.

"Something wrong?" Lena asks as I check my phone for the millionth time, like it will make Nash magically appear in the room.

I give her a tight smile. "Just, um, Nash. He's a . . . client. At the film festival. I told you about him."

"Do you need to talk to him?" she says.

"Yes." Not like she means, but this waiting and hoping is killing me.

"Do you want me to go to Bill's by myself?"

My head pops up, and I babble all the things I'm supposed to say. "Of course not. I couldn't ask you. It's your second week, and—"

But she's already logging off her laptop and slipping her phone into her pocket. "He liked me. I can go by myself."

I gape. "Really?"

Lena sneers. "He has a few screens. In Buenos Aires, at my old job, a server melted down the weekend before six hundred people moved into a new office building. I can help Bill if something isn't working."

She's so overqualified. If I'm lucky, she'll last a year then take her shiny new Canadian experience and get a job that will actually pay her what she's worth. If I'm really lucky, she'll buy half my equity and be my business partner.

I try to smile brightly as adrenaline floods my system. I'm going to see Nash. We're going to sort this out. "I won't be long at the film festival. If there's a problem at Bill's, text me and I'll be there in twenty minutes."

More like forty, assuming the streetcar is running on time, but I'm sure everything will be okay, and Lena has already won him over with her confidence and competence.

Everything is not okay with Nash, though. I can feel it in my bones.

The festival office is quiet as I walk in from the elevator. Nash's door is closed, but the meeting room is also empty.

"Is he in there?" I ask Patrick, who is still sitting at the long table in the middle of the room.

"Who?" He pushes his glasses up on his nose, looking nervous.

"Nash. Is he in his office?"

"Yes, but—"

I'm not here to listen to his objections. Nash has been cold-shouldering me for a week, and I am done waiting. Whatever the problem is, he can tell me to my face, and we will find a solution or we will part ways, but I am not going to spend the rest of my life wondering what the hell went wrong.

He's frowning at his computer when I shove the door open like I'm leading the SWAT team, and his head pops up, eyes wide.

"Brady, what—"

"IT service. Something's wrong with your phone. I'm here to fix it." I slam the door shut so hard it rattles in the frame.

"What? Nothing's wrong with my phone."

"Well, there must be, Nash, because you haven't been able to use it properly in a week."

I was grumpy before, but now that I'm in his office, I'm flat-out pissed. He looks the same as he always does. I'd expected him to look rumpled. Tired. Like something so dire happened that he hasn't slept in days.

Instead, his hair is neat, shining silver at his temples. Shirt freshly ironed. Tie in place. Cufflinks winking at his wrists.

"Where the fuck have you been?" I ask, hands on my hips.

"I told you, Jacob had some appointments."

"No." I shake my head. "An appointment. You mentioned one. Have there been more? Is he okay?"

"He's fine. He's having trouble reading."

"And?" I say.

"And what?" Nash looks genuinely confused.

"Well, I can't do math for shit, but that's why phones have calculators now. When we abandoned hope on my career as a mathematician, my dad didn't go AWOL for a week."

"It's a bit more involved than that. Dominic wants to get him into a private school before the year starts. We had to tour the school, and there were interviews for Dominic and me and Jacob."

I didn't think I was jealous. Nash has never been anything

but up-front about his marital status and history, but the way he keeps referring to Dominic so casually and using "we"—when he's kept his identity separate from Dominic's on every other occasion—grates at the thing that's been festering inside me for a week now, spreading the rot even further.

"And you couldn't have called me and told me all of this?" I ask.

He runs a hand over his face, and finally I can see the fatigue at the corners of his eyes and the way his tie isn't totally snug at his throat. He says, "It's a lot. It's going to be a lot for a while, I think. Brady, I—"

"I can handle a lot. What do you need?"

"Space. I—"

"What?" I want to scratch at my skin, like somehow I can let the agitation out.

"They need me. Dominic. The boys. Every trip to the school, every conversation about why things would be different devolved into bargaining and tears. Jacob knows something's up. And Karter's freaking out because he and Jacob won't be at the same school anymore. He bit Dominic one day last week so hard he nearly needed stitches. I don't know, I . . . " His hand trembles as he goes to his phone, then stops halfway there.

I rush to the desk. "I can help! Tell me what you need. My dad's a teacher. He got me tutors when we figured out numbers and my brain didn't mix. They had someone to work with me in class. He must know people who can—"

"It's okay." He holds up a hand. His smile is sad. "Karim's put us in touch with some good people."

"Karim? The boyfriend?" The very idea hurts. He trusts the boyfriend more than me.

"He's a doctor. The boys' doctor, as it turns out." Nash leans back in his chair, arms spread behind his head. I've fucked him on that chair, even if it wasn't awesome. I've kissed him in this office, watched as he took me into his mouth and brought me a kind of control and grounding I didn't know how to find otherwise. Right now, the space of the desk might as well be an ocean for how far away Nash feels.

"And you didn't feel like you could tell me any of this?" I sink into the seat opposite his desk. I sat here the first time I came to the office. I was surprised when they brought me to see him. In bigger organizations like the festival, I almost never meet the person in charge. And he looked me in the eye, and I knew I was going to have to really wow him if I wanted to keep this account. I threw everything I had at him. Every ounce of charm, every single thing I could do to make his life easier. And it worked. That first day, I could never have imagined what he'd be to me.

"It's a lot. So much. Dominic's been in overdrive all week, and Jacob's going to need help to—"

"He's not dying," I say. "I didn't die. For fuck's sake, Nash, I started my own business at twenty-five. You don't write kids off just because—"

"I'm not writing anyone off." For a moment, his cool exterior cracks and real emotion—*real fear*—leaches through. And I'm sorry he's struggling, but I'm also getting the very distinct sense that if anyone's being written off, it's me, especially when he says, "You don't get it. There's so much pressure."

"I can do pressure." If I can do the football phone, I can do this.

"You have too much already. I promised your dad I'd—"

"He worries about things he shouldn't." We don't need his concerns muddying the waters here.

"No, he's exactly right," he says. "This is going to need my full attention for the next while. The programs. The research. It's all so much."

"You're talking about this like you have one shot to deal with this. Like if you don't have a magic pill by the end of the month, it's all over."

"Dominic says—"

I don't know Dominic, but between this and the puckered look on his face at the restaurant, I don't like him. "This isn't an all-or-nothing game, Nash. You've got time. You can wait for the school year to start. Talk to his teachers. We can call my dad." I'll call the goddamned tooth fairy if it gets Nash to stop looking so fucking defeated.

"You're not—" He shakes his head, and the resignation on his face makes me go cold.

"I'm not what?" I say, gripping the arms of the chair. My toes are curled in my shoes.

"You're not their father. You aren't responsible for—"

"I'm not their father, but I'm your . . . " I fumble for the word. Shit. Why didn't we talk about this sooner? Why didn't I tell him? No time like the present, I guess. "Nash, I love you. Let me help." Even if I only make him dinners and keep his bed warm. I can do something.

But he only shakes his head again. "You're too young for this."

My head snaps back. "I'm what?"

"You have too much going on as it is. I mean, you can't even leave your phone alone for dinner."

Well, fuck you too. But my voice is small when I say, "You said that was okay."

"It is." He looks so earnest, and somehow that's worse. "It's what you should be doing. Run your business. Figure out who you are. Getting tangled up with me was a mistake. You don't need to be worrying about my kids. That's not for you to do."

A mistake? The word is a slap. "Because I'm too young?" He's never brought this up before. Never once made me feel less than an equal. And suddenly, now I'm too young? Not too young to suck his dick. Not too young to fix his computer. I'm not too young to take his abuse on the phone or take his body the way I know drives him wild. But to be an actual partner, when he needs someone to lean on, now I'm not ready?

"I'm sorry," he says. "I know this hurts. They need me right now. Maybe he gets into this school. If Dominic will . . . We can still get together sometimes. You and I could still—" He gets this pinched expression on his face, and before, when he was the asshole who called about his IT problems and we snarked back and forth, I would have laughed at how vulnerable he looks. Now I ache all over, and I can't take his pain too.

"You think I'd still want to have sex with you?" I hiss, rising to my feet. "You think you can ghost me for a week while you overreact to some family crisis I'm apparently too young to understand? You think I'm dumb enough to fuck you after that?"

He puts his face in his hands. "What? No. That didn't come out right. Brady. They're my family. I've never been good at being there for them, but—"

"But what? You're going to throw us away just like that? I'm sorry you're having problems. I'm sorry your kid isn't perfect. No one is. No relationship is."

"It's not about perfect, it's about—"

"It's about knowing where your priorities are. You're choosing them over me, and you have to. But I'm not going to wait around in case you text looking for a booty call. We were past that and you know it."

"Brady." He's aged in the last few minutes; I can see him clearly now. A family man with responsibilities, and when he looks at me, I guess he sees a kid not mature enough to handle life's big moments. Whatever.

I open the door to his office. My whole body hurts, and I don't think I can take anything for what's wrong with me.

At least my voice doesn't wobble as I say, "Consider our arrangement terminated. You'll have to find someone else to solve your problems for you. Make sure he knows you can't even be trusted to plug in your laptop. Don't want him charging overtime for after-hours calls."

"Brady." Only now is he rising from his desk. Too little, too late.

"Fuck you, Nash. We're done."

24

NASH

I stumble toward the office door. Brady is already halfway to the elevator.

"Brady. Wait."

I've said the wrong thing. So many wrong things. But I wasn't expecting him, and he was so angry. Dominic has been relentless since the night at the soccer game. I feel like I can barely keep up with anything these days, and then Brady stormed in demanding explanations.

He doesn't stop. Doesn't look back. He's carrying tension on his shoulders like a cross, and I'm to blame for that. I feel sick, like I'll never see him again. The look on his face said I went too far. He'll never forgive me.

"What's going on?" someone says behind me as I watch the elevator doors close.

"What was all that shouting?"

Doug and Harpreet are both leaning out of their office doors. Patrick is sitting at his workstation, obviously trying very hard to be inconspicuous. A few other heads have popped up over cubicle walls.

"It's nothing," I say. I need to leave. Go after Brady, maybe, but definitely get out of here, where everyone can see the impossible situation I'm in. For them, I'm supposed to be infallible. The fearless leader.

"Did you just fire Brady?" Harpreet says.

"No." Jesus. More heads appear. The whole floor probably heard us. I back toward my office.

"Then what was all that yelling about?" Doug asks.

"He quit." I think that's what he did. Fuck, I've screwed this up so badly.

"He quit?" Harpreet looks horrified. "Why would he do that?"

I open my mouth, but what am I supposed to say? I'd already told Doug and Harpreet I might need to take some time away to help Dominic and the boys. How do I explain how Brady fits into this? Or rather, how I can't figure out a way to make him fit, and now I've ruined everything. In the end, I couldn't invent more hours in the day, and this is what I'm left with.

"Because they were sleeping together, and Brady broke up with Nash."

The whole office goes quiet. Even the air conditioner rumbles to a halt. Slowly, every set of eyes in the place turns toward where Patrick is hunched at his table. He shrugs down even lower. "Did I say that out loud?"

"They what?" Harpreet says. "How would you know something like that?"

Patrick's gaze swings to mine, helpless and apologetic, but really, I'm the one who should be apologizing. I can't blame him for airing my dirty laundry at the office when I didn't even have the wherewithal to make sure everyone had gone home for the night before letting Brady fuck me here. I've brought this on myself in every imaginable way.

I jerk my head toward my office door, and Doug and Harpreet hurry inside. Patrick half rises, like he's been invited too, but my guilt-fueled charity only goes so far. I give him a quick glare, and he sinks back down to his seat. I'm sure his workplace harassment suit will be on my desk by tomorrow morning. Can't say it wouldn't be deserved. If they force me to resign, I'll have all the time in the world for both the boys and Brady. Two out of three.

Doug is sitting in the chair that Brady so recently occupied. I may have to get a new one. The disappointment, frustration, and the white-hot anger that rippled over Brady's face are going to be seared in my brain for a very long time, and even the sight of that chair will be enough to dig up old memories. Maybe I should just let Harpreet have this whole office.

Speaking of Harpreet, she's pacing behind Doug, hands on her hips as she shakes her head. "Seriously, Nash? You were sleeping with the IT guy? How stupid can you possibly be?"

I shrug, powerless as she stares me down. "I didn't exactly plan for it to happen."

"But you didn't stop it either. How long has it been going on?"

After so many poor choices today, what's one more? So I go for indignation. "I don't see how that's—"

"How long?"

I know a lot of people in this office find me intimidating, but they have never been grilled by Harpreet when she's upset. She is the real one to watch out for.

"Most of the summer." With every word and every passing second, my brain feels as if it's slowly being unspooled out the back of my skull, like dental floss being tugged out of its plastic casing. Brady is getting farther and farther away, taking his anger and hurt with him, and every second I don't go after him is another second in which I'm sure I've lost him.

Harpreet groans, and even Doug looks surprised.

"He could sue us," she says. "You know he could sue us for something like this. And we wouldn't have a leg to stand on."

"He's not an employee. He doesn't work for me. He won't

sue," I say. I couldn't stand it if he did. Another man I cared for, now shielded behind lawyers and paperwork.

"Employee or not, we still pay him," Doug says.

"They could pull our funding." Harpreet's working herself into a lather now. "If this got out. A lawsuit would kill us. You'd have to quit. No sponsor would fund us if we had a sexual harassment suit on our books."

"Brady wouldn't do that," I say. He said he loved me. Telling Harpreet that will not remedy the situation, but he did. And I love him too, but loving him isn't fair. Because I was kidding myself when I said we're at the same place in our lives. We aren't, and we never will be, and using him to make myself feel better after my divorce was inexcusable.

Brady needs to find someone he can build a life with, not someone who already has a life he will need to find a place in. He'll have to squeeze between teacher conferences and home-work, in the seconds when we're both not working and I'm not being a dad. I won't be able to give him the time and attention he deserves, and I can't be there when he realizes I've disappointed him too.

Harpreet is still catastrophizing. "We should be ready to talk to a lawyer. Even if nothing has happened yet. We should be ready in case it does."

"Calvin probably knows someone," Doug says.

"Oh God, no, we can't tell your fiancé." Harpreet shakes her head. "What if the bank pulls their sponsorship?"

"Hey," I say, though the word is strangled as the mental image of Harpreet's worst-case scenario continues to grow. Damn, I've been an idiot. I hurt Brady, and I hurt the festival, and for what?

"Calvin would understand. We're getting married. That's practically a conflict of interest."

"No, it's not the same, it's—"

"Hey," I say again, a little more loudly. Doug and Harpreet

both freeze as their attention swings back to me. I let out a long breath as I gather my thoughts. I spoke without thinking with Brady and look where that got me.

"First, I want to apologize. I've been extremely unprofessional. And inconsiderate. I was only thinking about myself, not about the wider implications for the festival."

"Nash." Harpreet's voice has dropped about an octave, reaching for the same soothing energy I'm trying to convey. "I know the divorce was hard, but—"

"Second," I say patiently. "Brady and I are both adults, and what happened between us was completely consensual, if maybe ill-conceived. He's angry with me as a person, not with me as the festival director."

"But he quit."

My hands are shaking, but I pull my crumbling composure together for the sake of the two people in the room whose trust I have also broken. "Brady leaving is unfortunate, and we will have to see if we can get him back. He can deal with you and Doug from now on. But I promise you"—I'm about eighty-five percent confident on this last part—"he's not going to do anything to hurt the festival. That's not what this is about."

Harpreet eyes me like she wants to say more, but Doug nods thoughtfully and says, "Let's hope you're right."

I am. What it's about is me. And him. And Dominic and the boys. I've been careful to keep all those worlds separate, instead of doing the hard work to find a way to fit them all together. I thought that division was important and relatively straightforward and, for a while, it was. When Brady and I were two people having sex, believing that he could exist outside the demands of my job and my kids was easy. But he's right when he says we were becoming more than that, and that I knew it too.

"Nash, I love you."

He did. But Dominic loved me and I let him down. And I let

Jacob down. And Karter, even. Loving me is not enough to get a happy ending.

The last week has been chaotic. Jacob is stressed, which means Karter is stressed. Dominic keeps asking these weird open-ended questions like, "What will we do?" and "What does this mean for Jacob?" and the teachers at this new school he's so keen on keep talking about milestones and outcomes and how much better students with strong parental support do. The email I supposedly never check is now full of articles Dominic keeps sending me. Some of them from news sources, but a lot are actual research papers that talk about different approaches to supporting kids with challenges like Jacob's. It's like he wants to drown me with a firehose of information. I haven't had a minute to think for myself before he's calling again, telling me about something new he read.

And, as I spent hours going over it all, I realized I couldn't ask Brady to do this with me. He didn't sign up for this. And he has enough going on. We've been dreaming airy, pie-in-the-sky dreams about dates and nights spent together, but how are we ever going to make that work? That day at his apartment, when he told the client he couldn't help right away then sat in my arms while his face went blank and his breathing got ragged . . . I can't put more on him. We have both been on the edge of balance for so long. I've fallen, but I don't have to take Brady with me.

But I handled it badly. I try to reach him. I call on Wednesday and Thursday. Hell, by Friday, I show up at his apartment, but he's not there. Or, at least he won't answer the door. I even consider going to his office, only to realize he never actually told me where it was, and the address on his invoices is a PO Box. That's how self-absorbed I've been this summer. Supposedly, I love him, but I don't even know where his office is.

Dominic calls me as I'm leaving Brady's building. The sound of the ringer is a shrill reminder my time is not my own. I can't run through the city streets calling Brady's name like a silver screen hero. My life doesn't work like that. The movie is over, and I'm back to reality.

"The boys want to come to your place again," Dominic says. He sounds stressed. In the background, a child is crying.

"Are you okay with that?" I ask. Jacob, who has an ingrained skepticism of authority figures, has not been pleased by the idea of new teachers and discussions about extra tutoring. The more we talk about it, the more desperate he gets. First he flat-out refused to go see the new school. Then he bargained for an hour. Then he went for tears that were still going by the time I had to drive back into the city for the night. And he is making everyone else's life miserable as a result, but Dominic's especially. I offered to take them last weekend, to give Dominic a break, but two weekends in a row makes me worry—and interferes with my plan to show up at Brady's yoga class tomorrow if I have to.

But the sound of crying is rising, and so is the pitch of Dominic's voice as he tells me to pick them up as soon as I can, so I say, "I'm on my way."

When I get there, Dominic has bags under his eyes, the boys are holed up in their room, and when I knock on the door, I'm met with an angry chorus of "go away!" which is not something we've ever dealt with before.

"Guys?" I say softly. "It's Daddy." And the door is pulled open, and the crying starts all over again as they wrap themselves around my knees, wailing into the fabric of my shorts. Dominic looks a little weepy too. "Okay," I say, smoothing a hand over Jacob's hair. "Okay. Let's get your pj's and some other things in a backpack and you can come to my place for the weekend."

If anything, Dominic looks weepier when the boys cheer and disappear back into their room to pack.

"I can stay," I say. "We can work this out."

"No." He shakes his head. "It's been the same all week. I'm sorry. I just can't right now. Maybe tomorrow. I'll call you in the morning."

The drive home is quiet and awkward. Karter actually falls asleep while Jacob stares out the window like he's on his way to prison. We order a pizza, and everyone goes to bed early. The boys sleep late, past eight o'clock, and we're finally getting peanut butter on toast at nine. I glance at the clock. Brady is at yoga. The studio isn't far. I could say we have to run an errand.

I send a text instead. *I have the boys this weekend. I miss you.*

I don't get a reply. I'm desperate to see him, but I deserve his silence.

"So!" I say, forcing some enthusiasm into my voice. "What do you want to do today? We could go to the science centre. Or take the ferry to the island and ride in the amusement park. What do you think?"

The boys give each other a look, and I brace for a whole new fight, but instead Jacob asks, "Can we stay here? We can do some puzzles and play some games."

The request nearly breaks me. God, even when Brady's not around, I'm still thinking about him. Before, the idea of not doing something special while Karter and Jacob were here would have sent me into a tailspin. Now, I stretch my smile a little farther and say, "Sure." Brady told me not to stress, and he is definitely the smart one in our relationship.

"He's not dying. I didn't die. For fuck's sake, Nash, I started my own business at twenty-five."

Jesus, I miss him. I miss his swagger and his confidence. He's so proud of what he's built, and he has every right to be. And he didn't need fancy schools. He managed even after his parents split. He's been amazing since the day we met, and there's a very good chance I blew it with him.

I try to teach the boys Monopoly, and suddenly Jacob's challenges are so clear. Before, I thought he got bored quickly. Now I can see how much he's covering for the words on each card that he can't read, while his brother marches over the board, snapping up properties with a confidence that would make even the most ruthless Toronto real estate maven proud.

"Do you want to be on my team?" I ask Jacob. "We can play against your brother together."

He looks skeptical. "Can I be on Karter's team?"

I have never been so glad to lose a board game to a pair of seven-year-olds in my life. They're unstoppable. Karter reads the cards, Jacob counts out the money, the houses, and eventually the hotels too. I take another page from Brady's book and teach them to use the calculator on my phone as the rents start to stack up. Jacob's gleeful "pay up, Daddy!" when I land on the Park Place hotel for the second round in a row is the best thing I've heard in a long time.

We go down to Sugar Beach in the afternoon, and things actually start to feel normal. The park is busy, but we find a spot under one of the pink umbrellas. Sugar Beach isn't actually a beach, just an urban park full of sand. The boys have fun chasing each other around the splash pad as the fountains shoot water in spurts.

I could have brought Brady here. The twins play pretty independently. Brady wouldn't have felt ignored. Now that I've had a second to breathe, away from Dominic and his questions and his emails, I realize Brady could have come with us today, and we could have talked through some of what's been going on.

Except there's still no reply to my text. I take a picture of the boys and send it to Dominic. He replies almost immediately. *Looks like fun. Are they doing better?*

I'll see if they want to come home tonight.

Dominic sends a thumbs-up. Hopefully he got some rest.

Karter flings himself down on his towel, lying in the sand next to me. Jacob has met another boy, and they're playing a complicated-looking racing game that involves going from one side of the splash pad to the other while keeping at least one limb touching a jet of water at all times.

"You don't want to play?" I ask Karter.

He shakes his head.

"Want a snack?" I say. I may not always feel like father of the year, but too many hunger-fueled meltdowns over the years have taught me the value of being prepared. I hand Karter a little string cheese. He wipes his sandy legs off with his towel, then opens the cheese and begins to meticulously peel it and lay the strings on his now clean thighs. I'm not sure how hygienic that really is, but the thigh-cheese hill isn't the one I'm going to die on today.

"Dad," Karter says.

"Yeah."

"Can I come live with you?"

Oh boy. "You don't want to live with Papa and Jacob anymore?" I do my best to hide all the nerves swirling in my stomach.

He shrugs boney shoulders. "You're all by yourself. Are you lonely?"

Is that a cheese string in my throat? "I'm okay. And don't you think they'd miss you if you lived with me?"

Another shrug. "Papa has Karim." His gaze hovers on his brother and the other boy. "And Jacob's going to make new friends at his new school. So then it's just you and me."

I thought Brady had ripped my heart out when he'd left my office, but no, it's still there, and now Karter doesn't even know how close he is to squashing it to tiny pieces.

"Are you worried about Jacob going to a new school?" When Karter doesn't say anything, I keep talking. "He'll still come home every night. He's not going away."

Karter's still staring across the splash pad. "But it won't be the same."

I speak slowly, brain racing. "We've had a lot of change this year, haven't we?"

He nods, and his eyes are decidedly watery when he looks up at me. "Can you move back with us?"

I sigh. He hasn't asked that in a long time. "You know that's not an option. Papa and I still love you and your brother very much, but we don't want to be married to each other anymore."

His lower lip wobbles. "But if Jacob makes new friends, then—"

No one ever tells you how your kids will always know exactly what to say to make you feel about three inches tall. I gather him up into my lap. He has definitely gotten bigger, and we're an awkward fit, but I don't care.

"Papa just wants Jacob to have all the help he needs at school."

"I can help him!" Karter begs. "I helped him at Monopoly. I did it at school before too."

"You have?"

He bites his lip and snuggles into me.

"Karter, I won't be mad if you helped him at school." I'm glad someone was looking out for Jacob, in fact. But it shouldn't have been his brother's responsibility.

"Sometimes, when we have to read something out loud, I count the lines, so I know what part he has to read, and then I whisper it to him so he can practice."

I'm going to start crying, right here in the sunshine on Sugar Beach. "That's really good. You're a good brother. A big help."

"I can help more," he says. "Please don't be mad at him."

Jesus, every word is a knife. "We aren't mad."

"But you're sending him away."

"We aren't mad at him, Karter. We haven't decided—" I almost say we haven't decided on anything yet, but Dominic is adamant. The more I talk to Karter, though, the more I finally have time to consider it all, and the more wrong Dominic's plan feels. Maybe he's already explored all the options, but I can't believe the trauma of splitting up the boys is going to be outweighed by whatever supports the private school can offer.

I check my phone. Nothing from Brady. I need to talk to him. He offered, and I wasn't in the right place to listen, but he can help. His dad, that client who does tutoring. Hell, even his own personal experience. There has to be an option for Jacob that doesn't mean taking him away from his brother. It might take longer to put it all in place, but that doesn't mean it's the wrong choice.

The boys allow themselves to be taken back to Markham early. If they aren't enthusiastic to see Dominic, at least we avoid the tears this time.

"Do you want to stay for dinner?" Dominic says.

I need to talk to him. I'd rather do it now, because then I have to go sky-write an apology to Brady, but the boys are watching me with expectant eyes, and I'd rather not start a fight the second we walk into the house, so I agree to stay.

"How's your boyfriend taking you having the kids again this weekend? Or have you not introduced them yet?" Dominic asks as we carry dirty dishes to the kitchen. Karter and Jacob have disappeared into their bedroom, but we can hear them laughing, so their door must be open.

"He's, uh . . . " I can't find the words. I haven't seen Brady in almost five days, and I feel like I have so little of him left there's no part of him I want to share.

"I'm sorry about some of the things I said about him. I was stressed and thought you weren't going to take Jacob's issues seriously."

"Right." My temper flickers to life. Dominic has always been like this. Quick to pick a fight, quick to apologize, like a simple sorry will wash all the hurtful things he said away. I let him do it too many times, but the divorce papers mean I don't have to stand for his manipulation or justify myself anymore.

"You should invite him over sometime. When you're both ready. We can have dinner with Karim and the boys," Dominic says.

I want to scream. A week ago Brady was an inappropriate choice, and now we're planning family dinners? I have done everything Dominic has asked, and he doesn't even acknowledge it.

"I don't think we should send Jacob to that school." I'm impressed with how calm I sound.

"Nash." Dominic sighs heavily. "We've been over this."

"No. No, actually we haven't. You decided it, and then you told me what you wanted to do."

He grips the edge of the sink. "Because you wouldn't—"

"I've been here."

"You were always working."

Yes. I worked too much to be the husband he wanted, but this is about our kids, and it's not all my fault. "Then you didn't try hard enough to tell me. I'm not an astronaut. You didn't have to send a message to the moon. Where were the emails? The voicemails?" Ridiculously, the image of Brady twirling in my chair, begging to fuck me, pops into my head. "If I worked too much, you should have come down to my office, locked the door, and forced me to listen to what you had to say. If you're so worried about Jacob you're willing to split the boys up, if you're so overwhelmed by all of this, then you should have told me months ago."

"But—" Dominic says, but I'm gaining momentum.

"The second you thought about having him assessed, you should have told me. You had no right to withhold that information."

"I—" He struggles for words.

"You and I should not be married. Me working too hard was the excuse we used to end our marriage, but it would have happened sooner or later. But I am not a bad father, no matter what you tell yourself, and I will not hurt this family more by tearing our boys apart before we know we have done literally everything we can to keep them in school together."

I've definitely caught Dominic off guard, because all he says is, "But Karim says—"

"He is their doctor. He is not a teacher, he is not a psychologist. And he is not their father." He is a boyfriend, just like Brady is—was?—a boyfriend, and in some ways Brady is more qualified to help. "Have you talked to Jacob's teachers?"

"Of course." Dominic straightens. "I told them we were having the assessment done."

He's still using "we" like I was part of that discussion, but unlike before, when I felt I had let them all down, now I'm angry at how much he's done in my name. "Have you talked to them since?"

Dominic scoffs. "They're a public school. We'd have to do so much on our own. What would they—"

"Brady went to public school, and he needed extra help." I feel bad bringing him, and especially his challenges, into this, but I need backup, even if he's not in the room. "They got him tutors, they got someone to help him in class. Do you know Karter has been helping Jacob pretend like he's reading?"

"He's seven. How could—"

"He's his brother." My voice cracks, but after the scene at Sugar Beach, I'm allowed a little emotion. "He knows him better than anyone else. And we can't do this to them, no matter how much you think it's the right decision. It isn't, Dominic, and I won't sign off on it. Not now, maybe not ever. I won't pay for tuition or anything else until I'm confident we exhausted all the other options that mean our sons can go to school together."

"Fine." He flings his hands in the air, spraying soapy water. "If you think you can do a better job, go ahead. Call their school. Set up the meetings. You can do the extra homework and vet the tutors."

"If you want me to do the homework, we'll have to renegotiate that custody agreement so I have them on more school nights."

He gapes, and I don't want to turn this into a power struggle, but I'm doing the right thing for my kids.

Dominic's eyes narrow. "Fine. Have it your way."

I don't delude myself into thinking this is our last fight, but I'll take it.

As soon as I leave Markham, I go directly to Brady's apartment.

"Brady! Come on." I bang on the door. "Please, I need to speak to you."

The door and the apartment remain infuriatingly silent.

"Please," I say one more time. I don't know which is worse. Either he's home and still won't answer. Or he's not and he's getting on with his life without me.

Neither leave me with any moves.

25

BRADY

M eanwhile, back on Tuesday . . .

I'm so mad as I leave the festival office that I'm shaking. Actually physically vibrating as I stumble out into the daylight and humidity.

Fuck Nash. Fuck his prejudices and his "you don't get to make this decision." I'll make my own damn decisions, and right now I've decided to walk away from him and the mess of his personal life and his sudden belief that I'm too young to be worth his time.

But goddamn I'm going to miss him.

I don't have too long to hurt about it, though, because my phone buzzes. It's Lena.

"Shit." A problem at the tutoring centre is the last thing I need today.

Except before I can even accept her call, another one comes in too. A client number I sort of recognize but don't hear from very often.

Turns out, we're in the midst of a province-wide internet

outage. And while I am not an internet service provider, that doesn't keep fully half my client portfolio from calling to find out what I'm going to do about it.

Sit on hold with the zillion other pissed off customers, listening to the automated message that says they're aware of the outage and technicians have been dispatched to address the issue, that's what I'm going to do. If I have any other problems, perhaps I'd care to visit their website, where more information can be found?

I would not, fuck you very much.

At least playing phone relay with clients keeps me occupied so I don't have to think about that awful scene in Nash's office. He looked so defeated and distant, like he didn't even want to fight. Like decisions had been made and no one cared what I had to say.

My fault for getting involved in the first place. For maintaining a professional relationship that bordered on flirting from day one, and for not backing down the first time he'd kissed me. I should have drawn a very clear line that we weren't going to cross. Instead, I got starry-eyed and started making bad decisions left and right.

Maybe I'm as young and naive as he thinks I am. Clearly his dick hasn't gotten in the way of his thought process, if he can tell me it's over with about as little emotion as he'd tell me it's time to upgrade his phone plan.

But fuck, I'm lonely as I go to bed. We aren't even in the habit of sleeping over—except for that night after the restaurant—but suddenly my bed feels big and empty.

When my alarm goes off the next morning, I spend a full twenty minutes staring at the ceiling, silently dreading the entire world outside.

At least the internet is back on.

Unfortunately, yesterday's outage and all the calls to the football phone have caused several clients I haven't heard from in months to suddenly remember I exist and can do stuff for them. One wants me to help him price and evaluate new billing software, which isn't even something I do, but he's adamant he needs my help. Another has an antiquated printer—*fucking printers*—that won't reconnect to his system since the outage. And a third is moving their office at the end of the month and surely I can help wire up a new thirty-seat space for them in Etobicoke with almost zero notice, right?

I'm not at all surprised when the panic attacks start midafternoon. I'm in the middle of walking Lena through troubleshooting a few of our less common but more complicated client issues, and when the phone starts to ring again, I have to excuse myself to the bathroom so I can ball my hands into fists and rest my head against the probably-not-at-all-sanitary subway tile on the wall.

My bed is not any more welcoming tonight.

Then Thursday is a shit show of follow-up calls, along with the bank phoning to tell me I've reached my credit limit because I maxed it out buying equipment for Bill Immerchuk, while he's not required to pay me for the install until the end of the month. I suck up my pride and call Bill to beg for money. I tell myself I'm using it as a lesson for Lena on how to deal with cash flow issues.

I nearly break down and call Nash that night. He's called, but he never leaves a voicemail, and the one time I happened to be at my desk long enough to see his name come up on the screen, I was only seconds off the phone with the bank and waiting for the spiraling drain feeling to stop in my head. Not the ideal time to have a heart-to-heart with the guy doing his best to break yours. So I spend Thursday night staring at the ceiling again.

By Friday morning, I haven't slept in thirty-six hours, feel like I'm going to throw up, and might be getting a migraine even though I've never had one before. And the football phone has rung twice before I even get on the streetcar.

I take my last resort and call the only number I can think of.

My dad picks me up from the office at three o'clock on Friday afternoon. I've left Lena with detailed instructions on how to reach me if anyone calls with something that can't be put off until Monday. She rolled her eyes as I went through the plan for the third time. She probably thinks I'm control freak or that she's made a terrible mistake working for me, and both could very possibly be true. I feel guilty leaving her in charge on her second weekend, but she assured me she was up to the task, and I'm only an hour outside the city. But the panic attacks are basically a continuous thing now. Something is throbbing behind my right eye, and the look on my dad's face says it all.

"When was the last time you ate something?" he asks as we pull onto the highway.

We don't talk much as we drive, which takes a while, even though we left early in the afternoon. Everyone trying to get ahead of traffic, instead creating the traffic they wanted to avoid.

Dad's got a buddy with a cottage at the south end of Lake Simcoe. No idea where said buddy is this weekend, but I'm so past the point of caring right now. I sounded about five years old when I called Dad this morning.

"Can I come over?" was all I said. Instead, he said he'd come get me and we'd take the weekend away.

"Go fishing. Drink some beers. You sound like you need it."

Fuck, do I ever. I made some kind of protest about work and Lena and the football phone, but my dad wasn't having any of my bullshit.

"No. Pack your things. Do whatever you have to do, but I'm coming for you and we're leaving."

Dads, man. I don't call, I don't write, but when I need him, he'll drag me out of the office kicking and screaming.

The cottage is exactly what I want. Basically plywood. It smells like mice and vinyl. Pretty sure the mattress in the room my dad gives me has been on that bed frame since before I was born. But the place has a cute porch that faces the lake, which washes toward us on a small beach.

We could take Nash's kids to the beach.

I must make a noise, because my dad, who has just handed me a beer, says, "You want to talk about it?"

"About what?" I say, trying to drown myself in MGD. I cough as I finish swallowing.

"Whatever made you call me." He sits down in an old folding chair that creaks but holds together.

"No." I finish the beer. He doesn't say anything about it.

No one must call the football phone, or else Lena truly is the saintly miracle worker I want to believe she is. The plan is, if she needs me, she'll call the cottage's ancient landline. The old phone can't be more than six months newer than the last of the rotary phones. And it stays silent all through Friday night and into Saturday.

Dad finds a few fishing rods and some tackle. We take a tippy aluminum boat out on the lake. I'm not much for fishing, but I'm all for sitting on an open body of water in silence, feeling like the world is a million miles away.

We could take Nash's kids fishing.

They're probably city kids, like their dad. They think fish come on foam trays from the grocery store.

The boat wobbles. I sit suddenly.

My dad says, "You want to talk about it?"

I glare at him, pulling my hat down low. "No."

We don't catch anything. Dad cooks up dinner—pickerel he buys in town. It comes packaged on foam trays. We play cribbage under a lamp with a stained-glass shade that was probably the height of fashion fifty years ago but is now vintage in a delightfully tacky way. I beat my dad at the first two games. He beats me at the next two. We're neck and neck on the last one as we cross the skunk line.

Dad looks at me over his cards and says, "If I win, you tell me what's wrong."

I peg like hell and beat him by two points.

We don't talk about it.

Lena doesn't call. I start to believe maybe I can escape the football phone after all.

I dream about Nash. I've never bottomed for him, but in the dream he's deep inside me, moving like I know he would. But no matter what we do, I'm always reaching for a climax. He's with me, but he won't let me come.

I wake up hard and aching, so I jack off into a tissue. It should be hot, but it only leaves me empty and lonely. The cottage is stuffy. I feel like I'm sticking to my bed. When it becomes clear sleep has left the room, I wander through the dark little house and out onto the front porch.

The stars are out. I need to get out of the city more. We're only an hour away, and I'm amazed at how dark it is here and how much clearer the stars are.

We could take Nash's kids camping.

I wonder if they've ever been. We could sing songs and toast marshmallows, collect bugs and tell scary stories. When the kids go to bed, Nash and I could sit under these same stars. We could talk about our week and plans for the future. We could give each other blow jobs by the campfire, trying to stay quiet enough the kids don't hear us.

I sigh at how much I miss something I've never had. Not the blow jobs. All of it.

My dad asks, "You want to talk about it?"

I say, "Holy fuck!" and tumble backwards off the porch, because it is fucking dark out here. So dark I don't see the first step as I flail, and especially so dark that my dad comes out of nowhere—this disembodied voice that floated over my shoulder with no warning that he was outside.

"Are you okay?" Dad asks.

At least I land on soft grass. I glare up at him from where I'm sprawled on my ass. He's this dark outline, the sort of thing that haunts your nightmares.

"What are you doing?" I ask.

"I heard you get up."

"And you thought scaring the shit out of me was a good way to bond?"

He helps me to my feet. I'm going to have a bruise on my hip. I stagger to the porch, but at the last second, I sink down onto the old wooden steps because going back inside feels confining.

My dad stays where he is on the grass.

I say, "I don't think I can do it anymore."

Dad asks, "What part?"

I don't want to talk about this, but the words tumble out like vomit. "The business. All of it. It's too much. I don't sleep, I'm never home. I have no friends."

"You do work a lot," my dad says. "Must be hard."

"And I don't know why I'm doing it anymore."

Dad sits next to me. The stairs aren't wide, and we're a tight fit, but I don't mind.

"Have you talked to Nash about this? He seems like a smart guy."

Hardly. "Nash and I broke up." My voice wobbles. I miss him so much. Stupid uptight asshole.

"Oh." Dad doesn't sound very surprised. "That's a shame. You two seemed to get along well."

I snort. "Yeah, except for the part where he likes making decisions about our relationship without talking to me first."

He's quiet for a long time. Crickets fill in the silence. Finally, Dad says, "If he doesn't want to be with you anymore . . . "

"Not like that. He had—one of his kids is having problems at school. He's so scared of letting them down. He said he needed to spend more time with them."

My dad sighs heavily, leaning back on his elbows. "You can't ask a man to choose between his children and you. That's not how—"

"I know, all right?" I swipe at my nose and my watery eyes. I'm not crying. I'm not. "I would never do that. I just wanted him to talk to me instead of deciding it was over on his own. Or treating me like another kid he has to deal with instead of someone who could help."

"You're your own man, Brady."

"I am. I don't know why he couldn't see that."

"Maybe he did. You've accomplished so much these last few years. I'm really proud of you, even if I worry about how busy you are."

I wipe one cheek on my sleeve. "Thanks, Dad."

"He might not want to get in the way of everything else you could achieve. Raising kids, even part-time like he's doing, is a lot of work, and you don't have a lot more room on your plate."

Wow. My dad is really smart when he's not being a creepy lurker in the dark.

I, on the other hand, am a stubborn asshole. Nash and I are so well suited for each other. "I could, though. I'd find room. I'd figure it out."

"Brady." Dad puts a hand on my shoulder. "You looked like you were an hour away from a nervous breakdown on Friday."

"Well, if Nash hadn't—"

"You were too busy, even before you met Nash. Your mother and I tried to talk to you about it in the spring, but you couldn't even put down your phone long enough to listen."

Oh. Right. He has a point.

"You've always done your own thing," he says. "Even when you were a kid. I think that's why you managed as well as you did when your mom and I weren't doing so hot and then after, when we were sharing our time with you. Because you went ahead and did what you wanted anyway. And I know you didn't like working in an office, and I'm not saying you should go back to that, but I think you need to ask yourself if this business you're running is really giving you what you want."

I want Nash. I want to meet his kids. I can't exactly say I want to be a dad, not yet, but I want to be the kind of partner Nash believes he can count on so *he* can be a dad. And if that means finding a way to spend less time working, I guess that's what I'll have to figure out.

"I don't know what to do," I say, feeling as lost as I did when I called my dad forty-eight hours ago. Because the idea of disentangling myself from work seems completely overwhelming.

"If it's about work, there are people who can help with that. Heck, I can probably be a sounding board for some of it. Or Nash."

Nash. God. He's so smart, and yet so dumb at the same time. Maybe I am too. The way my dad's telling it, I probably am at least as naive as Nash said I was. Trying to have it all and ignoring the ticking countdown flashing the seconds until I completely crashed and burned.

But I want Nash. Everything else will have to work around that one truth.

"Dad?"

"Yeah," he yawns.

"Can we go back to the city?"

He laughs. "It's four o'clock in the morning."

"We can stop for breakfast along the way. Please?"

He's quiet for a minute like he'll say no, and if he does, what am I going to do? I can't exactly leave him up here with no car.

Finally he says, "Okay, but you're driving."

26

NASH

I am dead asleep when the phone rings. As I stretch for it, my shoulder spasms in a charley horse that radiates from my back up over my neck and behind my ear. For a second, I think I'm going to pass out, but then the pain recedes.

The phone is still ringing, the screen flashing in the dark of my bedroom.

"Hello?" My voice is thick and heavy. The other end of the call is quiet for a long time. "Brady?" My heart wakes up before the rest of me is fully alert, and it beats so hard I'm having trouble swallowing.

"I'm downstairs." His voice is flat, so I can't tell if his presence is a good or bad thing, but I don't care.

"Downstairs?"

"Can I come up?"

Yes. Yes, anything he wants. I press the button to unlock the building's main door. The call disconnects, but I can't stop staring at the phone.

He's here. He's on his way up.

I'm naked, except for my underwear, and while that mode of dress would have been more than enough for his arrival in the past, today, I need more. Also, I should brush my teeth. Christ, what time is it? I check my phone. A few minutes after six in the morning. Early sun is filtering through my curtains. It's Sunday, right? Today is Sunday, and without the boys here, I wasn't going to—

Brady's coming. Right. He's in the elevator right this second.

I rush out of bed but only succeed in pulling on sweats and a wrinkled T-shirt before I hear the soft knock at the door. Even that hurts. He shouldn't have to knock.

But never mind the tooth brushing, he's here. I am going to make this right.

When I open the door, I'm so relieved he's okay that I don't say anything at first. His face is the best thing I've seen in days. I stare, taking him in. The unruly hair. The flash of his earring. He's dressed down, in an old Blue Jays T-shirt and a pair of cut-offs.

He says, "I want to take your kids camping."

"What?"

"And take them to Jays games. I want to teach them how to build a computer from scratch, and I want to be there the first time one of them downloads a virus thinking it's porn."

"Brady." I am not ready to think about my boys discovering porn. Especially not at six o'clock on a Sunday morning.

"And I will cook meals and go to parent conferences if that's what it takes." He pushes his way into the apartment, and I have to take a step back, and one step becomes two, and two is three as he strides in without ever taking his eyes off mine.

"I won't work weekends. I'll be home for dinners."

Oh, Jesus. I've given this speech before. So many times. Made all the promises. And now I've forced him into it too. I'm so glad to see him, but I hate that I've pushed him to this point of desperation.

"Brady, stop."

"No. Listen." He shakes his head fiercely. "I want them. All of it. I don't care what it takes. I'll do it. I can handle it."

"It's not always that simple."

"It has to be!" He grabs at my shirt, halting my retreat. "It has to, Nash. Because I want you. I love you so much I can't breathe without you. Please. Whatever it takes. Please." His voice breaks, and I can't help myself when I pull him into my chest. His tears soak through my shirt, and I don't care.

"No. No, hey. Shh. It's okay." Words I use when the boys have a bad dream or they skin a knee. "It's fine."

"I love you," he says again. "That has to be enough. I'll do anything you want."

We wind up on the couch, him half in my lap. He's stopped crying, but he won't sit up either. I can't say I mind, really. He feels so right in my arms.

"I'm sorry for sending you away," I say, threading my fingers through his hair. The curls feel softer today, like he hasn't styled them in a while. "I was overwhelmed and—"

"I can help." He turns his face up to mine. "Whatever is going on with your son, if it's about school, I can help. We'll talk to my dad. I'll call my client Bill and see if he knows anyone who—"

"I know. I'm sorry I didn't feel like I could accept your help before."

"Really? Okay." He nods eagerly. "Whatever you need, I can do it. Don't worry about work. I just went away for the weekend and nothing bad happened. I can leave the phone at home."

"You went away? Without the football phone?"

"My dad and I went to a friend's cottage. I needed some time to think. This week was . . . " He sighs. "Business was not good this week."

I hold him tight against me. "I'm sorry I wasn't there."

"I don't think I can keep going the way I have been. Even before we first got together . . . It's not healthy. I need to step back more."

"I can't ask you to give up your business."

"I'm not giving up. I'm reorganizing. Lena will be running my operation in six months. We can do this. Nash. All the time we were carving out to be together, we'll give it to your kids. But we'll still be together. I promise. It's going to work. We already had the time. We'll just be naked less and parent more."

I want the picture he's painting so badly. The two of us on Sugar Beach while the boys play in the sand. Lying next to each other in the dark, talking about work and school, making love until we fall asleep. I had that with Dominic, for a while anyway, and then it fell apart, but maybe it fell apart because we didn't work together, not because I can't have it all.

Three out of three.

He kisses me. His lips stay closed, but the heat under them is painfully clear.

"I love you," he says against my mouth.

"Brady."

"No. That's it. I love you. I love you." He punctuates each declaration with another kiss. "Nash, I love you."

"I love you too, but—"

"But nothing. I demanded your time this summer and you made room for me. Now we're going to make room for your kids. I mean, what we have will be different, and I am okay with that, as long as I'm doing it with you."

I promised the kids we'd be okay, even if we spend less time together. Somehow, I think Brady is trying to tell me the same thing. And maybe our life won't look the same as it has this summer, when we thought we could keep ourselves separate from the rest of the world. Instead, we'll both work too much and spend all our free time bickering and chasing after my kids, but if that's the life we want, why shouldn't we have it? If our nights are leftovers in the kitchen instead of sex in my office, who says that's not enough?

He takes one of my hands and puts it on his chest, palm

down. "You get me, Nash. More than anyone else I've ever met. And I get you. Tell me I don't."

I laugh a little, dropping my forehead to his collarbone. "Yeah. Yeah you do." Every touch, every look he has ever given me says he knows how I tick, and every flash of his eyes and brush of his hand says he loves who I am.

He wraps himself around me, gripping me fiercely, the way the boys used to do when they were small and learning to give bear hugs. Brady says, "It doesn't matter how old I am. Doesn't matter that you were married. We are it for each other. I know this, Nash. In my bones. We've been making each other better, helping each other find the time for the important things all along."

"Blow jobs?" I say.

"Shut up. A healthy sex life is important. But priorities change, and your priority is your kids. My priority is you. So we will find tutors and help your kids any way they need. I don't care how many T-ball games I have to sit through and how much macaroni art I have to make on rainy weekends."

"They're a bit old for macaroni art," I say.

"You haven't seen my macaroni art. I'll make you a fucking macaroni mosaic. Macaroni Mona Lisa. We'll have a whole macaroni gallery, and you will like it."

I groan. He and Jacob can never be in the same place together. They will meet their match when it comes to negotiation, and the rest of us will get sucked into the vortex of their debate. Breathlessly, I say, "There's that smart mouth again."

Brady's on me in a second. He might even roar as he wrestles me onto my back. I have a split second to think I never did brush my teeth, but Brady doesn't seem to care. His kisses are no longer restrained, and his hands work on my clothes with determined purpose. My head is wedged at a weird angle against the arm of the sofa, and I don't even have time to shift before he's pulling at my T-shirt, practically lifting me with his intensity to get it off.

"Brady," I groan as he presses kisses down my sternum. I thread my fingers into his black curls, holding them tight. "I'm sorry. I'm so sorry." He dips his tongue in my belly button, and I moan. "I'm sorry. I love you."

"Damn right you do." He kneels between my legs and runs his hands up and down my thighs. His eyes are dark, his lips swollen. When his thumb brushes over my thickening cock, my whole body ripples with the contact.

"Yes."

"You're mine," he says. "You know that, right?"

I swallow hard. "Yes."

He strokes me through the fabric of my sweats. "And being mine means you don't get to make decisions without talking to me first, okay?"

"Okay."

"No more of this bullshit where I'm too young or you can't make me do something. You're right." He lets go of my erection, and I thrust on reflex, trying to find his hand again. "You can't make me do anything."

"Brady." I urge him on, rocking my hips, but he pins me down, spreading his whole body over mine. He's hard too, and I want to cry as our dicks rub together, separated by too many layers of fabric. But he holds himself rigid against me, and I can't get the friction I need. I know what he wants. He's asked for it so many times before. I take a deep breath and let myself relax, melting under him. He smiles, nipping at my skin.

"Good."

"Brady, please, I need—"

"I love you." He's back to kissing.

"Brady." I shift restlessly under him.

"Say it."

"I need you, please, I—"

He takes my chin between his thumb and forefinger, holding me in place until I meet his gaze.

"I love you," he says again, like he's sounding each word out in a picture book.

I shiver as I realize what he's asking me for. "I love you."

His smile is wicked. "In the future, I will not be an ass and make stupid decisions without talking to you first."

"But—"

He gives my chin a little shake. "Say it."

"Jesus, are you going to make me pinky promise next?"

Brady rises off me. He's got one foot on the floor before I manage to grab hold of him and pull him back down.

"I promise to talk to you before making decisions—"

"Stupid decisions," he says.

Smart-ass. "Stupid decisions in the future."

He pats my cheek, sliding the rest of him back into place, fitting us together. "Was that so difficult?"

"Listen, if you think—" But my words are cut off when he slides a hand under my underwear and strokes me hard and fast. "Jesus, Brady."

"More apologies later," he says. "Orgasms now."

I can get behind this plan. In fact, I come embarrassingly quickly. He only needs to flip my cock out of my waistband and take me all the way to the back of his throat and I'm shooting off. "Brady. Fuck. Jesus."

His hair is in his eyes, and he gives me a lazy smile that says he has always known what he does to me. When I wipe a smear of come off the corner of his mouth, he sucks my thumb back between his lips, and I start getting hard all over again.

"Bedroom," he says. It's not even seven o'clock in the morning. At the rate we're going, I'll be comatose by eight. "On your hands and knees."

I slide out of my pants and do as he says. Despite having had an orgasm in the last five minutes, I'm suddenly nervous, but

Brady somehow knows, and he rubs gentle circles over the small of my back while he fishes through my nightstand for condoms and lube.

He's not as thorough as he usually is with prep, but I want him too much to care. He takes his time sliding into me, waiting for my body to open and welcome him. It hurts, but the sting is like his hands on my body, holding me to the earth while he claims me inside and out.

I groan when his pelvis and balls brush against my ass. He plants wet, open-mouthed kisses on the back of my neck while I tremble, getting ready for him to move.

"I love you." The brush of breath over his saliva on my skin makes me shudder, and only then does he pull back and plunge in again, making me shout.

"Brady!"

He plants one foot next to my knee, rocking in and out of me with a rhythm that makes me burn.

"We are it. The beginning and the end. You feel me moving inside you?"

I do, Jesus, I do. He fits so perfectly, knows exactly what I need.

"That's all you have to know. Understand? This. Everything else, we do it together. Okay?"

"Yes," I sob. When he's like this, I will give him anything. Blindly, I reach behind me until I find his hand. I pull it against my chest, holding it to my heart. "Yes."

"Good." Our pace slows until we're rolling against each other, finding the motion that moves us together in just the right way. "Now come." The only warning I have is the click of the lube cap before a cool slick hand closes around my dick and works me hard, stroking, twisting as he reaches the sensitive head.

"Brady." I gasp.

"Come on, Nash." His voice is rough in my ear, and his hips

are moving again, pounding into me, finding my prostate and setting my nerves on fire.

"Oh God." I reach for him, finding the back of his neck and holding him against me as he takes everything he wants and leaves me only feeling blazing white heat as my balls tighten.

"You can do it, Nash. For me. Come on."

The second orgasm is almost as intense as the first. Brady's dick on my prostate gives me the stimulation I need to arch and shudder, spurting white come over his fist. Behind me, he growls once more, and his teeth graze over my neck before he stills, leaving only the pulse and spasm inside me as he spills into the condom.

We crawl, naked and spent, back into my bed. I let Brady arrange us so he's wrapped around my back. The little spoon is not my favourite place to be, but today I will be anyone—any spoon—he wants.

"I got your text message. This morning when we got closer to the city," he says.

My whole body is sluggish, and my brain is not much better. "My text?"

"You missed me."

I pull his hand to my mouth so I can kiss his palm. "I did. Missed you so much."

He snuggles against me and purrs. "You should have told me sooner."

"I didn't know how. I'm so sorry for everything I said."

"I think you have to admit you're basically helpless without me."

I reach around awkwardly and smack his bare ass. "I am an adult and a very capable human being."

I'm half asleep when I feel his lips on my shoulder. "You already told me no one is ever a grown-up. We're all just pretending."

As long as I can pretend with him, everything will be fine.

BRADY

Seven months later

The phone rings and a surge of adrenaline spills through my heart. I have to stab at the screen twice to pick up the call.

"Hello, Brady speaking."

"Hi, it's me, I'm so sorry," Dominic says.

I breathe out a sigh of relief and shoot a glance to Nash, who is currently losing his fourth round of Uno to his children. His raised eyebrow is the question he has asked me over and over for the last hour, and I nod.

"Okay!" Nash shoots to his feet, scattering cards over the table. Karter and Jacob both whine, but Nash shakes his head. "Nope. Papa's here. Get your stuff. Time to go."

Not that we're hustling them out of the apartment.

Except we totally are.

Dominic is almost two hours late to pick them up. I smooth down the lapels of my suit jacket. We were on the verge of me staying here with them, and as much as they're sweet and entertaining, and most nights I'm totally happy to crash on the couch and watch *Star Wars* or play more card games, I have plans for tonight.

"Come on." Nash claps his hands as the boys doddle around the living room. "Bags are by the door. Get your shoes on."

"I can't find Henry," Karter says.

"He's in your backpack," I say, ignoring the virtual steam ready to pour out of Nash's ears. Karter loses Henry more than he and his brother are losing teeth these days combined. I was prepared. No missing raccoon is going to delay our rainbow carpet moment.

"Where's my toothbrush?" Jacob says.

"Your toothbrush stays here. You've got another one at

Papa's," I say. And we have four extras under the sink, just in case the one in the cup mysteriously gets slipped into a backpack and makes the trip to Markham.

The front door swings open, and Dominic rushes into the apartment.

"I'm sorry. I'm so sorry." He's breathless, and his shirt is untucked on one side.

"It's fine," I say. "Can't be helped."

"The Don Valley Parkway was closed. Accident. Three cars and a tractor trailer. Can't have happened more than twenty cars ahead of me. No way around, so I had to wait until the police arrived and started turning people back to the off-ramp. Everyone was trying to find another route and—" He shakes his head. "I hate driving in this city."

He's told us this already on the numerous updates he sent us while completely stalled in traffic.

"It's fine," Nash says, handing Dominic a backpack and turning to the boys. "Okay. Bye, guys. Have fun at the aquarium."

The plan had been pretty solid. The boys were off school today. Nash took the day from work to spend with them, and I worked a half day. We passed the afternoon playing at home, and Dominic was supposed to pick them up at five, take them out for dinner somewhere, and then go with them to a sleepover at the aquarium, while Nash and I go celebrate the opening of this year's festival.

Except Toronto traffic is a fickle mistress, and Nash and I were chewing on our fingernails for the last two hours, silently staring at the clock and Google Maps, willing Dominic to get here so Nash didn't have to go solo to the opening.

Nash's phone rings. "That's probably Harpreet wondering where I am." He strides back up the hall. His departure couldn't be better timed, because I haven't even turned back to Dominic and he's sliding the small velvet box into my hand.

"I am so sorry," he says, this time in a whisper. "I know you were waiting."

I can't say Dominic and I are BFFs, but we're coming to an understanding. Nash has been hard-core in his efforts to help Jacob with school through the fall and winter, and it's paying off. We've found Jacob an amazing tutor who really seems to understand how to break things down for him. He's still struggling with his words, but he's not hiding it from us, and that's progress.

And Dominic . . . well, he's still got a propensity to freak out whenever something hits a road block. This winter, Karter got sent home with a stern note from his teacher after he pushed a kid into a snowbank on the schoolyard. Dominic treated it like Karter was one step away from a criminal record, even after Karter explained the other boy was giving Jacob a hard time for needing extra help in class. I have no problem with the boys sticking up for each other, but I let Nash take the lead when Dominic starts overreacting.

"Okay, time to go," Dominic says, gathering the boys and their bags.

"Bye, Brady!" Karter says, giving me a big smile that shows off all his missing teeth.

The boys are awesome. Sweet and hilarious. We've already booked a campground at the Pinery Provincial Park this summer. It's going to be great.

"Bye, guys. Nash!" I call down the hall, sliding the box into my pocket. "They're leaving, say goodbye."

"Bye!" Nash rejoins us, kissing the boys and promising to see them again soon.

Dominic and the twins hustle out and the apartment descends into a brief silence.

"Okay. Get your coat," he says, still sounding like he's talking to the kids.

Instead, I give myself a second to take him in. I want to

remember how he looks tonight forever. He's like James Bond—if Daniel Craig weren't exhausted and bleeding all the time. The crisp white of his shirt glows against the deep black of his tuxedo jacket. His lapels are satin and gleam under the lights.

"What?" He scowls as he catches me staring while he adjusts the rainbow cufflinks that peek out of his sleeves. I gave those to him at Christmas, but he's been waiting until the opening night of the festival to wear them. He wanted it to be special, he said. As impeccable as he looks right now, I can't wait to help him take them off later. I'm pretty good at it now; we've only lost one cufflink under the bed this month.

But first, I'm going to make tonight as special as I possibly can.

"Your tie is crooked," I say, throat suddenly tight.

"What?" His hand goes to his collar, and he swings around like he might go for the mirror inside the hall closet. It's not, and if he sees it, he'll force us out of here before I can finish what I have to say.

"I'll fix it for you," I offer.

"I've got it." He takes a step back.

"No, here, I've—"

"Brady, I'm—"

"I know what—"

"Stop, I—" But he's too slow, and my finger snags a loop and pulls it loose. He scowls at me, but I feign innocence and take a step forward.

"It will just take me a second. Hold still."

He grumbles but submits as I go about redoing his tie, hoping he doesn't notice the way my hands shake.

In fact, my first attempt is a lumpy lopsided disaster and I have to undo it.

Nash grumbles. "Do you know how to tie one of these damn things or not?"

Of course I do. One of the advantages to being my age is

bowties are legitimately fashionable and not just ironic. But I didn't realize how hard it would be to concentrate in this moment.

"Sit down." I push him back up the hall toward the chairs around the dining table. He grouches some more but settles as I loop the tie around his neck. "Hold still." I have to come around the back side of the chair so I can tie it from behind. "There."

Before I can pull away, he tangles his fingers in mine, pulling me forward until he can reach my lips. "Thank you."

"Of course." I smile at him. "Gotta look our best tonight." For more reasons than he knows.

"We're going to be so late." He stands and goes to head back up the hall.

"Nash," I say, panic rising. Now. Now. I have to do it now.

"What?"

"I—" My brain is blank.

He turns. "What?"

I love him. His sharp eyes, his stubborn mouth. I love how much he loves his kids and also how passionate he is about making the festival a major Canadian film event. I love him when he stays up late working on PowerPoint slides and when he drags me away from my computer so we can make love in our bed.

He loves me too, no matter how hard I work or how sometimes it feels like I understand his kids' pop culture references better than he understands mine.

So, with all the same grace I managed that first time at hot yoga, I more or less collapse onto my knees then remember I'm only supposed to be on one knee and wobble as I get my foot planted again.

"What are you doing?" he asks.

With shaking hands, I pull the little velvet box from my pocket and open it to reveal the plain band inside. I had a

229

speech planned and everything, but for a long minute, all I can do is breathe while sweat breaks out down my spine.

"Brady?" Nash says. His voice doesn't sound particularly steady, which is good, because I have to swallow three times before I can get any words out.

"Nash O'Hara. You're it for me. I've known it since the first day we met. I love you. Will you marry me?"

The apartment goes dead silent. Nash looks stunned, and what if I've misread this? It's fast, I know it is, but why wait when you know?

"I—" His mouth drops open.

"Please?" In the fitted suit pants, my range of motion isn't awesome, and my quad is cramping. "Nash. Will you—"

He moves so fast he really could be an action star. Before I can say anything else, he's pulling me to my feet so he can cup my cheeks and press his lips to mine. Nash shudders against me, and even all these months later, that contact is enough to set us both on fire.

"Yes," he says against my mouth, voice rough in a way that brings tears to my eyes. "Yes, I'll marry you. Jesus, Brady. Yes."

I exhale slowly. "You had me worried."

He laughs, holding his hand out so I can slide the ring over his finger. "Had to think about it for a second. That's not what usually happens when you're on your—"

I pinch the back of his hand. "We're going to be late."

"Let them wait."

"You don't mean that," I say, but then he's kissing me again, and all the hesitation is gone.

"How long have you been planning this?" he asks.

"About a month. The boys helped me pick the ring out. Do you like it?"

Something like wonder passes over his face as he stares at the band again. "They know?"

I had to basically promise them my soul to get them to keep

it a secret, but they do. "Karter wants to be a flower boy at the wedding. Do you think we can make that happen?"

I can't wait. Can't wait to marry him. Be his husband. Be a stepdad and be part of his family. Our family. For real. Forever.

"Flower boy?" Nash says.

"He didn't see why it had to be a girls-only job. I said it was a little non-traditional, that I'd talk to you."

"Definitely workable. You're a smart guy," he says against my lips. "You'll figure something out."

With him, it doesn't matter. We'll find what works for us. Everything else is details.

THANK YOU

Thank you so much for reading *Work-Love Balance*. Next up is Doug's happily ever after in *Honeymoon Sweet*. Get ready for cruise ship shenanigans, seduction via trivia night, and the best *Newlywed Game* ever!

Follow me on Amazon to be notified of new releases, or come join my Facebook readers group (facebook.com/groups/allisonsalist).

Or sign up for my monthly newsletter for new releases, give-aways, and recommendations, at allisontemplebooks.com/newsletter.

The kindest thing a reader does for an author is read their book. The second kindest is to recommend it. Please take a minute to leave a review on Amazon or Goodreads, so other readers will know if this story is for them!

ABOUT THE AUTHOR

Whether I knew it then or not, I've been a writer since the second grade, when I wrote a short story about a girl and her horse. My grandmother typed it out for me and said she'd never seen so many quotation marks from a seven-year-old before. I took that as a challenge and have tried to break that record in all the stories I've taken on since then. It's good to have goals, right?

I live in Toronto with my very patient husband and the world's neediest cat. I try to split my time between writing, community theater stage management, and traveling anywhere that has good wine. Tragically, this leaves no time to clean the house.

ALSO BY ALLISON TEMPLE

The Seacroft Stories
Top Shelf
Cold Pressed
Hot Potato

Standalone
The Pick Up